HOUSE OF HOMICIDE

Early Readers say...

Cindy Fairbank is a force to be reckoned with. She needs to be. Fighting to save her family and solve murders that span over forty years, she must uncover an evil that has destroyed families for generations. In her spectacular debut, Magill has created a smart, resourceful heroine and a world that honors the living and the dead. --M.P. Cooley, author of *Ice Shear* (July 2014), *Faint Trace* (April 2015) and *Flame Out* (May 2015), published by William Morrow/ HarperCollins

You wouldn't want to live in the House of Homicide, but a visit there will thrill you. Eileen Magill's debut novel is suspenseful, scary, and satisfying--well worth a reader's while.
-- Margaret Lucke, author of *House of Whispers*

A taut, well-paced horror story with serious creep factor!
--Kirsten Weiss, author of the Riga Hayworth series

Magill's superb blend of urban legend, paranormal activity, and twisty turns, enhance a story chock full of engaging characters. Grab some holy water, lock your doors--*enjoy the read!*
--Dänna Wilberg- Producer/Host PARANORMAL CONNECTION TV, Author of *The Red Chair* and *The Grey Door*

HOUSE OF HOMICIDE

By

Eileen Magill

Oak Tree Press   Hanford, CA

Oak Tree Press
Publishers Since 1998

For information, address Oak Tree Press, 1820 W. Lacey Boulevard, Suite 220, Hanford, CA 93230.

Oak Tree Press books may be purchased for educational, business, or sales promotional purposes. Contact Publisher for quantity discounts.

First Edition, June 2015

ISBN 978-1-61009-188-6
LCCN 2015940457

To my beloved Aunt Bernadine

ACKNOWLEDGMENTS

My deepest and undying gratitude goes to Janice, my muse, who countered my tears with laughter and my uncertainty with hope. And to Tom, the brightest part of my life, who gave me the inspiration and confidence to attack this dream. Berni, my pillar of strength, who has always believed in me. I could not have made this journey without the three of you.

One of the best moves I made in writing was joining Sisters in Crime. The connections and friends I made there have had a tremendous influence on my writing and my courage to continue my dream. Every person I met at SinC had an impact on me and my story, but I want to specifically thank Terry Shames, Michelle Gagnon, Camille Minichino, Sheldon Siegel, Martha Cooley, Dana Fredsti, David Fitzgerald, Kelli Stanley, Andrew MacRae, Simon Wood, JJ and Bette Lamb, and Susan Shea. Each of you at different times boosted my spirit, gave me hope that my dream could come true, and unselfishly shared your time and knowledge, putting up with my incessant questions.

This story would never have even been conceived if it weren't for my friend and real estate agent Dawn Thomas. Together we shared our first look at the real House of Homicide, and unlike Cindy, we ran away. Dawn, you are an angel.

When it came time to delve into the mysteries of the paranormal, psychic mediums Laura Lee and Jackie Barrett were my go-to ladies. I took a lot of liberties in the telling of this story, and any errors are solely mine. I can never thank the two of you enough for all the support you gave us, both in the story and in the ordeals we faced in our own lives. I am forever in your debt.

And, of course, everyone at Oak Tree Press. You all have put up with my continual questions and held my hand while giving me the freedom to be the control freak I am.

Prologue
Spring, 1967

Francine Bell glared at her husband. He was sprawled on his favorite leather armchair with his feet up on the table. His business
suit was wrinkled, the tie loose, and the first few buttons open. He
was drunk again. She loathed his drinking, but there wasn't much
she could do about it. If he wanted to drink, he would do it, no matter
what she said. Bringing it up would only anger him, and she'd made
enough visits to the emergency room. The police had been called several times in the few months since they'd moved into this new house.
The higher his stress, the more he took it out on her small frame.

Larry had a vision. He wanted the small farming community of
Santa Clara to become a thriving city, a rival to San Francisco, its
grand neighbor forty miles to the north, and San Jose to the south.
He'd been buying up the land all over Santa Clara when the farmers
couldn't make their mortgage payments. He owned Valley Bank, the
bank that held their notes, so he knew when they were in trouble.
The farmers were given a choice: sell to Larry or lose the land
through foreclosure.

His biggest completed project to date was the development of the housing tract where they currently lived, with a self-indulgent name of Bell Tract. An even larger tract just a mile away was due to break ground in the next few months. He'd grandly named that one after the President of the United States: the Johnson Tract. It disgusted Francine how he celebrated when he bought the land all over the city – stole it, really. He wiped out the farms and started building. She'd peeked at his plans for the south end of the city. After he finished these two housing developments, he would start on a business district. "Modernizing the city," he called it. Destroying it was more like it.

There were still a lot of empty houses in this tract, and until the rest of the houses sold, he claimed they needed to be frugal. He only gave her a pittance to run the household, but it didn't stop him from spending money on his clothes and furnishings. He liked to say that he needed to look successful if he was to be successful. He was juggling a lot of financing, and she suspected that it wasn't all legal. But she needed to be careful about what she said and did; he was quick to fight.

Larry was staring at the television through drooping eyes. Francine knew it would only be a few more minutes before he was asleep. He wouldn't stay that way for long. She silently slipped from her chair and headed to the bathroom. Her face flushed in panic when she didn't see her Valium in the cabinet right away. It had been pushed behind the aspirin and his shaving cream. Relieved, she swallowed one pill. She would need the cloudy state the drug gave her when her husband eventually came to bed and started his pawing.

Within minutes the relaxing fingers of the drug spread through her body. She sat at her vanity with a pleased sigh and started her nightly ritual of brushing her long brown hair. Between the slow *whisk whisk* of her strokes, she heard movement outside. She walked over to the window and cupped her hands around her eyes to see into the dark. She couldn't see anything, but she heard a faint mewing sound, like a hurt animal making soft, pitiful cries. Francine hurried to the front door. A gasp escaped her lips when she opened it. The faint porch light revealed a woman laying on her side at the bottom of the porch steps, her stomach distended in pregnancy. Francine struggled with the lock on the screen door, her fear for the woman and the drug-induced haze making it difficult to maneuver the small pin that held the screen shut.

Her husband's sharp voice stopped her just as she got the lock open. "What the hell are you doing?"

Francine cringed and shrank away. Her voice quivered. "There's a woman outside. She looks like she's in trouble. I think she's pregnant."

Despite his intoxicated state, it only took Larry a few moments to hoist himself out of his arm chair and stagger to his wife's side. He held onto the door frame with one hand, while his other hand had a tight grip on his highball glass. The smell of the whiskey from his glass mingled with his sour breath. He took another sip, pondering the situation.

"I think she's our neighbor, the cop's wife," Francine whispered. She looked up at her husband towering over her and then back at the poor woman. The porch light sparkled off the sweat beaded on the woman's head even though this was a cool spring evening. The spreading stain below the woman's belly told Francine that her water had broken. She again reached a trembling hand towards the screen door but Larry swept her hand aside.

"The cop's wife? Well isn't that just too bad. He should have kept his nose out of our business. We keep out of theirs. She's not our problem." He gripped his wife's bony shoulder, his finger digging into her skin, and yanked her back. The *boom* of the door slamming was a fist hitting her soul.

Francine hovered by the closed door, her hands clasped, tears filling her eyes. She could hear the woman calling her name. Most of the houses were still unoccupied, and she had met the neighbors who had already moved in, but the Valium was fogging her memory, and she couldn't remember this lady's name.

The woman's cries turned into the screams of a woman in the midst of a troubled delivery. Francine's stomach cramped at the sound, and her knees threatened to give way. She couldn't leave her out there, but if she disobeyed her husband, she would pay. Dearly. She looked at her husband who had collapsed back onto his recliner, clenching his drink. His calm, drunken face was at peace, as though nothing had happened. Francine couldn't stay still; she had to do something for the woman. She tiptoed into the kitchen and with shaking hands picked up the phone. She dialed the police, chewing on her lip with worry that the sound would carry above the laugh track on the television.

"There's a woman on my porch," she whispered into the phone. She gave her address. "I think she's hurt. She needs an ambulance. Please come get her."

"Yes, ma'am. We just dispatched a unit to your area for a call for help, but we can't find the person. We'll redirect–"

Francine didn't wait to hear the dispatcher's explanation; she just hung up. She'd done what she could, but tears streamed down her face.

Francine went into the living room to check on Larry. He was passed out in his chair. The highball glass was balanced precariously on his knee. She took the drink and put it on the table. His snoring didn't stop when the sirens announced the arrival of the police and medics a few minutes later.

She pushed the curtains aside just far enough to see the medics working on her neighbor. *Karen.* That was the woman's name, she thought with triumph. But her moment of happiness at this success was fleeting. Karen wasn't moving and didn't seem to be responding to the medics. She watched as one medic placed Karen on her back and pushed her knees up. Francine held her breath as the medic slowly pulled the infant from the unresponsive mother. He cradled the baby in his arms, wrapped a blanket around its tiny body, and dashed towards the open doors of the ambulance. Francine couldn't hear any crying. Was the baby alive? She gripped the curtains in her hand. Emotions raged through her body: fear for the woman and the baby; rage at her husband for not letting her help; embarrassment, self-loathing, and humiliation that she couldn't stand up to Larry. An aching pain went through her chest as the other medic enlisted an officer to put Karen on a gurney and covered her with a sheet, pulling it up over her face.

An officer approached the front door. If he knocked, Larry would wake up. Her eyes wide in fear, she franticly shook her head, waving the officer away, but he didn't seem to understand. She sent a panicked glance over her shoulder at her husband, and opened the door just enough to slip out and ease the door closed behind her. In a whisper, she told the officer that she couldn't be involved. He nodded as if he had heard this before, but the disapproval in his face hammered her.

"We'll need you to come to the station tomorrow to give a statement, ma'am."

She nodded. "Tomorrow morning, then." Larry would be at the bank and wouldn't know. He wouldn't remember that anything unusual had happened here tonight.

Francine slipped back into the house and gently closed the door. Her husband was still in the same position as before, completely unaware of the horrible drama that had just taken place. She hurried to her room and sat on the bed. Sobs wracked her body, and she put a fist in her mouth to stifle the sounds. She believed in karma and knew this would come back to haunt them.

Chapter 1
July, 2011

"What does 'good bones' mean?" Cindy Fairbank was reading from the property description that her realtor and friend, Dawn Thomas, had given her.

"It means the house has a good structure," Dawn said, "but that's about it. When you see it on a property listing, it usually means it's a fixer." She pulled up in front of 1492 Almond Way, the next house on the printout of possibilities. "And 'a mess' would be a good description of this one."

The two-story clapboard ranch-style house, built in 1967, was on a large corner lot. It was listed as having five bedrooms, three bathrooms, a recreation room, gourmet kitchen, and two-car garage. On paper, it was exactly what Cindy wanted: a bedroom each for her, her aunt, and her two children, with the fifth bedroom to be used as her work office, and a recreation room for workout equipment. But she could see that there would be a lot of repairs needed. The pale green paint was peeling off, showing deterioration of the boards underneath. The roof was missing tiles and the rain gutters hung askew. Despite the dilapidated appearance of the house, Cindy was drawn to the covered porch with intricate patterns carved into the wooden posts. She could see a house that was once lovely; she could bring the beauty back with some hard work. As the daughter of a contractor, she had spent her youth learning the construction trade. Cindy was short, 5'4", and had a round figure, but she was strong. Her silky blonde hair, blue eyes, and smooth, light complexion made people notice her face, not her weight. She looked younger than her thirty-eight years, and no one would ever suspect that she could wield a hammer with as much skill and finesse as she could a typewriter. She focused again on the price. It was quite a bit lower than the others on the list, low enough that she would be able to afford it and still do the work it needed.

Dawn shifted her tall frame uneasily in her seat and smoothed her Lauren Ralph Lauren dress. "The price is pretty good for this area of Silicon Valley, and since it's been on the market for a while, we may be able to bring it down further. But it's not my favorite."

"Yeah, it definitely has a sad look to it. But I could probably do some of the work."

"You don't need a money pit." Dawn shut off the car and got out. She pulled her leather briefcase from the back seat. She glanced at the dark clouds and put on her Burberry hooded trench coat. She frowned slightly at Cindy's aging windbreaker that would do little to protect her from the weather.

The first raindrops of a rare summer storm began to fall as the two women hurried up a brick walkway that wound its way through a weed-choked yard. As Dawn worked on the lock box, a cold wind blew against their backs. Cindy pulled her jacket close around her neck.

The front door groaned as Dawn opened it, and they quickly entered to get away from the chill and rain. Thunder sounded in the distance.

Dawn flicked on the light. "Well that's a good sign," she said. "At least the bank left the power on." She crinkled her nose at the musty smell of a home that had been closed for a long time.

The front door opened into a large living room, lit by an ornate ceiling light. The beige walls were in desperate need of paint, and the carpet was worn. One worn path led straight from the front door through an open doorway to what appeared to be a hallway. Another path led to the kitchen to the left. But Cindy was drawn to the right side of the living room. Through a layer of dust, the golden veins of the marble fireplace glinted. Cindy ran her hand over the marble and cleared away a bit of the dust. The fireplace gave her a warm, inviting feeling. An immense picture window that spread the length of the room would brighten the room on a sunny day, but today it showed the dark clouds and pouring rain.

"I like it so far," she said. She turned to look at Dawn and saw the agent had her back against the front door. Dawn's face was pale, and her eyes were wide. In the three years they'd been friends, Cindy'd never seen the woman this shaken.

"Hey, are you okay?" Cindy asked. When Dawn didn't respond, Cindy returned to her side and reached out to touch her arm. The realtor jumped. "What's wrong?"

"I don't know" Dawn whispered. "Look, I've got goose bumps."

"It *is* kind of chilly in here."

"Yeah. Maybe that's it. Or maybe it's just because the house has been empty for so long and with the storm coming in, and the wind." Dawn took a deep breath and headed through the arched doorway to the kitchen where the disclosure binders were usually kept in houses that were up for sale.

From beyond the doorway, she shouted, "Cindy, you've got to check out the kitchen!"

The kitchen was huge. All of the appliances were top quality. When the pair discovered a walk-in pantry, Cindy's excitement went up a notch. A large pantry was an item on her "perfect house" list.

The two had looked at dozens of houses and had developed their own routine. Dawn reviewed the disclosure and inspection documents while Cindy explored. Cindy returned to the living room and turned to the hallway. The hallway appeared to run the entire width of the house with several doors in each direction. The first door, in direct line with the hallway entrance from the living room, led to a decent sized bathroom that needed updating. She turned left down the hall and found a good-sized bedroom. It was perfect for Cindy's seventy-three year old aunt who would be moving in with the family. Her Alzheimer's was becoming more of an issue, and the retirement community where she was living was wonderful for elders who needed light assistance, but the facility was not equipped to handle dementia. Having a room where Aunt Gloria could spend private time without being cramped was ideal. Gloria was part of the reason Cindy wanted a house. She hated Gloria's tiny room in the apartment she shared with two other older ladies in San Diego. Every time Cindy visited her, she felt guilty at the cramped quarters. If Gloria moved in with Cindy, she would have company and supervision, but she'd also have some independence. Cindy also hoped that diet, exercise, and mental stimulation would keep the disease from spreading past intermittent memory loss and decreasing cognitive skills – or at least slow it down.

She continued down the hall to the garage. It was large with plenty of room for storage, and it would still fit two cars inside. They only had the one van right now, but Cindy's daughter, Marti, was fifteen and would be driving soon. Cindy could envision a workbench – something she would surely need if she were to do repairs by herself. She silently thanked her father for bringing her along on his construction jobs when she was growing up.

Retracing her steps back down the hall, she passed a short passageway with a door that led to the backyard. At the end of the main hall, the stairs to the second story were on her left and another room was straight ahead. This must be the recreation room, she thought. Her stomach dropped when she entered the room. It was in shambles. There were several areas where the floorboards were torn up, and gaping holes exposed the crawl space underneath. The odor of damp, musty soil wafted into the room from below. The few areas of drywall that weren't missing completely had holes. It looked like someone had deliberately cut portions away. The windows were cracked and taped together. Cindy stepped into the room, testing each footing to be sure it wouldn't collapse. She crouched down to take a closer look at the floor beams. They appeared to be in good condition. She'd helped her father put in subflooring, hardwood floors, and drywall throughout the years, so this work wouldn't be a problem, especially if she could get some of her construction friends to help. What the hell had happened in here? A flash of lightning flooded the room with light for a moment, giving the room an ominous feel.

She felt rather than heard Dawn come into the room. She stood up and turned towards the door. But the doorway was empty. Cold air encircled her and she shivered. A cloud appeared in front of her face, startling her. She inhaled sharply and stepped back. Her foot slipped on the edge of a hole. She shifted her weight and scrambled forward. Her heart was pounding, and each breath caused another cloud to appear. *How had it gotten so cold in here?* She turned back to the floor boards and swept her gaze across the room at the damaged walls and exposed support beams. She spun around at the screech of unoiled hinges, followed by a loud *bang*. The door to the rec room had slammed shut.

Cindy sidestepped one of the holes in the floor and sprinted to the door. She tried to pull it open, but the doorknob wouldn't turn. She fumbled with the lock and got the knob to move, but the door wouldn't budge. Trapped. She stepped back, breathing fast and heavy, but her breath was no longer a cloud in front of her face. As suddenly as the cold in the room had appeared, it dissipated. A strange warmth enveloped her. She tried the door again, and this time it opened without protest.

She looked around the room, taking in the broken windows and holes in the floor. The summer storm had brought a heavy wind with it. Could that have been what caused the cold air? A draft caused the door to close? She stepped outside of the room and pulled the door shut. Other than protesting hinges, the door closed smoothly. She looked at the door jamb, but it appeared fine, and the door sat evenly in it. Opening the door again, she looked for signs of wear on the paint where the door might have stuck before, but there were no rough spots. She opened and closed the door again several times, but couldn't get it to stick. Could a breeze have caused the door to close and create a vacuum-like seal for a few moments? It didn't seem likely, but she couldn't think of any other reason. She pushed nervousness away and continued her tour of the house.

Upstairs there were three medium-sized bedrooms with a spacious full bathroom at one end of the hall. At the other end was an immense master bedroom suite. The master bathroom was all marble. She felt a wave of heartache that she couldn't share this room with her husband. She would be alone in this beautiful room. *Will I ever find someone to share it with?* She shook off the impending melancholy thinking of her deceased husband and yelled, "Dawn! You've got to come upstairs!"

"Nope, you need to come down here," Dawn hollered back. There was an edge to her voice that bothered Cindy, and she hurried downstairs.

Standing at the kitchen counter with the disclosure documents in front of her, Dawn's face was drawn and pale. Cindy considered Dawn to be one of the strongest, most stable, and unflappable people she knew. Cindy's husband, Keith, had died from a fall from a roof while installing solar panels three years ago. Dawn had stepped in as an agent to help her sell the house and pay off the mortgage – and as a friend to get her life in order. Now Cindy was leaning on her again. She was desperate to get out of the dingy apartment. Keith's insurance payoff was finally going to allow it to happen, *if* she could find the right place at a decent price. It meant that she was going to have to make some concessions, like fixing up a rundown house. The schools in this area were excellent, and Santa Clara was where she really wanted to be. But most of the houses they'd seen that would work for her family were too expensive. The money from the insurance would pay for a mansion in most places of the country, but not in this area of California. Even with the recession, a modest house cost nearly a million.

"What is it?" Cindy asked, looking up at Dawn.

Dawn pointed to one of the documents in the binder. "You know how you have to disclose if anyone has died in the house within the last three years?" The agent looked directly at Cindy. "There aren't any details, but someone died of heart failure here."

Cindy rolled her eyes. "Heart failure? That could mean *anything*. The final cause of death is *always* the heart failing to beat. The question is really what caused the heart to fail."

She took a deep breath and closed her eyes, letting herself feel the house. She sensed an urgency, a longing, and wasn't sure if it came from her or the house. Her mind went back to the torn-up rec room and what she'd experienced there. Was that where someone had died?

An old friend from high school was a psychic medium. She'd once told Cindy that there were spirits everywhere; the average person just couldn't sense them. If a person suffered a sudden death, they were more likely to have difficulty passing over. Maybe that's what Dawn was feeling. Cindy would get in touch with the psychic and see what she thought.

She looked at Dawn and shrugged. "Death is an inevitable part of life, and the death in the house was probably just an old person dying of illness or natural causes, which would explain the ambiguous 'heart failure' cause of death."

With Dawn doing her magic with the price of the house, Cindy might end up with her dream home for a great price. The fact that someone had died here really didn't bother her; if anything, it added character to the house. Growing up with a psychic friend had opened Cindy's eyes to the paranormal, and although she couldn't feel, see, or hear what a psychic could, she kept an open mind and believed her friend. Her son would think it was cool. At eleven years old, Randy would enjoy thinking his house was haunted. It might make up for having to move to a new school. Marti would be a different story. She was still torn up about her father's passing and shunned anything that had to do with death.

Cindy looked at the inspection reports while Dawn explored. This was far more house for the money than anything else on their list. Other than its sad history of a recent death and the work that needed to be done, it was exactly what she wanted. The neighborhood looked respectable, and the master bedroom had an unobstructed view of the not-so-distant Santa Cruz mountains.

Cindy nearly collided with Dawn at the bottom of the stairs. She reached out a hand to steady her friend. "I want it."

"Are you sure?" Dawn asked. "Look. I wouldn't tell you this except that we're friends. I've been in a lot of houses, and I can honestly say I've never had such a bad feeling about a house. There are a dozen more properties on the list. Let's keep looking."

Cindy's stubbornness kicked in. "The house is beautiful. A bit run down but a gem. It's more than I could ever hope to have. It's got almost twice the square footage of the other houses we've seen, and it's a corner lot on quiet streets. I know you hate the idea that someone died here. But I see a neglected house waiting to come alive again."

"It's not that someone died here. I've been in plenty of houses like that. This is different. I feel a heaviness. Can't you feel it?"

Cindy searched for the right words to describe what she was feeling. "You know, it's like I share something with the house. I lost my husband, and it lost someone, too."

"Will you at least look at the rest of the houses we have on our list?"

Cindy sighed in resignation. She would look, but this house was the one she'd buy in the end. It was speaking to her, calling her. She had to have it.

Chapter 2
November, 1967

Despite the dark and cold, the three boys needed only moments to scale the chain link fence and drop into the construction area. Roger Duran, the tallest of the three, took off at a jog towards the first house. The streets in this part of the development had already been paved, and the sidewalks were mostly completed. The house the boys liked to hang out in was on the corner of Almond Way and Grove Road. Most of the houses were just frames, but this house had its roof and exterior walls up. Although the windows were only framed and the glass hadn't been installed, the boys had more privacy than in any of the other houses. It was a perfect place for an after-game celebration.

Freddie Dellman followed Roger, right on his heels. They'd been best friends for more than ten years, starting when they met in pre-school. They were inseparable. If one was in trouble, their parents knew without a doubt that the other was involved, too. Freddie was just an inch shorter than Roger, but outweighed him by a good twenty pounds. Freddie worked his father's farm and had built a strong, muscular body, very much like his father's. Roger, on the other hand, took after his mother, a magazine model. One look at his eyes, and the high school girls swooned. Freddie, ever the opportunist, followed behind his friend to sweep them up.

The third boy was a newcomer. Enrico Martinez's family had moved to the area four years ago, when his father took a position in the management of the local bank. Mr. Martinez worked directly for the bank owner, who also owned this development. It was hard for a Hispanic boy to fit in with the other kids. It took him several years to be treated as anything other than an immigrant farm worker, even though his family had never been on a farm. He wouldn't know how to pick fruit or vegetables if his life depended on it.

It wasn't until he made the football team that he was noticed by the popular Freddie and Roger. Freddie used his size to block the attackers, and Roger took advantage of the extra time to get perfect passes to Enrico. So far their team was undefeated. Though the three boys were just freshmen, the coach had indicated they would probably make the varsity team next year.

They shielded their flashlights as they ran to the house, using only as much light as they needed to avoid construction debris. Creeping into the house, they put their backpacks down and peered out through the window frames.

"Looks like we made it here unseen again," Enrico said, a note of triumph in his voice.

"Heck yeah," Roger said. "Break out the beer."

Freddie dug into his pack and came up with three cold Pabst Blue Ribbon beers that he'd liberated from his dad's stash of alcohol in the garage refrigerator. They opened their cans and crashed them together, spilling beer on the plywood floor.

"We really kicked ass today," Freddie said.

The other two boys whooped in agreement and guzzled their beers. They tossed the empties in the general direction of the masonry shell of the fireplace. Roger let out a burp of heroic proportions, and the other two boys did their best imitations.

Opening their second beers, they settled themselves on the floor, leaning against the bare wall beams. The dim moonlight came in through the window frames, and only Roger kept his flashlight on. He set it in the middle of the floor.

"Did you see Carolyn?" Enrico asked. "I think she's got a thing for Roger."

"Moving in on the varsity quarterback's girl?" Freddie said. "You'd better be careful."

"Oh, I noticed," Roger said, ignoring Freddie. "She found a way to come stand by me when the defense was on the field."

Roger reached into his backpack and pulled out a bottle of tequila. "Look what I found."

"Break it open and pass it around," Freddie said.

Roger took the first swig, held it out to Freddie, but stopped short. "Shhh. I hear something. Someone's here."

Freddie took the bottle from his friend. "Yeah, right. You just don't want to share."

"Hush, I mean it. I saw something. Out there." Pointing out the framed window, he stood up, staggering as the beer and tequila hit him.

Enrico crawled to the window and peered into the dark. "I don't see anyone." Roger and Freddie were used to getting into trouble. It had happened so often that their parents barely said anything anymore. It helped that they were the darlings of the football team, but his own father would have his hide. Being a star receiver on the team wouldn't help. His father wouldn't think twice about yanking him out of sports.

Concluding that Roger was just seeing things, Enrico crawled back and took the bottle of tequila. He took a small mouthful and sputtered. The other two laughed at him.

"Look at him," Freddie said, "a Mexican who can't handle tequila! Maybe you should stick with this stuff." He tossed another can of beer at him.

"Ha ha ha! Very funny," Enrico said, catching the beer.

"Shhh," Roger whispered. "Now I *know* I saw someone." He got up and walked unsteadily through the doorframe and out onto the porch area, out of sight of the other two.

A loud grunt and thud came from the porch. Freddie and Enrico looked at each other.

"Hey, Roger. You okay?" Freddie called out. When he got no answer, he stood up and walked slowly towards the door. He stopped midway when a scraping sound came from outside. "Come on, Roger. Knock it off." There was a tremor in his voice.

Enrico got into a crouch, ready to run if someone was out there. His heart was pounding at the thought of getting caught.

Freddie started moving forward again, and when he reached the door, he peered out. "Come on, Roger, stop screwing around." He walked back into the room and grabbed a flashlight. He was shining it out the door looking for his friend, when suddenly Enrico was at his side, making him jump.

"Put that down!" Enrico hissed. "We don't want people to see the light and come check it out. And keep your voice down."

Freddie's flashlight was aimed at the flooring of the porch. The light reflected off something wet, and Freddie stepped forward to look at it. "Look, Roger spilled his beer."

Enrico stepped back farther into the house. "No. He wasn't carrying a beer when he went out."

"Then he's out taking a piss."

"Where is he then?"

"Good question." Freddie went down the steps, his flashlight still pointing at the ground. "There. Something's moving by the forklift."

"I'll stay here and protect our stuff," Enrico said. We don't want someone running off with it."

"Yeah. You do that." Freddie moved off in the direction of the forklift. The flashlight cast shadows that moved with his shaking hand. What was hiding in the dark? He guessed Roger was just messing around, but his rapid pulse told him that he wasn't so sure. He again thought he saw movement behind the forklift. He slipped up to it and held the flashlight like a gun in both hands, imitating what he'd seen on *77 Sunset Strip*. He quickly stepped around the forklift, swinging the light in front of him. He was expecting to find his friend, but the figure in front of him was bigger. Much bigger. He was so startled, he didn't move when the figure swung something at his neck.

* * *

When Enrico guessed that five minutes had gone by without hearing from either Freddie or Roger, he decided it was time to go home. *Screw them.* If they wanted to be jerks, they could do it without him. He considered the bottle of tequila and the other cans of beer, but decided to leave them.

He picked up his backpack and flashlight and stepped onto the porch. He knelt down to see the puddle on the wood. Up closer, it didn't look like piss; it had a coppery smell to it. He reached out and dabbed his fingers in the puddle. It was thick and sticky on his fingers. He shined the light on his hand and stumbled back, falling on his ass when he saw that it was red.

"What the fuck!" he moaned in a hoarse whisper. "Oh, shit. Oh, shit. What the fuck's happening?" His pulse raced, and he was breathing fast. Adrenaline shot through his body. If that was blood, then something bad had happened. He frantically wiped his hand on the porch, desperate to get the blood off. As he stood up, his legs were shaky, and the backpack felt like it weighed a hundred pounds on his back.

"Freddie? Roger?" Enrico called out. "Where the hell are you guys?" Worried that his friends were hurt, he no longer cared if someone saw his light or heard him.

He headed off in the direction he'd seen Freddie go. He played his flashlight over the construction equipment. There was something wet and gleaming on the forklift. It looked like a dark, thick liquid dripping down the side of the equipment. He got close to the forklift and moved the flashlight beam over it. Definitely blood. His flashlight beam followed the dripping blood to the ground. The dirt was wet. Something had been dragged through the dirt, leaving twin trails of blood. The drag marks went around the end of the forklift, but he didn't move to see what was there.

"Fuck this, I'm outta here," he said under his breath and hitched his backpack higher on his back.

As he started toward the perimeter fence, he heard laughter coming from the house. A wave of relief spread through his body. Jerks. I can play that game, too, he thought. Figuring that he was hidden from view, he shielded his light and slipped around the back of the house, intent on sneaking up on his friends.

Fake blood, he thought. They got me. What a fool! Well, he'd show them who the fool was.

Enrico moved silently up the back stairs and entered the house. He crept into the main area. Sure enough, the guys were there, waiting for him. Except there were three. It took him a few heartbeats to realize that two of them were hanging by their ankles from the exposed beams overhead. One looked wrong, somehow.

The head was missing.

He staggered backwards, his legs going weak.

The third figure turned towards Enrico and laughed—the same laugh he'd heard outside. It was a large man, over six feet tall, wearing dark overalls with a long-sleeved shirt. A straw hat was pulled low, hiding his face. The man bent down and picked up a round object off the floor and tossed it at Enrico. Out of reflex, Enrico caught it. The fingers of his right hand slipped in a warm wetness; his left hand gripped tighter to something stringy. He looked closer at the object. It was Freddie's head. He dropped it and gagged. He was paralyzed with fear. The dark figure moved towards him, still laughing. The bodies swung as he shouldered past them.

Enrico shrugged the backpack off his back and swung it in front of him. He threw it as hard as he could at the man. He didn't wait to see what happened. Turning, he ran face first into a wall stud, knocking himself out cold.

Chapter 3
August 1, 2011
Day 1

"Are you two ready to go?" Cindy Fairbank called out from the front door of the tiny apartment, her car keys clenched in her fist. She glanced at her watch again. It was already 9:45. "We have to be at the house in fifteen minutes."

"I'm ready," Randy replied as he swaggered into the living room from the kitchen where he'd finished cleaning up their breakfast dishes. He had a soccer ball tucked under his arm. "But you know Marti. She's *trying* to look pretty." Randy started humming the theme to *Mission Impossible* loud enough for his sister to hear.

"Shut up, you little rat!" fifteen-year-old Marti yelled from the bathroom. She was applying makeup. Her naturally long and dark eyelashes were the envy of most of her girlfriends. They highlighted her ice blue eyes so that very little mascara, eyeliner, or eye shadow was actually needed. Taking one last look from all angles, she made sure that her blonde hair was securely tied back and decided she was ready to go. Maybe she'd meet a cute neighbor — there certainly weren't any in this dumpy apartment complex. The new house *had* to be better.

* * *

Cindy was anxious as they pulled into the driveway. The traffic on the way to their new home was light, but it still took twenty minutes to get there, and they were ten minutes late. She waved to Dawn who was standing on the porch.

"I was starting to wonder if you'd gotten cold feet," Dawn said. She gave Cindy a hug and ruffled Randy's blonde hair. He pulled away and stood next to his sister. He dropped the soccer ball and rested his foot on it.

"Are you kidding? I haven't been able to sleep." Cindy's eyes lit up at the sight of the house keys in Dawn's hand.

Holding the keys out, Dawn said, "Here you go. It's officially yours! The new Fairbank residence."

As Cindy had expected, Dawn had been able to get the house for an unbelievable price. Everything had come together: after years of bickering between the insurance company and his employer, Keith's life insurance payout finally came and his pension had kicked in. With a room that she designated as an office, she was able to work from home as the editor at the magazine. With the insurance covering most of the price of the house, she was able to have only a small mortgage and still have funds left to make most of the improvements she wanted. She couldn't believe that things had worked out so well.

Cindy opened the front door with a trembling hand. At the loud creaking noise it made, she had a flashback to the door in the rec room slamming closed. She pushed aside the twinge of fear that something wasn't quite right. "Come on in," she said to the kids. She swept her arm in a grand arc with a welcoming bow. Both kids rolled their eyes.

In a practiced move, Randy used his foot to pull the ball back and kick it up into his waiting hands. He pushed past his mom into the house. He turned and looked at his sister, who was still hanging back. "Let's pick our bedrooms. Race you upstairs," he said and tossed the ball at Marti. He took off down the hall to the staircase with his sister right on his heels, the soccer ball in her hands.

* * *

Randy opened the door to the first bedroom, and Marti opened the door directly across the hall, which turned out to be to the bathroom. Next to the bathroom, she found a bedroom that drew her in. One wall had a huge window that looked out over the backyard. There was a walk-in closet on the right side, enough room for all of her clothes.

She went back out into the hall to check out the other two bedrooms. Randy was still in the first bedroom, staring out the window over the street. "Do you like this room?" Marti asked. When he nodded, she continued, "The one across the hall is great for me. Let's go check the other one."

Marti let him lead the way. When he got a few steps ahead of her, she tossed the soccer ball at him, nailing him in the back of the head. The two scuffled, and Randy ended up with the ball in his possession. Laughing and out of breath, they went down the hall to the third bedroom. The door at the end of the hall opened to the master suite. They both poked their heads into the room and then moved back to the third bedroom. "I like the one I first went in," Marti said. "What about you?"

"I don't know," he replied. "You can have that one. I like looking out over the street. Either would be cool."

"Why don't we leave this room for Mom's office since it's closest to her room? Besides, we can be louder if we're farther away," Marti said.

Randy gave her a knowing look. "And closer to the stairs if you want to sneak out. Let's check out her room."

Their mom came up the stairs. "Did you two decide which rooms you want?" Cindy asked. They showed her their choices, and when she agreed, Randy put the soccer ball in his new closet. "Start thinking about what colors you want for the carpet and paint. We'll go to the hardware store in a bit and get supplies." Ignoring their protests, she gathered them in a hug. "When you've decided, come back downstairs. I need your help figuring out what to do about the rooms down there. We've only got a week to get out of the apartment, and there's lots of work that needs to be done here before we can move in. So 'chop chop' as my dad used to say."

By the time the kids finally came downstairs, Dawn had left to meet with other clients. Cindy took them to the recreation room. She warned them to be careful of the holes in the floor. They both poked their heads in. "What the hell happened in here?" Marti asked, her eyes narrowed and her lips pursed. "It looks like someone got murdered."

"I don't know," Cindy said. She decided that being upfront and honest was the way to go. "The paperwork said that someone died in the house, but there weren't any details. It didn't say anything about this room, though."

Randy piped up. "I'll bet someone was murdered in this room." His voice squeaked as he warmed up to his story. "The floor and walls were covered in blood and had to be removed."

Marti made a sound of disgust and glared at her mom. "That's gross! How could you buy a house where someone was murdered?"

"Oh, come on," Cindy said. "Your brother's just making up stories."

"Whatever. I'm going outside. This room stinks." Marti left the room, and a few moments later the front door slammed. Cindy started after her, but stopped.

"What a bitch," Randy muttered under his breath.

"Hey! Watch your language. And I don't need you making things worse with your imagination. Keep that stuff to yourself."

Cindy thought about his attitude with a touch of worry. She'd worked hard to foster a loving relationship between the two kids. She and Keith had played games with them, teaching them to be competitive, but always supportive of each other. They'd tried to instill the belief that you can admire your opposition, not hate. When he died at work, leaving Cindy with the two children, she saw how much these lessons had helped. The two were supportive of each other. A tragic event of such magnitude could tear a family apart, but instead, they were drawn closer together.

At the thought of her late husband, she felt his arms encircling her from behind, giving her the comfort and support he'd always shared. She closed her eyes and breathed in deeply, hoping to smell his cologne. There, just a touch of fragrance before it drifted away. She turned her thoughts back to her boy. Now that Randy was eleven, she was seeing more independence... and a lot more attitude. But he was still her little boy, and always would be.

*　*　*

Marti stopped on the sidewalk. Her pulse pounded in her ears, and she realized how angry she was. *How could Mom buy a house where someone died? It's gonna be hard enough starting at a new school, but I'll be seen as a freak living in that house.* "So unfair!"

"What's unfair?" came a female voice from behind her.

Marti spun around. She hadn't realized she'd spoken aloud. Nor had she heard the woman approach. She opened her mouth to reply, but nothing came out.

"Are you moving into this house?" the lady asked. She was old, and Marti guessed that she was maybe a bit older than her mom, forty-ish? There was a touch of gray in her brown hair.

"Yes," Marti said.

"I'm glad someone will be moving in. It's been vacant for a couple years now, so it's looking pretty run-down. It used to be one of the nicest houses on the block until..." Her voice drifted off.

"Until what?"

The neighbor looked closer at Marti. "You haven't heard about the Fremonts? It was terrible. The whole family was killed."

"What? A whole family? Mom said that _someone_ had died."

The woman's face flushed and she stammered, "I'm sorry." She held her hand out. "I'm Nicole Wilson. I live three houses down with my two sons." She pointed to a house down the street.

It was the first time Marti really looked at the other houses and compared them to her own new place. Most were similar in size and shape, and a few, like hers, had second stories added on. Her house was the only one that looked neglected. Her heart sank again. Not only had people died there, but it was by far the ugliest on the street.

Nicole broke into Marti's reverie. "Would you like to meet my sons? My oldest, Peter, looks to be about your age. He's fifteen."

"I am, too," Marti replied. Things were looking up. "Yes, I'd like to meet him."

"Why don't you tell your mom where you're going, and I can introduce you to Peter."

"She's sorta busy. She knows I'm checking out the neighborhood."

They stopped in front of the tan and brown house. The front lawn was surrounded with rose bushes, cannas, and other flowers Marti didn't recognize. Her eyes were drawn to the trim back of a guy pulling weeds in the lawn. His brown hair and T-shirt were damp with sweat, accenting his athletic build and great tan.

When Peter turned around, Marti couldn't breathe. He was hot! He took off his gloves and stood up. He looked Marti over for a beat and a smile spread across his face.

"Hi." He stepped onto the pathway and walked over to her.

Marti held her breath as he took her hand to shake it. Her knees felt weak, and she couldn't look away from his deep blue eyes. "Hi," she breathed. *Yes, things are definitely looking up. This guy has potential. A lot of potential.*

* * *

Cindy's heart lifted when Marti returned from checking out the neighborhood. Her daughter was smiling, and there was no greater feeling for a mother than to see her children happy. The smile and Cindy's elation didn't last long, though.

"Mom," Marti growled. "I can't believe you bought this house. Didn't you know a whole family was killed?"

Cindy's eyes widened. "What? Where did you hear that? I was told one person died. From heart failure."

"Nicole Wilson. She lives down the street. The Fremonts were killed. All of them. Dead."

Cindy's heart sank. No wonder the bank was so happy to drop the price. She felt anger welling up. If it was true, then the bank lied by saying only one person died here. They should have disclosed that the whole family was murdered. Would she have any recourse? She'd been so busy getting things ready for the move and preparing for her aunt's arrival, she hadn't looked into the house's history like she should have. She chided herself. She'd been an investigative journalist, and she hadn't done her homework on a very important decision in her own life. She also hadn't called her psychic friend like she'd promised herself.

Marti stomped her foot and pouted. "You could have at least asked us if we were okay with it."

Jolted out of her introspection, Cindy reacted harshly. "You don't have to like or approve of my decisions. This isn't a democracy." As Marti stormed away, Cindy called out to her, "Go figure out what you want to do with your room. We're leaving for the hardware store to get paint and carpet in fifteen minutes."

After Randy described what he wanted for his bedroom, she asked his opinion of how they should redo the rec room. Her own father had started her construction education even younger, and she remembered how good it felt when he asked her to imagine a completed room from one that was in shambles. How could the space be used? What would the walls and the floor look like? What supplies would they need? Pride flowed through her as she watched Randy's face. His eyes took on a distance as though he was seeing a room that didn't currently exist. Was he visualizing the room as they might make it? Or was he seeing it as it had once been – the room where a murder took place. The gleam in his eye said it was the latter.

It was early evening by the time they left the hardware store with construction and paint supplies. On the spur of the moment, she put in an order for a special door with a large dog door in it to replace the one leading to the backyard. It would take nearly a week to be delivered, so she wouldn't install it until everything else was done. A puppy would help soothe her daughter's hurt feelings.

Chapter 4
August 2, 2011
Day 2

There was a lot of work to be done before the Fairbanks could move into the house. Randy and Marti began bickering immediately over who had to do which jobs. Cindy let them snivel and then gave them "the look." She dreaded the day when that wouldn't work anymore. Marti chose to get started on painting while Randy would help Cindy with the construction-type jobs.

On the morning of the second day in the house, Cindy made a frustrating discovery as she and Randy were tearing out the damaged flooring in the rec room: if they wanted to have workout equipment, she needed to install a much stronger subfloor.

Many older houses in California had basements, but more recent ones like this were built on dirt with pillars pounded deep into the ground. The floor stood several feet off the ground, sometimes as little as two feet, but as much as four feet, leaving a space to crawl under the house to access pipes, vents, and wires. Cindy was happy that this house's crawl space was on the deeper side, a little more than three feet, but wished it was a full basement instead. Crawl spaces were places that Cindy never liked; they were always cold and dark, and this one was no exception.

She dropped down into the space and inspected the beams and joists by flashlight to determine what supplies she would need to replace the subfloor. It was difficult for her to breathe. The air was oppressive, as if the dark had substance. She knew it was her imagination, but she got out as fast as she could.

"What's the matter, Mom?" Randy smirked as he helped her out of the hole.

Cindy scowled at him and shuddered. "Damn, that place gives me the willies. I think you'll do all the work down there."

A stray, disconcerting thought hit Cindy. There had been a recent news story about a suspect fleeing the police and hiding in a stranger's crawl space. The entrance to the crawl space for this house was a set of horizontal double doors, reminiscent of a Midwest storm cellar. They were raised about two feet above the ground in the backyard, and when opened, there were four stairs leading down into the dark. The thought that someone could easily get under her house from outside bothered her. She looked around the rec room. This could be the perfect place to put a new entrance and seal the outside doors. She wasn't keen on making more work for herself – she was worried enough about finishing everything before they had to vacate the apartment – but once the safety idea was in her head, she was compelled to do something about it.

"Looks like I'll be going back to the hardware store," Cindy said. "Want to join me?"

"Can I stay here instead? I wanna explore under the house."

"Sure. The inspection report said there was some debris down there. Would you mind cleaning it up?" She handed him the flashlight. "I'll get a bag for you." All Randy wanted to do was to explore, but she might as well get some extra work out of him while he looked for treasures.

"I'll let your sister know where you're going to be. She's in charge while I'm gone, so listen to her and do what she tells you."

"Yeah, yeah. I know the drill."

* * *

Randy pulled the knee pads on over his jeans and slipped his hands into work gloves. He peered into the hole. It looked a lot scarier when he was the one going down there. It seemed to have gotten darker and deeper. He suddenly didn't want to go down there. He sat on the edge of the hole and let his feet dangle. Even through his jeans, he could feel the colder air down there. He held the flashlight and plastic garbage bag in his left hand and gripped the flooring with his right. He jumped into the hole. The ground was harder than he expected, and he grunted when he landed. He stood up and cursed. At 4'7", his shoulders were barely above the flooring. He was going to have a struggle getting out.

He dropped to his knees, and the cool air enveloped him, raising goose bumps on his sleeveless arms. He shined the flashlight around. Wires and cables were stapled to the beams, and strange silver foil-like tubes spanned the length of the house with branches reaching up to the floor above. He scooted closer to one and poked it. It dawned on him what it was: a heating duct. Proud that he'd figured it out, he moved on. He scouted out a pile and went to investigate. He found a pile of paper, candy wrappers, and soda cans. Someone else had thought this was a cool spot to hang out. He put everything in the garbage bag and moved on to the next pile of junk. He set the flashlight down on its side, the wide beam pointing back the direction he'd come. The first item in the pile was a set of denim overalls. It looked really old and had rust-colored stains. A costume? Weird, but cool. He set that aside and went back to the pile. A black denim shirt with long sleeves was folded neatly. He shook it out to look at it, and bit back a squeal when a spider dropped onto his lap and disappeared. He dropped the shirt, grabbed the flashlight, and scrambled backwards. The spider was on the ground next to him, and he smashed it with the flashlight. *Gross.* He set the flashlight back down and went back to the pile of debris. Next was a straw hat that reminded him of the pictures of farmers. There were a bunch of towels that were stiff and dirty. He imagined they'd been used to clean up blood. Were the stains on the overalls actually blood? Suddenly weirded-out, he shoved the towels in the garbage bag. His eyes widened when he saw what was hidden under them.

A gun.

Randy pick up the gun. It was a semi-automatic like in the cop shows, the kind that ejected the cartridges out. It was heavier than he expected, and the dark metal was cold. Maybe the people who died here really were murdered. Could this be the murder weapon? Holy crap! That would be cool to show off at his new school. A flush of guilt ran through him. He knew he should give it to his mom, but *damn* it was sweet to have his own gun.

Excited, he stood up. His head banged against the boards. He swore, rubbing his head. He shined the flashlight up at the offending boards, long planks of wood in alternating rows. He caught sight of a small square section that didn't quite fit the pattern. He crawled over and inspected it. He put the flashlight down on the ground with the beam pointing upwards and pushed up on the square. As the board moved up, he found himself with his head above the floor in a dark room. *A hatch!* He could hear his sister nearby. He guessed that he was in the closet of the downstairs bedroom, his aunt's room.

Without a sound, Randy set the hatch cover on the floor of the closet, grabbed the flashlight, and tried to figure out how to get out. Without anything to brace his feet against, it was going to be tough, especially while trying to be quiet. He pulled the bag of garbage over and stepped on it. It squished down and was unstable, but it raised him up about six inches, just enough to get his arms in a better position to lever himself out. With a silent heave, he lifted himself up and scrambled onto the floor of the closet. Careful to be silent, he opened the door into the room. Marti was engrossed in painting the wall near the ceiling, her back to him. She was standing on a paint-splattered tarp using a paint roller on a long rod. She was singing along to the radio and hadn't heard him. He hated the pop music that she liked. He preferred rock like Muse or Breaking Benjamin, or even harder stuff, like Disturbed. Struggling to hold back a snicker, Randy snuck up behind his sister and said, "Boo!"

Marti screamed and dropped the paint roller. It splattered paint on her legs and she swore. She spun around as her little brother made a run for the bedroom door. "I'm gonna kill you, you little rat," she snarled.

He ran as fast as he could, but she finally cornered him in his room upstairs. He was laughing so hard that he could barely breathe. His laughter was infectious, and Marti joined in. She wrapped her arms around him and gave him a harsh rub with her knuckles on the top of his head.

"Ouch!" he shrieked.

"You deserve it!" She probably thought he deserved more than that, but they'd learned long ago to avoid leaving bruises.

When Marti returned to painting, Randy went to the garage and grabbed the folding stepladder and took it to the rec room. He laid on his stomach at the edge of the hole in the floor and lowered the stepladder down. It was just tall enough that he would easily be able to pull it back out when he was done. With the ladder positioned, he climbed down under the house and scurried over to the hatch door under his aunt's room. He replaced the hatch. He had to stifle a laugh. Having a secret entrance was going to be fun.

He put the overalls, shirt, hat, and gun in the second garbage bag and hurried out of the crawl space to hide the stuff in his closet before his mom got home.

He filled up three garbage bags with the debris he found under the house and was just bringing the last bag up into the rec room, when Cindy arrived home with new supplies and lunch. He pulled the stepladder out after him and set it in the far corner of the rec room.

"Find anything interesting under the house?" she asked.

"Nope, just cans and wrappers and odds and ends," he said. He felt the guilty flush in his face. "Nothing good."

Cindy sighed. "I guess it was too much to hope that you'd find something to make us rich."

They ate their lunch on the front porch. Randy stood, playing with the ever-present soccer ball with his feet while he ate. He saw his mom watching him, a puzzled expression on her face. He turned away and sat down on the porch step, keeping his back to her. *I really suck at lying.*

Chapter 5
August 5, 2011
Day 5

"Oh, my God," a voice whispered in her ear. "Why are you doing this to us?" Cindy turned her head and saw a woman with wide, terrified eyes. Cindy looked around, confused. She was in a room about the same size as the rec room, but there was an air hockey table, a dartboard, and a piano. She looked back at the woman. She was in her forties, just a few wrinkles around her brown eyes and no gray hair yet in her black hair. The woman stared past her. Cindy turned and saw a shadowy figure in dark clothing with a hat pulled low over his eyes. The man was holding a gun.

"No!" she screamed.

"Mom! Are you okay?" Marti asked.

Cindy sat up, the sun blinding her. She'd fallen asleep next to Marti on the blanket that her daughter had spread out on the backyard lawn.

"Just a dream," she said. "Guess I'm more exhausted than I thought." Even with the kids working every day and her friends coming over in the evenings, the twelve-hour days were getting to her. But they needed to be out of the apartment in just a couple days.

Marti stretched and yawned. "I wanted to work on my tan, but I fell asleep, too. I was having a great dream. I'm excited about school starting and making new friends here."

As they walked into the house from the backyard, Randy burst in the front door. His face was flushed with excitement. "I gotta play roller hockey with the guys at the park. I played goalie. I've gotta find my skates before next week."

"Roller hockey goalie? That's dangerous. Where will you get the gear?"

"I guess they get the stuff from the city's Parks Department. Everything but the skates."

Cindy nodded, happy that her son had already made friends and would be getting exercise with them rather than just playing computer games. "I've got some good news: tomorrow morning you both can sleep in. I'll be here with the contractors. I'd like you to get things ready at the apartment for the movers. They're scheduled to arrive at noon."

As Cindy expected, the idea of being able to sleep in brought a smile to Marti's face. But she wasn't prepared for the look that crossed Randy's face. She wasn't sure, but for the briefest moment, he looked worried.

What the hell's going on with him? What's he hiding? Cindy hated being suspicious, but she remembered being a teen and getting into trouble.

* * *

The next morning, Cindy arrived at the house before seven, only minutes before the carpet layers arrived. They started with the upstairs. One group of men took out the old carpets, followed by the other who put the new carpet in. The last room they did was the living room. One of the workers called out, "Wow! What the hell happened in here?"

Cindy walked into the room and saw a dark brown stain covering the center of the room's floorboards. She knelt down beside it. "I don't know," she said.

"Looks like blood," another of the workers said with a heavy Spanish accent. He backed away making the sign of the cross.

To make a stain that large, it had to have been a significant amount of blood or whatever. Cindy felt a chill down her spine. Whatever it was, it was old. "Don't worry about it. Just install the carpet as planned," she said in a low voice.

The foreman stepped up to where she was squatting. He looked at the stain closely and then motioned to the workers. "Let me see the carpet and the padding you just pulled out of here."

The Hispanic worker led the foreman outside. Cindy followed.

The foreman examined the old carpet and pad. "No sign of blood on the carpet, but there's a stain on the pad." He pointed out a faint brownish outline on the underside of the pad. "I'd guess the blood's pretty old. Looks like water seeped through the carpet and padding when it was being cleaned. The staining on the boards underneath was picked up by the pad." He shrugged.

Cindy was partially relieved. "So you think this is fairly old?"

"The carpet looks like it's at least a decade old, probably more than that, going by the style and workmanship."

Even if the stain was old, how did it get there? Cindy stayed behind, looking at the carpet while the foreman ushered the workers back. The Hispanic man was reluctant to return, and crossed himself again before stepping through the front door.

The crunch of a leaf made Cindy jump. She spun around and found a teenage boy standing a few feet away.

"Hi, Mrs. Fairbank? I'm Peter Wilson."

So this was the neighbor boy that had caught her daughter's attention. She could see why Marti was smitten. He was all Marti had talked about over the last few days. A guy this good looking was going to be trouble.

"Nice to meet you, Peter. I've heard a lot about you. Thanks for making Marti feel comfortable in the new neighborhood."

"I'm glad she's moving in. I mean, you're all moving in."

"She tells me you're a pretty good gardener."

Peter took a deep breath and stood up straighter. "My uncle has a gardening business. I've been able to work with him. I'm hoping you might want to hire me to work on your yard. Marti said you might need some help."

"She did, did she? Let's walk around, and you can tell me what you think you could do."

The two walked around the front yard and into the back. The entire back yard was enclosed by a six foot wooden fence with a gate that faced the side street, Grove Road. There was a magnificent pine tree that cast a beautiful fir scent throughout the yard. Peter suggested clearing out the ivy under the tree and putting in a small rock garden with a fountain. Cindy liked the idea. A table and chairs, maybe a couple chaise lounges. It would make a peaceful retreat area.

Cindy mentioned that her aunt was a rose fanatic, and Peter indicated an area along the side fencing that got just the right amount of sunlight for roses.

They worked out the details, including how much she would pay him and shook hands on the deal. He would start work immediately.

Cindy watched him leave with mixed feelings. Good looking, smart, creative, and a head for business. He'd been polite, although a bit stiff in his attempt to impress her. Even though he was the type of guy that she'd like her daughter to date, she wasn't ready to lose her little girl to a boyfriend. Marti had gone on a few dates — school dances and parties—but Cindy had kept a tight rein on her. She wanted to see her daughter grow into a woman, except she was terrified to let go.

* * *

Shortly after noon, the movers arrived at the apartment. Randy noticed that his sister was staring at the foreman. He was huge, all muscle. He wondered if girls would ever look at him like that.

Marti saw his gaze and smacked him on the back of the head. "Come on, slowpoke, get a move on," she said. "Mom just got here. We'd better look like we've been working hard all morning."

Randy helped his mom and sister fill their minivan with boxes while the movers took the furniture to the truck. He was amazed that their whole apartment fit in the truck. It took less than an hour to clear it out. It was still weird to know that this was the last time he would see the place.

On the way to the house, Randy's nerves were jangling, and he shifted in his seat, unable to get comfortable. Would his stash be safe? What if the workers discovered the gun?

When they arrived at their new home, Cindy backed the van into the garage, and the moving truck pulled up in front of the house, blocking the driveway. Randy leaped out of the minivan and as he got to the door from the garage to the house, his mom's voice called him back. "Take a box, Randy!" He dashed back, pulled a box labeled with his name, and stumbled his way up to his room. His heart was beating fast as he opened the closet door. The floor of the closet had been carpeted, along with the rest of the room. He didn't see the bag. He dropped to his knees and finally saw it. It was pushed back into the corner in the shadows. He'd chosen a dark brown carpet, and the garbage bag was camouflaged by the dark. He grabbed it and rifled through it. Everything was still there, even the gun. He let go of the breath he'd been holding and sat back against the wall, relieved. Then another thought hit him: if they'd put carpet in his closet, had they done the same in Gloria's room? They might have covered up the hidden entrance to the crawl space.

Taking two steps at a time, he raced downstairs and sprinted to her room. He threw open her closet. *Damn it, they'd put carpet in here, too.* But as he looked closer, he saw they'd cut around the crawl space opening. As he ran his hand over it, he found a tiny handle. He yanked on it, and the cover came up. He held his breath and didn't move as he heard his mother and sister pass by the room in the hallway. He waited for a few seconds before he gently put the cover back in place. *Perfect.* It would still be his secret, provided that Gloria didn't notice it. He didn't think she would.

* * *

It was finally time for Cindy to share the gift she'd been hiding.

The movers had left, and while the kids were unpacking their rooms, she installed the door to the backyard on the existing frame. It was later in the afternoon than she had hoped, but they'd worked hard. They deserved this treat. She called them down to check out the new door.

"What's this?" Randy asked, pointing to the lower half of the door.

Cindy slid the cover off to reveal a rectangular hole in the door with a swinging plastic flap that snapped into place with magnets. "You want your puppy to have a way to go outside to play, don't you?" Cindy replied.

"Puppy!" both kids yelled.

"If you aren't too tired, we can go to the animal shelter." In answer, Marti and Randy ran to the van.

The Humane Society had dozens of dogs, and each pair of eyes bore into Cindy's heart. But when Marti saw the male basset hound/spaniel mix, she announced, "It's a done deal. This puppy is coming home with us."

Randy was standing down the hall, admiring a female husky mix, and the two kids started bickering. Cindy looked at the paperwork on the puppies. Both dogs were around six months old, fixed, and supposedly already housebroken. She couldn't eliminate either dog on those criteria. The adoption specialist suggested that they take both dogs to the play area.

The basset's white legs were short, typical of the breed, but his legs and tail had the long fringes characteristic of a Brittany Spaniel. His long brown ears flopped wildly as he ran around the grass. Randy tossed a ball to the husky, and she leaped high in the air to catch it with her mouth. She pranced around the yard as though she was doing a victory dance before coming back to drop the ball at Randy's feet. Her one blue eye and one green eye stared at the ball with the intensity that only a dog can match, waiting for the boy to throw it again. But as he started to reach down to grab it, the basset jumped in, snagged the ball, and ran away. The chase was on. The husky caught the basset, and the collision sent both puppies rolling. The ball was momentarily forgotten by the dogs as they playfully wrestled until Marti grabbed it. Both dogs turned their attention to her. She threw the ball hard, and it hit the chain link fence and bounced into the shrubs that lined the edge of the play area. The husky ran back and forth in front of the shrubs, but the basset followed his nose and squeezed into the bushes.

"And he finds the ball!" Marti exclaimed. "My little detective, you have a new name: Sherlock."

"Yeah, well, after the tackle this dog did," said Randy with his arms wrapped around the husky's neck, "we'll have to find a good warrior's name for her."

Cindy stood back, watching her kids' interactions with the dogs and couldn't help but feel a warmth of happiness mixed with worry. The husky was already strong and would continue to grow. The dogs were going to need some good training. But she couldn't shake the feeling that both dogs were meant to join the family. They both felt *right*. It wasn't simply that she was already falling in love with them, but a deeper, intuitive feeling that they were an important for her family's safety. "We'll take both dogs," she said to the adoption specialist.

Chapter 6
August 19, 2011
Day 19

"What movies did you bring?" Randy said to Peter as a greeting as he entered the front door.

"*Friday the 13th, Halloween H2o, Saw IV*, and *Fast Five*," Peter said, distracted by Marti who just entered the living room wearing jean shorts and a tight blue crop top that showed her flat abs.

"Cool!" Randy said, not noticing his sister's entrance. "Lee and Steve will love these!"

"I can't believe you've got all the work done on the house and completely unpacked," Peter said to Marti, already forgetting Randy. "It's only been, what, three weeks? We had boxes for months last time we moved."

"Mom's like a slave driver," Marti said, slipping into his arms. "But the good side is that now that it's all done, and we showed her we're *responsible*, she agreed to let us stay here alone instead of going with her to San Diego to get Aunt Gloria." She stepped out of his embrace and pulled on his hand. "Let me show you what I did in Gloria's room."

"You know it's not Gloria's room I want to see," Peter whispered and shot a glance at her little brother. Randy was still engrossed in the movie selection.

"Oh, God, don't tell me you're one of those that wants to see where the Fremonts were murdered," she replied with a scowl as she led him in the direction of the downstairs bedroom.

"No, I've seen that room. Which room is yours?"

Marti opened the door to Gloria's room. They stepped inside the room, and Peter looked around. "Wow," he breathed. "Just wow. You did all this painting?" He moved over to the window to look closer at the rose vines painted around the window.

She stepped up behind him and put her arms around his waist. She rested her head on his back, his black T-shirt soft against her cheek. "It was kinda strange," she said. "It was like I was compelled to paint these roses. But it was fun."

He turned in her arms and pulled her into a hug. "You're amazing."

"When did you see the rec room?" she said, her voice muffled by his chest. The top of her head just barely met his chin.

"About a year after the murders. It was seriously twisted. The room was blocked off. I guess because the floor was torn up."

Marti shivered. "Is it just me or does it feel cold in here?"

"You're cold," Peter said. "Why don't we go up to your room?"

The dogs' barking alerted them that Randy's friends had arrived, and she made her decision. "Come on, let's go up before the guys see us."

They slipped down the hallway, peeking into the living room as they passed. Sherlock saw them and broke away from the boys to follow them up the stairs. As she closed her bedroom door behind them, Peter murmured in her ear, "I like your room a lot better than Gloria's." He moved past her desk to the window, nearly tripping over Sherlock. "What a great view. Must be *some* gardener you've got," he said, an impish smile lighting his face.

"Yeah, I like to sit up here and watch him working his ass off. Especially when he takes his shirt off."

"Oh really? Perhaps you'd like to see that up close?"

* * *

The revving car engines and wreck scenes in *Fast Five* shook the floor of the living room. The boys felt like they were in a theater with the big screen TV and surround sound system. Steve and Lee sat on opposite ends of the reclining couch like bookends. The two boys had been friends since elementary school and looked enough alike with cropped brown hair, brown eyes, and lanky limbs to be mistaken as twins. As the credits rolled, Randy held up the other movie selections. "Wanna watch another one before I order pizza?"

"How about we go outside and kick the soccer ball around," Steve suggested. "And by the way, Randy, why'd you need me to bring mine? What the hell happened to your ball? You lose everything."

Randy shrugged. "No clue. I'm positive I put it in my closet last night when I went to bed, but this morning it wasn't there."

"Xena probably took off with it," Lee said.

Shaking his head, Randy said, "No, the closet door was closed."

"Can we check out the rec room instead?" Lee asked. "I want to see where the family was killed."

"Yeah!" Randy hurried towards the rec room, the husky, Xena, right on his heels. He opened the door to the rec room and stepped inside. He described how the room was torn up when they moved in and how much work he and his mom had done. "But my favorite part," he said, "is this." He moved to the corner of the room and knelt down next to the new crawl space trap door. "Since there were a bunch of holes in the floor, I put this in."

"Yeah, right," Lee snickered as he sat down on the weight bench. "I'll bet you did it. All by yourself."

Randy flushed. "Mom helped. Her dad used to be in construction and taught her, so now she's teaching me. Dad was in construction, too, before he..." Randy felt tears threatening and turned away. He took a deep breath, and with his back still to his friends, he said, "What do you guys know about what happened in here?"

"I don't know much except what Steve told me," Lee said. He looked expectantly at Steve who was sitting sideways on the recumbent stationary bike.

Steve looked down. "I'm not supposed to talk about it." He tilted his head and said in a conspiratorial voice, "But I've heard about another murder in the 80s."

"No way! Others were killed here, too?" Randy's eyes were wide, and when he looked at Lee, he saw his friend nodding his head.

"So who's ordering the pizza?" a deep voice said from behind them. Randy spun around. Peter and Marti were standing in the doorway. "How about if we order the pizza, and while we wait for it to arrive, I'll tell you what I know about what happened in this room."

Marti rolled her eyes. "Really? I'll go call for the pizza while you...*boys*...talk about dead people." She huffed and left the room.

Peter watched her leave the room with a lopsided smile on his face. He moved over to the window and rested his tall frame against the sill. "I overheard my mom talking to the babysitter about the Fremonts a couple weeks after they were killed. So that was in 2008."

"Wait," Lee interjected with a snorting laugh, "that was three years ago, so you were, what, thirteen? How come you had a babysitter?"

Peter glared at the younger boy. "Not for me, stupid. For my little brother. I was going out with friends and my mom had to work." He walked across to the door and peered out, looking for Marti. With her nowhere in sight, he turned to the boys and said, "The oldest girl in the family was Whitney." He whistled softly. "What a looker! She was about three years older than me and had babysat us years before. She still babysat my little brother sometimes, the lucky kid." He moved back to his perch at the window, and his voice took on a storytelling lilt. "So check this out. Whitney had stayed home while the rest of the family went on vacation. They were supposed to be gone for the weekend, but she had some big school project to do and couldn't leave. The father was some big guy in the fire department and got called back from vacation for an emergency. But he never showed up and didn't answer the phone." Peter stopped and looked closely at the boys. Each was wide-eyed, leaning forward, intent on every word of the story. "The fire department sent someone to the house to get the father. No one answered the door, so he went around to the back of the house, looking in the windows. When he got to this window..." He stopped and patted the window sill. "He saw the whole family." He dropped his voice to a whisper. "All dead. Except Whitney. They never found her."

"Dude, no way," Randy breathed. He looked over at Steve. "Is that what your dad told you?"

Steve nodded solemnly. "Pretty much, but..."

Peter snorted a laugh. "Oh right. Your dad didn't want you to talk about it. That's because the police screwed up and shot some homeless dude and then said he was the killer."

Steve jumped to his feet. "Did not! That was a good shoot! They found some of Whitney's stuff in the guy's tent."

"Yeah, well, since the guy's dead, there's no way to prove it."

"So if it wasn't him, who do *you* think did it?" Randy asked.

"I bet it was a drug lord," Lee interjected. "You hear about those guys killing whole families as examples."

Steve scoffed. "That's just in the movies."

"Bullshit," Lee retorted. "I've seen it on the news, too."

"My money's on the guy across the street." The three younger boys looked at Peter. "He's pretty creepy...watching everyone out his front window. Whenever I'm in the front yard, I can feel his eyes on me."

"The old guy?" Steve asked. "Nah, he's too old."

"How old is too old to shoot people?" Peter retorted. "He looks like he's in pretty good shape to me. Anyway, the guy creeps me out."

Randy looked to Steve. "What do you think?"

Steve was silent, his eyes distant. Finally he answered. "My guess... I don't think I could pin it on one particular person. There's a few in the neighborhood who're kinda strange. It could be any of them."

"Your dad's a cop," Randy said. "Who does he think it is?"

The doorbell rang and broke up the conversation, keeping Steve from answering.

* * *

Peter took one of the pizzas and followed Marti up to her room with Sherlock dancing around their feet hoping for handouts. When they'd come up to her room earlier, he'd felt like someone was watching them. He'd pulled away from her and suggested playing cards or a board game. He'd seen the relief on her face, too. Was she getting the same eerie feeling? Or was he moving too fast? They'd sprawled on her bed and played gin rummy for a penny a point. After two hours, he owed her more than two dollars. While they were playing cards, the creepy feeling had disappeared, but now it was back. As they sat on her bed again with the pizza, plates, and napkins between them, he started to get that feeling again. He couldn't decide if it was malicious or just disapproval, but he was getting more uncomfortable. The air felt heavy, ominous.

"Are you okay?" Marti asked as she put a slice of pepperoni pizza on her plate.

"Yeah, but the murders here bother me." He took a mouthful of pizza and waited to speak until he was finished. "It's fun to scare your brother and his friends, but the house is freaky." He met her eyes. "Do you feel anything strange here?"

"No, not really. It's gross that people were killed. I was really pissed when I found out. I couldn't believe Mom bought the house."

"Me and a couple friends broke in here one night, before the house was first put up for sale. About two years ago. The murders were about a year old by then. We thought it'd be cool to see. The power wasn't on, and it was dark. We just had our flashlights, and one of the guys fell through the floor in the rec room."

"Was he okay?" she asked in alarm.

"A few bruises, but he was okay. We all laughed about it, but I couldn't wait to get out. I felt like someone was watching us. I still don't like being in this house. The feeling is still there, and it gets stronger the longer I'm here."

Marti leaned over and kissed him. "Even now?"

He moved the pizza debris out of the way and pushed her onto her back. He pressed his body against hers and nudged her blouse up, his hands getting closer to her breasts. She moaned encouragement. He had never gone this far with a girl, and his groin stirred. Suddenly, he felt the hair on the back of his neck stand up. He pulled away and looked around the room, certain someone was there. Nobody was, just Sherlock lying on the floor near the end of the bed, impatiently eyeing the pizza remains.

"What's wrong?" Marti asked.

The mood was broken for him. "I'm sorry. I just can't stay here. Let's go over to my house."

Chapter 7
August 19, 2011
Day 19

The lights were out, and two flashlights were on the living room table, providing the only light. Steve, Lee, and Randy sat on the rec room floor in a circle. Xena settled down with her head on Randy's lap, and he entwined his hand in the thick fur around her neck. Sherlock was waiting at the front door for Marti to return from Peter's house.

In a low voice, Steve said, "So back in the early 80s–"

"Okay, so wait, how do we even know you're telling the truth?" Lee asked. "I mean your dad's like forty, right? Even I can do the math. He wouldn't have been there."

"No, dummy, cops always share stories about their cases. My dad's FTO–"

"FTO?" Randy said. "What the hell is that?"

Steve sighed and glared at Randy. "Field Training Officer. It's the guy that shows the rookie cops the ropes. You know? Like in *Training Day?*"

"Oh, right! Okay."

"Anyway, my dad's FTO was one of the cops that responded. It seriously freaked him out. Two kids and the babysitter had been sliced up."

Randy's jaw dropped open, his eyes wide. "No way! Here? In this house?"

Steve nodded. "The Eriksons had three kids. I don't remember their names, but one was a little girl, and two boys. The oldest boy was about our age. He was always in trouble, getting into fights. Oh, Randy, you'll like this. The little brother was just in preschool, but was always playing with his soccer ball."

"Sweet!"

"Then there was the babysitter. Suzy Dudley."

Lee snickered. "You remember her name, but not the kids?"

"Hell yeah, after what happened to her... So the parents go out to the movies–"

Lee interrupted again. "Did they *really* go to a movie?"

"How the fuck would I know that? And who cares, anyway?"

"Well, you know, maybe they're the ones who killed the kids."

Exasperated, Steve asked, "Why would they kill their own kids?"

"Maybe they don't like them," Lee answered. "Ya know, they think having kids was a mistake. A lot of parents hate their kids – beat them up, kill them." He muttered, "I wouldn't mind killing my parents."

"Dude, you are seriously fucked up." Steve took a deep breath and continued, his voice taking on a dark storytelling timbre. "Okay, so, it's a hot night and all the doors are open. The oldest kid is in the backyard with his little brother when this tall guy comes in through the back gate. The guy is big, wearing dark clothes, but a hat hides most of his face. All the kid can see are the whites of his eyes and the knife and a menacing sneer. He can't move; he's too terrified. The man moves closer and closer, not saying a word, but the kid can feel his doom approaching, and he's powerless to do anything. He picks up his little brother and turns to run when the knife slams into his back." Steve slammed his fist down on the table, pantomiming the stabbing. Lee and Randy jump. One of the flashlights tipped over and spun to the edge of the table by Steve, sending shadows swirling around the room. "He screams in terrible pain and drops the little boy and falls to his hands and knees. He uses the last of his strength to kick backwards and hits the killer's leg. He hears a grunt, but then the knife slams down again, this time into his neck. He can't move, the pain is too much, and he can't feel the rest of his body, just the excruciating pain, and the life spilling out of him. His blood is spreading around him in a red, sticky, hot pool. The little brother runs into the house, and the guy follows, slowly, taking his time. The little girl is—"

"Wait." This time it's Randy who interrupted. "How do you know what he was thinking and stuff?"

Steve picked up the fallen flashlight and held it below his chin, giving his face a ghastly shadow. He put on an evil grin. "Because the kid lived. For a little while. He died in the hospital, but he was able to describe the man. And what happens next they figured out from the bodies and the blood. Forensics, you know? And stop interrupting.

"So the killer follows the boy into the house, and finds the little girl in the hallway." He points toward the back door. "He picks her up by her neck with one hand, and with a huge swing of his arm, he jams the knife into her stomach. She's so small the blade goes all the way through her. He drops her on the floor and goes after Suzy. He finds her at the front door. She struggles with him, but he keeps stabbing her. Again and again. Then he guts her. When they found her body, she was propped with her back against the wall by the front door. Her hands were on her stomach like she was trying to hold everything in, but it was all spilling out anyway. Her insides were all over the floor. The first cops that responded slipped in the mess."

"Gross!" Lee made a face.

"No way!" Randy said.

"The blood trail showed that the killer went upstairs after the little boy. There was a huge puddle of pee under the boy's bed, and it looked like the boy was dragged out from under the bed, through the pee. There was more blood there."

"Was he dead?" Lee squeaked. "What did his body look like?"

"That's the thing. There was blood in the room, but the boy was gone. He's never been seen again."

There was a tremor in Randy's voice. "Um, which room was his?"

"Yours."

* * *

At 9:45 Lee's cell phone rang, and Randy paused *Halloween H2o*. It was Lee's mom. After speaking for a moment, he turned to his friends with wide eyes. "Uh oh, guys, we gotta bounce. My parents are already on their way home. They'll be at Steve's house in a couple minutes to pick me up!" Since Lee's parents hadn't met Randy's family, he wasn't supposed to go to Randy's house yet. They thought he was at Steve's. Steve and Lee bolted out the front door.

Randy tried to finish the movie by himself, but sitting alone in the dark seemed to make the movie even scarier. When he turned the TV off, the room went totally dark. He reached out a shaking hand towards the lamp on the table next to him and nearly knocked it over. He turned it on and slumped in his chair. The table lamp didn't provide much light, and as he looked around the room, he saw too many places where a killer could be hiding. He suddenly just wanted to be in his room. As he moved through the house, he turned on every light, forcing the shadows back. He wished his sister was home. He paused in the doorway to his room and thought about the story Steve had told. The little boy was missing, assumed to have been killed in this very room. Randy shuddered. Were Steve's and Peter's stories true? Or were they just trying to scare him? He sat down at his computer to search the Internet for anything he could find on the house. He found an old website with a blog that gave some gruesome details of crimes that had happened in Santa Clara. Some of the posts described some murders that had happened in his neighborhood, but didn't specify the address. He was just about to close the site when a name popped out at him: Suzy Dudley. Wasn't that the name of the teenager? The hair on his arms stood up as he read the story. It was pretty close to what Steve had said, but no address was listed. Instead, it said the house was on the corner of Almond Way and Grove Road–just like his house. There were more details about the victims:

"Chuck told the police he'd tried to fight back and thought his little brother, Aaron, had gotten away, but he could tell from the screams in the house that his baby sister, Barbie, just seven years old, hadn't escaped. The last words he whispered to his parents before he died were, "Find Aaron. He had to make it. Please find him."

Randy's breath caught. What had happened to the little boy that shared this room? A cold chill made the hair on his neck stand up, and he spun around in his chair. No one was there, just Xena at the end of his bed, watching him with tired eyes, and Sherlock sleeping in oblivion on his pillow. He scrolled down the list of blog posts and pulled one up about some teenagers who were killed in the late 60s during the construction of a housing development. A muffled bang made him jump. The dogs leapt off the bed and dashed down the stairs. Randy followed. He heard the dog door rattle as each dog plowed through at full speed. He stepped out to the backyard and spotted the dogs at the side fence.

The latch on the gate wasn't closed, and as the dogs pawed at the gate, it clicked shut. Randy wished he was tall enough to see over the fence; he was too scared to open the gate. It was a warm night, but he was shivering. Scenes from the movie ran through his head. A terrible thought hit him: *while I've been outside at the gate, could someone have gone around to the front of the house and entered through the front door?*

Randy ran through the house with the dogs trailing him. He stopped dead in his tracks in the front room.

The front door was ajar.

He jumped forward and slammed it shut, throwing the deadbolt home. He tried to remember if he'd actually seen the door close when Steve and Lee ran out. It was possible that they hadn't shut it completely. The air was still, so it couldn't have been a breeze blowing the door open. With his hand still on the deadbolt, he worried that someone might be in the house with him. Should he run out of the house? Maybe go to the Wilsons and get Marti? He wished she had a cell phone or that he had the Wilsons' phone number. Should he call the police? Or go to Steve's house and get his dad, the cop? He didn't want to look like a baby. He crossed the room and grabbed a fire poker. He held it in front of him, ready to jab or club an intruder.

"Okay," he said aloud. His voice in the quiet made him jump. He looked at Xena and Sherlock. "We need to find out if anyone is in the house." He flicked the lights on in the kitchen and stuck his head in. The room was clear. His eyes settled on the walk-in pantry. What a great place to hide, he thought. Shaking, he crossed the kitchen and slowly reached out to grasp the door knob. As his hand gripped it, a loud bump made him jump and spin around. The noise had come from upstairs. He left the kitchen and headed up the stairs. As he turned at the midpoint landing, his soccer ball bounced down past him and came to a rest at the bottom of the stairs. He turned and fled to the front room. He fumbled with the lock on the front door and jumped when the phone rang. Marti had left the portable phone on the end table after ordering the pizza, just inches away. He grabbed the phone and went out onto the front porch.

"Dude, we made it just in time." It was Steve. "His parents never suspected a thing. But they were kinda pissed–"

Randy broke in. "I think someone's in the house!"

"What? Man, you're just freaked out by the movies. I thought you had more balls than that. Stop being a pussy."

"No way, dude. You know my soccer ball was missing? It just re-appeared. It came rolling down the stairs."

"Really? That's awesome! Ya know what? The ball was probably at the top of the stairs all along. Maybe we just had a small earthquake or something. That made it roll."

"I didn't feel an earthquake." Randy remembered from science class that the Bay Area had tiny quakes all the time that were too small to be felt. Maybe Steve was right. Logically it was a good argument, but inside, Randy didn't believe it. *I would have seen the ball if it had been at the top of the stairs earlier.*

Still shaking, he turned the phone off and dropped it in his pocket. Fighting back tears, he took a deep breath and said aloud to himself, "I'm not a pussy, dammit. If someone's messing with me, they're gonna pay."

Grasping the fireplace poker again, he slowly went toward the stairs. Resting at the bottom was his soccer ball. Randy stared at it, afraid that it would start moving again on its own. He pressed himself against the wall as far away from the ball as he could and slipped onto the stairs. As he went up the stairs, he stayed close to the wall to avoid the squeaky spots in the center of the steps. By the time he was a few steps from the top, his heart was thundering in his ears. He stopped before he rounded the corner into the hall. If someone was on the other side of the wall with a weapon, he'd expect Randy to be standing and would aim for the body. He knelt down so his head was near the floor and peered around the corner into the hallway. The only light in the hall was from the street light in front of the house, shining through his bedroom window and into the hallway. He didn't see anyone — or anything. On shaking legs, he stood up, took a deep breath, and got ready to make a run for his room.

Something touched his leg.

The breath he was holding escaped in a scream. He bolted towards his room, but tripped over the husky. Xena pounced on him, licking his face. Relief battled with annoyance and he pushed the dog away and went into his room. Xena followed him, while Sherlock sat down in the hallway. Randy closed the bedroom door and leaned against it, taking deep breaths. He looked at his closet door, and remembered the gun. The gun! That was much better than the poker. He moved to the front of the closet and reached his hand out towards the handle and stopped. *Could someone be hiding in there like the boogeyman Michael Myers from* Halloween*?*

He willed his hand to open the door, but it didn't move. He backed away from the door until his legs bumped against the edge of his bed. He dove into his bed and pulled the covers over his head, the fireplace poker next to his body. He laid there, too afraid to move, but he knew that hiding in a bed wasn't going to help him. Minutes ticked by with no sounds of movement in the house. He started to relax, but he couldn't get the appearance of the soccer ball out of his mind. Where had it been? What made it roll down the stairs? He really didn't think there'd been a quake. Wouldn't it have had to be pretty strong to make the ball roll? And he'd heard a loud bump, then nothing until he'd made it halfway up the stairs. If the ball had started rolling down the stairs when he was in the kitchen, it would have reached the bottom long before he'd gotten there. The hair stood up on his neck. *Who made it roll down the stairs?* His chest was tight with fear, and he could barely breathe.

The minutes ticked by, each taking a lifetime. Randy poked his head out from under his blanket when he heard muffled curses outside. He looked at the clock: 11:10. Had less than a half hour gone by? He hoped it was Marti returning, but what if it was someone else trying to break in? He gripped the poker tighter as Xena went to the bedroom door and whined. Randy heard Sherlock's heavy feet pounding down the stairs. Relief went through him when he heard his sister crooning to her basset hound.

There was a bang, and Marti swore loudly. She came up the stairs and paused outside his bedroom door. "I'm home," she said through the closed door. "And I found your damn ball."

He tried to sound irritated, not relieved. "Did you lock the front door?"

"Of course. Thanks for not leaving the porch light on for me, jerk," she replied.

"Yeah, well, you should have turned it on as you left," he shot back. Feeling more secure with her home, he went to his closet. In a fluid move, he yanked the door open and jabbed the poker in. No one was there. He sank to his knees in relief and grabbed the plastic bag. He wrapped his hand around the butt of the gun hidden there and took it back to his bed. He felt much better with a weapon. As he drifted off to sleep, he wished that he'd shown his new friends the gun. They would have been impressed.

Chapter 8
August 21, 2011
Day 21

"I'm sure you're going to love your new home, Gloria," Cindy said to her aunt as she pulled the car onto Almond Way. She slowed down to a crawl as she approached the house so Gloria could take it in. The painting contractors had done a good job replacing the damaged siding, and the color scheme of light gray with dark blue trim and burgundy accents was striking, better than she'd envisioned. The new roof of dark gray composite shingle was a perfect finishing touch.

Peter had worked hard in the yard. The hedges were trimmed, and the flower beds had a variety of colorful plants that he'd wrangled out of his uncle's supply. He had killed off most of the dandelions in the lawn and had put more grass seed down. There wasn't much he could do about the crabgrass except to keep cutting it back and pulling the runners.

When the garage door rolled up, Randy ran out to the garage to greet them. Behind him, Marti stood in the doorway between the garage and house trying to look bored.

Xena and Sherlock pushed past her to see what all the excitement was about. Randy and Marti had been training the dogs over the last two weeks, and even though their tails were wagging their whole bodies, they didn't jump up on Gloria. They waited impatiently for her to greet them.

As Cindy expected, Gloria loved her new home. She was taken with all the effort they had put into her room. With her finger, Gloria traced the rose vines that Marti had painted around the window. With tears in her eyes, she said, "I love roses."

"Marti remembered that you always had roses at your house when she was little, so she painted them here for you," Cindy said.

Marti slipped her arm around Gloria's waist and hugged her tightly. "I just want to be sure that every morning when you wake up, you see the flowers and know that we love you."

"I picked out the chair." Randy pointed out the brown, overstuffed recliner, not wanting to be ignored.

"Well, then, let me check this chair out." She sat down and ran her hands over the soft microfiber upholstery.

"Look, the feet kick up," Randy said. He showed her where the release lever was. Her feet popped up as soon as she tugged on it.

"You picked out a good one, Randy," Gloria said as she nestled into the chair. "I may never get out of it!"

After inspecting the bathroom, they moved on to the rec room. Light was streaming in through the windows giving the room a warm glow, so different from the feeling it had harbored when Cindy first saw the room. She'd been dreaming often about this room and the woman begging for help, her eyes wide with desperation. And then the tall man with a gun.

"Look at all of these gadgets!" Gloria exclaimed.

Marti spoke up. "Mom checked with her doctor's office to find out what the best exercise would be for you. We're hoping Mom will get back in shape."

"Oh, come on now, I'm not that bad." Cindy grimaced. "Do you want to set up a daily time to exercise in here? We can watch movies as we work out."

"I think that's a fine idea," Gloria said. She turned to the children. "You know, I used to be a pretty good ballroom dancer. I'd love to teach you some steps."

Randy looked mortified, and Marti cracked a smile, more at Randy's discomfort than the thought of dancing with Peter.

They crossed the hall to the stairway and went up to see the upstairs bedrooms. When they got to Cindy's room, Gloria elbowed her and whispered, "Perfect for entertaining."

Cindy felt a flush go through her at the thought. "And the same could be said for you and your new room," Cindy whispered.

Gloria linked her elbow with Cindy's and said, "Hmm, maybe we can go out hunk hunting together."

"Hunk hunting? Really? I can't believe you said that!"

The kids helped Gloria get settled into her new room, and Cindy went to the back patio to start the gas grill. While it was warming up, she sat at the table and took in the beauty of the yard. Peter had done a fabulous job with the plants. She turned back to face the house. The only area that she still disliked was the entrance to the crawl space. She looked at the doors and tried to think of what she could do with them to make them more attractive. There was cement surrounding them, so putting in plants wouldn't help. Perhaps potted plants? Watering them would be a pain, though. Sighing, she went into the house to get the meat.

She poked her head into Gloria's room. All three were busy setting up the room and unpacking. As she went back into the kitchen, a thought hit her: Marti had done a beautiful job with the detailed painting around Gloria's window. Maybe she'd like to paint a mural on the crawl space doors. Humming to herself, Cindy took the meat outside and put it on the grill. The sizzling sound and the smoke always lightened her spirit. She turned and looked at the crawl space doors and gasped, her heart stopped.

One of the doors was not fully seated in position. She was positive that they'd been flush minutes before.

Chapter 9
August 29, 2011
Day 29

"Cindy? Can we talk for a minute?" Gloria took Cindy's elbow and steered her away from the sink where she was finishing up drying the breakfast dishes to a chair at the kitchen table.

Alarmed, Cindy said, "What's wrong? Are you feeling okay?" This was the first time since Gloria had arrived the previous week that she seemed anything less than completely happy.

Gloria nodded as she sat down and picked up her coffee mug. "Something feels off...I don't know how to really explain it." She noticed the concern in Cindy's eyes and continued. "Don't worry, it's not about my health. It's about the house. I just feel something... wrong. The dogs feel it, too, especially Sherlock. He's the one that drew my attention to it. He sometimes jumps up from where he's sleeping at the foot of my bed and spins around, like he's trying to find something...elusive. I don't really know how to describe his actions. Then the dreams started." She dropped her gaze to the table. "I bet you think I'm just losing my mind. I swear it's not the Alzheimer's."

"No. Funny you should mention dreams," Cindy replied. "I've had my share of strange ones, too. What're yours about?"

"There's a man, and I'm afraid of him. I can't see his face or anything clearly. He's always in the shadows, waiting. Then when I wake up, I feel like I'm being watched. I swear the man from the dream is still around." Gloria shuddered.

"But you don't think it could be a symptom of Alzheimer's?" Cindy asked.

Gloria shook her head. "Well, paranoia can be part of Alzheimer's, but you know I did a lot of research on the disease when I was first diagnosed with dementia. I saw what my roommate went through, too. I don't think I'm that far along." She noticed Cindy's downcast eyes and bristled in irritation. "What are you thinking? I'm making it up? I'm not crazy."

Cindy touched Gloria's hand. "Listen. It's not you. I should have told you, but I didn't want to bother you with it." She told Gloria what she knew about the family being killed in the rec room. "I wonder if you're feeling something left over from that trauma. Kind of like there's a negative energy hanging around."

Gloria's eyes narrowed. "You bought a haunted house? Why would you do that? Why would you put your family in danger?"

Cindy rolled her eyes in exasperation. "Oh. My. God. Why do people keep saying that? I only knew that someone had died in the house. Big deal. A lot of people prefer to die at home instead of in a hospital."

"Okay, you're right. I'm sorry. Listen, have you talked with your friend—damn, what's her name—the psychic medium?"

"Laura Lee? You know, I thought about contacting her when I first found this house. But then I forgot all about it."

"Do you think she'd come over?" Gloria asked.

"No, she moved out of California right after we graduated from high school. Last I heard, she lives in Illinois."

"Oh. Hey, didn't she do something with the police? I seem to remember you saying something about that."

"Yeah, she did. I'll bet Randy would love to hear her stories, they're pretty intense. She also has a radio talk show and 'reads' people over the phone. We could see what she has to say. Want to call her right now?"

Much to Cindy's surprise, Laura answered the phone on the second ring. Cindy put the phone on speaker so Gloria could join in the conversation. Cindy started to describe what she knew about the family being killed, but Laura interrupted her.

"Oh, Cindy, I wish we'd talked before you bought the house. I feel there's more to the story than what you've been told. I'm getting conflicting signals that are hard to separate." She paused then said, "Who else is in the house with you right now?"

"It's just me and Gloria, plus the two dogs. Marti and Randy are at school."

"No, I feel something—someone—else there. A man. There's a lot of anger. You're sure no one else is in the house?"

Worried, Cindy got up from the table. "You two stay on the phone, and I'll go check around the house." She looked at the two dogs lounging a few feet away. "Xena, stay. Sherlock, come." Going from room to room with the basset hound by her side, Cindy looked in all closets, under beds, checked windows and doors, but found nothing amiss.

"Nope, no one else is here," she said as she sat back at the table.

Gloria whispered to Cindy, "Could she be feeling the man from my dreams?"

Cindy's brow furrowed. "Hmm, maybe. It kind of supports what I said about negative energy."

"Okay, then let's move on," Laura Lee said. "There's definitely more to the house than you've been told. I see several spirits trying to get your attention." She fell silent for a few moments. "I don't think I've ever sensed such turmoil over the phone. It's a more tenuous connection than being there in person. But I'm being bombarded. It's hard to separate all the voices."

"Voices?" Gloria asked. "How many?"

"It's hard to say, but I feel more than just the family of six you mentioned."

Cindy paled. "More than six? I don't understand."

"Yes, there're more." Again, Laura paused. "Please remember: just because the spirits are there, doesn't mean they'll interfere with your lives. Most spirits are benign, even positive, beings. They're angels or guides watching over their loved ones. And it doesn't mean they died there, either."

Cindy felt warmth embrace her. A wonderful thought hit her. "Keith? Is my husband here?" It wasn't the first time she'd felt his reassuring presence but was afraid she was imagining it.

"Yes, I hear him. His voice is weak compared to the others, though. He sounds concerned."

Cindy's fear came back. At the look on her niece's face, Gloria intervened. "Laura, would you be interested in coming to visit?"

"You know, actually, I would," Laura replied. "I'm sensing spirits that need help moving on. Maybe I can help with that."

"Oh, I'd really like that!" Cindy chimed in. "It has been years since we saw each other. I know the kids would love to see you, too."

The women worked out the details of the visit. Laura would come the next weekend over Labor Day, but would only be able to stay on Sunday and Monday. She needed to be back on Tuesday for her radio show. She asked Cindy to make a hotel reservation for her.

"You don't want to stay here?"

Laura paused for a moment. "No, I feel like when I get there, I'll need some distance. Otherwise I won't be able to sleep."

Laura encouraged Cindy to research the house in the meantime. "Compile a list of previous owners and any suspicious deaths in the area, especially related to the house. But keep the list to yourself. And Cindy, pay attention to your dreams. They're trying to tell you something."

When Cindy hung up the phone, Gloria gave her a look. "What dreams are you having?" Cindy hadn't mentioned them.

Cindy shook her head. "They're gruesome. Let's not talk about them right now. It looks like I've got some homework to do to research this house. Where can I even start?"

"The County property records could at least tell you who all's owned this house. Could one of the investigators from your magazine help?"

Cindy grimaced. "Unfortunately, reporters do their own investigations, so unless I want to bring one of them in for this as a story, I can't ask them to do any work for me. I'll just have to do this as though I were back being a reporter. I'll check the local newspaper morgues to see if there are any articles that haven't made it to the Internet." Cindy put her head in her hands. "Where am I going to get the time? I thought being the magazine editor and working from home was going to give me plenty of down time. Not so."

Gloria changed the subject. "As much as I don't want to, we need to talk about my Alzheimer's. I am relieved Laura senses spirits here. I was afraid it was just another symptom of the disease, but it really didn't feel like it."

Cindy looked closer at Gloria. For the first time, she noticed the tension in the older woman's face. "It must be scary for you, knowing your memory is failing."

"I thought these were supposed to be the golden years. I think the gold is actually rust. I feel so powerless."

"You're not powerless. You know what you're facing. We can take precautions." Cindy held up her hand and counted off the points on her fingers. "Your neurologist gave you medications, and your support group is there to help. We're getting exercise, eating right, and keeping our brains active. We're in this together. We're a team. I will be with you."

Gloria blinked back tears as she struggled to find the words to explain her worries. "Do you think it's possible..."

"Possible?" Cindy prompted.

"I feel like I'm losing my grasp on my mind, on my reality. Is it possible for the spirits here to use that?"

Cindy scoffed. "Do you mean like possession?"

Gloria shook her head. "Oh, no. I just mean they might have a way to focus their energy."

"I have no idea. I'm not even sure who we could ask. Your neurologist would want me to start taking the medications, too, if we asked him. He'd think we were both losing it." She indicated the phone. "Until we talked with Laura, I wasn't completely sold on the idea that the spirits are here. I guess we'll have a lot of questions to ask her when she gets here. Until then, let's continue to work on the memory exercises the doctor recommended, along with the workouts and food." She winked at her aunt. "And if you come out one day acting like a former deceased tenant, I'll just tie you up in your room."

"Well, that's a relief," Gloria said. "It's good to know that you'd be so considerate."

"Any time!" Cindy looked at her watch. "And speaking of time, I've got to get some work done or we won't have to worry about the house because I won't be able to pay the mortgage."

"Just tell me what I can do to help," Gloria said. "We've got the barbecue party this Saturday, and Laura will be here the following day."

Cindy put her head in her hands, overwhelmed. "Oh, boy. I'd forgotten about the party. Maybe I *do* need to see your neurologist."

"Not funny. Don't worry about it. Go up to your office and start working, and I'll earn my keep."

Chapter 10
August 30, 2011
Day 30

Cindy arrived at the County Assessor's Office before nine on Wednesday morning. The office was well lit with workers toiling away behind a counter with bullet-proof glass. On the public side of the counter, there were two rows of tables. Each table had four work stations with a keyboard, mouse, and computer screen; the computers themselves hidden under the tables. At the end of one table was an old microfiche machine.

Cindy sat down at the closest computer and started by plugging in her address to see who the previous owners were. The online property records showed only the last few years for Santa Clara County; a red box flashed on the screen telling Cindy that the rest of the records were on microfiche. She headed up to the counter and got the attention of an elderly clerk. The woman had her gray hair pulled back in a severe bun, and her tortoise shell glasses were propped at the edge of her nose. Her mouth was pinched as she scowled at the paperwork in front of her, but she smiled when she looked up. Cindy explained that she was looking for all possible records dealing with her address and those in the neighborhood and would like to talk with anyone who knew the area.

"Oh, I remember that development," the clerk commented.

"Really?"

The clerk sighed and leaned against the counter. "The land in Santa Clara was all farming back then. I don't remember who the land belonged to, but you should be able to find that out through the records. I'll get those for you." She made a note on her steno pad. "Anyway, during the '60s, a lot of farmers lost their land to the local bank." She shook her head trying to remember. "It's been too long. Someone from Valley Bank bought everything and built a new housing development. I remember the construction going on. I was a senior at Santa Clara High School at the time, so it must've been 1967. Two guys from the football team were killed there."

"A construction accident?" Cindy asked.

"That was the line we were given." The clerk's eyes narrowed. "The school was in an uproar. All the kids were upset. Imagine having the football stars killed! The principal called an assembly and told the student body that the guys were messing around with the construction equipment at the new housing development one night after a football game and got crushed. Two of them died. The third was missing. Everyone figured the kid who was missing was responsible and had run away. He was a Mexican," she said in a conspiratorial whisper that made Cindy cringe.

"Did you know any of them?"

The clerk nodded. "My boyfriend at the time was the varsity quarterback, and I was a cheerleader, so we were at all of the games." She gazed off. "Roger Duran was the JV quarterback. A real bad boy. Good looking. All the girls had a crush on him. Today, I suppose he'd be called a 'player.'" She straightened up. "So what's your interest in the development?"

Cindy wasn't sure what to say. She didn't want to admit that she thought the house was haunted. "I bought one of the houses there. I'm a bit of a history buff, so I thought I'd check it out."

The clerk nodded her head. "Santa Clara has quite the history. From the times of the Native Americans at odds with the Catholic

Missions to..." She shrugged off what she was going to say and extended her hand through the small window in the glass. "I'm Carolyn, by the way."

The ladies chatted for a few moments more before Carolyn excused herself to go find the microfiche films. Cindy set up her laptop next to the console and linked to the Wi-Fi. Something Carolyn said struck a chord within Cindy's investigative instincts. She wasn't sure where she was going with the line of thought, but it had always served her well in the past to follow up on random thoughts and gut feelings. And right now she was getting a peculiar feeling about the bank buying up peoples properties. That kind of thing can create a legacy of mistrust and festering anger that can manifest in surprising violence. Valley Bank's historical data showed that Larry Bell was the owner from the early '60s until it was bought out in 1990. Cindy expanded her search of the microfiche to other parcels in the area that had passed through Larry Bell's or Valley Bank's hands. She came up with twenty-two names of families in Santa Clara who'd seemingly lost their homes to the bank, although the records didn't clearly state that. For some, the land started out in one name, was transferred to the bank's name, and then again to Larry Bell within a short time. For others, the land went straight to Larry Bell. Fifteen of the properties were within a mile of her house. One name caught her attention: Wilson. Peter's family? That boy was just a little too perfect. Wouldn't it figure that his family was linked to this somehow? She sighed. Her daughter would never forgive her.

Cindy asked Carolyn how she could find out about the people she'd written on her list, and the older woman directed Cindy down to the County Recorder's Office in the basement.

As Cindy started to leave, Carolyn called out to Cindy. "I've done a lot of research of this area over the years. I've got a lot of historical books and documents at home that cover the Santa Clara Valley in the 1800s and early 1900s. Would you be interested in seeing them?"

The two exchanged phone numbers, and Carolyn agreed to try to come to Cindy's party on Saturday.

The basement offices were dull, dingy and depressed, and the workers at the Recorder's Office reflected the same attributes. Her request for microfiche films of birth and death certificates from the 1930s through the 1990s was met with dejected sighs as though it would take a monumental effort to fulfill the request.

The public area computers were set up in a similar fashion to the Assessor's office. Cindy sat down at the end of one of the rows of computers where she could use both the microfiche and a computer. She inserted the first film into the microfiche machine and started working forward from the 30s. She spread out her sheets of notes from the Assessor's office. She scrolled through the documents on the machine looking for any records of births or deaths for any name on her list. The records were in date order, and Cindy was getting a headache from looking back and forth from the microfiche to her notes comparing the names. Like many farming communities, families were large, most with four to six children. One family, the O'Conners, had seven children, and another, the Franklins, had a full dozen. Cindy shook her head. She couldn't imagine raising that many.

When she got to the late '50s, she started to see a terrible pattern. Births were followed with death certificates days or a few months later. In the mid '60s, the births of the children were succeeded immediately by the death certificates of the mothers. She recognized one of the names: O'Conner. She looked back at her notes. This was one of the families in the '30s and '40s that had many children, but the next generation in the '60s was cut short when the mother died shortly after giving birth to her first son. She counted six other families that appeared to have been devastated by this type of tragedy.

Other citizens came and went, but Cindy barely noticed until a woman sat down next to her with two small children,. One was a boy still in diapers. The older of the two kids, Cindy estimated she was about three or so, went on a noisy journey around the room, sweeping keyboards to the floor. She ran by Cindy and grabbed the mouse from under Cindy's hand and tossed it to the length of the cord. Exasperated, Cindy turned to the mother of the children. Before she could say a word, the boy in diapers knocked over his bottle. The lid popped off, and the bright red drink splashed across the desk, splattering the keyboard his mother was using. She snatched the bottle and screwed on the top and tossed all of her possessions into a plastic shopping bag. She hoisted the little boy onto her hip, grabbed her little girl's hand, and made a beeline to the door.

Cindy hurried up to the counter and asked for a towel and explained what had happened. A spry woman on the older side of 50 stormed out with a roll of paper towels and a bottle of cleaner. Cindy helped her clean the mess up, sopping up the fluid that was dripping off the table and was soaking into the worn utilitarian carpet.

The clerk thanked Cindy and eyed her notes as they finished the cleanup. "How's your research going?"

"I'm actually kind of puzzled by what I've found." She launched into an explanation of the births followed by the deaths of the mothers.

The clerk sat down on the edge of the table she'd just cleaned. "You know, I seem to remember something about pesticides causing problems back in the '50s and '60s. Some caused deformities to the fetuses, but others affected the mothers." She pursed her lips. "One of my cousins was born with deformed arms. My aunt and uncle tried to sue the chemical manufacturing plant that was about a mile away in San Jose, but no luck."

The clerk stood up in a huff and strode away without saying another word. Cindy thought about the woman's story for a while. She remembered reading about teratogens in her college biology class more than a decade earlier. Chemicals that were used in the agriculture and manufacturing industries were only now being discovered to have long-lasting and detrimental effects. Perhaps that could be a good investigative report for the magazine in the future: a look at the aftermath of pesticide usage many years later.

She spent a small fortune copying the death and birth certificates just in case something occurred to her later.

Cindy's next stop was the newspaper morgue in San Jose. She loved newspaper archives: the smell, the cumulative knowledge, the peace and quiet. During journalism courses in college, the morgue was her favorite place to study. No one bothered her there, and the morgue librarians tended to be quiet and introspective.

But things had changed. At this morgue, where she'd hoped for solitude, she found interns busy digitalizing the many stories penned years before. It was a tremendous undertaking, one that would put another proverbial nail in the print media coffin. File cabinets were open with their contents in stacks that were threatening to topple off tables and chairs. Individual papers were strewn across the floor. Within minutes, Cindy realized that there was no way for her to find what she needed in the disarray. Disgusted and disheartened, she headed to the police station to get a copy of the report on the Fremont murders.

Chapter 11
September 3, 2011
Day 34

Cindy set the tray of drinks down on the folding table on the front lawn for the boys, a moment of fear gripping her. Steve's wrist shot sent the roller hockey puck whistling towards the goal and her son standing in front of it. Randy, showing none of the fear she felt, got his blocker up and knocked the puck away. The puck careened past the goal post and sped down the street. Cindy's relief gave way to a new fear. The puck was still moving fast down the street, straight towards the feet of an elderly man. The man was holding a potted plant that was decorated with a bow and a colorful, hand-printed sign that proclaimed "Welcome to the neighborhood."

"Watch out!" She started running towards him, hindered by her long flowing skirt and heels. She was surprised when he deftly stopped the puck with his foot. With an agility that contrasted with his apparent age, he kicked the puck onto the stick of the hockey player that flew by Cindy on his skates.

The man moved the plant to his left hand and held his right hand out as he neared her. "You must be Cindy. I'm John O'Conner. I live just a few houses away." He pointed to a house across the street from

Peter's home. "Thank you for inviting me to your housewarming party. I see your daughter spending a lot of time at the Wilsons' house." He winked at Cindy and whispered, "I keep an eye out for them. We wouldn't want these teenagers getting into any trouble, would we?" He linked his free arm with hers and turned towards her house. They walked to her house, crossing the lawn to avoid the boys playing roller hockey.

As Cindy opened the front door, she felt John pull back and take a deep breath. His eyes were wide and had a look that she couldn't quite place. She turned to see what he was looking at. Gloria. Her expression matched John's. Her eyes were full of wonder with a glow that spread to her expanding smile. *So this is what love at first sight looks like.* Cindy accepted the plant from John and introduced him to her aunt.

The first guests showed up just after three, and by four, the living room and kitchen were crowded, with every couch and chair occupied. But the majority of people spilled out into the backyard where Cindy had set up tables with platters of fruits and vegetables, dips, chips, and nuts. Marti had hooked up her iPod to the sound system in the rec room and brought the wireless speakers outside. They had compromised on the type of music with jazz fusion bands like the Yellow Jackets, Dixie Dregs, and Brand X. More people showed up for the party than Cindy had expected – or planned for, and most of the food was already gone. She was afraid that she didn't have enough burgers and buns.

She found her daughter in the kitchen mixing up a batch of punch made from lemonade, cranberry juice and club soda.

"Mom, this is the last of the club soda. Want me to run to the store?" She tilted her head at Peter who was standing at her side. "He can drive."

Relieved, Cindy nodded and started scrawling a list of supplies. She'd planned on just having cheeseburgers, but her budget would go further if she added hotdogs and buns and far less hassle without needing to slice more tomatoes, lettuce and onions.

As her daughter went out the front door, a friendly laugh caught

Cindy's attention. Her realtor and friend, Dawn, had arrived. Cindy rushed to the front door where she saw Dawn on the porch talking with Nicole Wilson, Peter's mother.

"Dawn! It's so good to see you!" She threw her arms around her friend.

Dawn squeezed the hug tighter before pulling away. She pulled a bottle of white zin from her bag that was slung over her shoulder. "I'm sorry I can't stay, dear, but I've got a meeting to run to."

"Beringer Brothers white zin?" Cindy said as she took the bottle. "You know that's my favorite local wine."

Dawn blew her a kiss as she headed down the path to the sidewalk and waved to Randy and his friends playing hockey. Cindy linked arms with Nicole and they went into the house. Cindy put the wine in the refrigerator to chill for later.

She suspected that many of the guests had come to satisfy their macabre curiosity about the house where murders had taken place. As she left the kitchen and headed towards the backyard to catch up with Nicole, she glanced down the hall towards the rec room and the crouched shadow of someone in the room. Curious, she went to the room and stood in the doorway. A man she hadn't yet met was kneeling, inspecting an area of the wall that she'd replaced. He was on the north side of forty with black hair and thick glasses. He was holding a camera in his hand. When she stepped up to introduce herself, he mumbled something and made a quick exit.

While Cindy was still puzzling over the strange man's actions, her new friend from the county offices came into the room.

"Hey, Carolyn! I'm so glad you made it."

The older woman looked unhappy. She was holding a stack of books and a thick binder. She didn't say anything.

Cindy stepped up to her. "Carolyn? Are you okay?"

Carolyn slowly met Cindy's eyes. "No. Not really. You didn't tell me you lived in *this* house."

"What about this house?"

"This is where the guys were killed when the tract was being built." She thrust the armload of books at Cindy. Without waiting to be sure that Cindy had a good grip on them, she spun on her heel and left the room.

"So this is where it happened, huh?" A man's voice pulled Cindy out of her shock. He was tall with distinguished silver hair and neatly trimmed mustache.

"I'm sorry?" Cindy said.

"The murders? The Fremonts?"

"Oh. Yes. Are you from around here?"

He nodded. "Yes, I live three blocks over." He held out his hand. "I'm William Kentcher, and this is my wife, Tabby." He nodded his head to the beautiful, curvaceous, white-haired woman standing on his right.

Cindy shifted the books she was holding and shook his hand. "What do you know about what happened?" The police report she'd obtained earlier in the week didn't have much information.

Tabby shuddered. "If you two are going to talk about that, I think I'll go mingle."

William watched her go with a gentle smile on his face before turning back to Cindy. He was a handsome man with a strong jaw peppered with a five o'clock shadow. His prominent cheekbones, sharp, straight nose, and golden eyes gave him a predatory look that bothered Cindy. "Nothing much. Just the usual rumors."

"Like what?" Cindy prodded.

He lowered his voice and leaned his six-foot frame towards her. "It's said that the house is haunted, and everyone that lives here will die a violent death or run away. Either way, people don't stay here for very long. The house always sits vacant for a while before someone else moves in."

Cindy straightened her posture. "I don't plan on running away, and I'm certainly not going to let anything happen to my family." She spoke with bravado, but the hair was standing on the back of her neck and she fought the urge to run away from him.

* * *

Cindy was distracted by what she had learned from William

Kentcher about the rumors surrounding the house. Was the house haunted? She thought back to the day that she had first seen it. When she was in the rec room, the room had suddenly gotten cold enough for her to see her breath, and then the door slammed shut. She remembered the panic when she couldn't get the door open again, and then the warmth that settled around her and the door opening. And what about the crawl space door being open the other night? Had someone opened it when she'd gone back inside the house? Someone...or something? Human or ghost? Was the door opened to get someone in or let someone out?

"Earth to Mom!" Marti's voice startled Cindy out of her thoughts. "The hot dogs are on fire."

"Oh! Guess I wasn't paying attention."

"Ya think?"

Cindy grimaced and pulled the dogs off the barbecue. They were snatched up as quickly as she set them out. She looked around for her aunt. She spied Gloria sitting in the shade with John. They looked rather cozy. Cindy filled two plates with hot dogs, potato salad and fruit and brought them to the couple. They both thanked her, but it was obvious that they really didn't want to be interrupted.

* * *

"Are you okay living in this house?" John asked. He and Gloria had finished their food and were enjoying Marti's punch.

"Oh my, yes," replied Gloria. "My niece is wonderful. It's been a long time since I was this happy."

"She seems very nice. But I meant the house. How are you dealing with this house?"

"What do you mean?" Gloria asked, feigning confusion. "The house is perfect."

"You mean you haven't seen or heard anything strange?" John shifted his position on the chaise so that he was on his side and facing Gloria.

"Strange? No, nothing unusual. The days are quiet except for the dogs following me around." She stared off for a moment, and when she looked back at his face, his eyes were full of intense concern, as though her wellbeing truly meant something to him. She decided to trust him. "Yesterday afternoon when I was in my room reading, both dogs were stretched out on my bed. Xena sprang up and started growling for no reason. Then Sherlock went to the closet door and growled. His hair was standing up on his back." She cocked her head. "Is that the kind of thing you mean?"

John considered her words for a moment. "The dogs may be sensing things that you can't."

"Sensing things? Whatever do you mean?"

"How much do you know about the history of this house?"

Despite a gut feeling that she could trust him, Gloria decided to play dumb and see what he'd tell her. She rolled onto her side to face him, tucked her feet up, and looked him straight in the eye. She shrugged and tilted her head. "Well, I know that just five weeks ago, my niece bought it and fixed it up. It'd been vacant for a couple years. But that's not surprising in this economy. Beyond that, nothing."

"Ah, my lady, I have a lot to tell you then. But the stories aren't for the faint of heart. Perhaps we can steal away some time together and I can tell you what I remember."

"I would be most pleased," she replied, a blush rising on her cheeks.

The jazz fusion music that had been playing at a low volume in the background changed to pop rock dance tunes, and the volume was turned up. "Look," John said, "they're clearing the tables out of the way. Care to take a spin with me?"

John took Gloria's hand and led her to the lawn. Gone was the aging woman with aching bones; in her place was a beautiful silver-haired lady moving with grace and fluidity. Each sweep of her arms extended to her fingertips, and her feet glided across the grass like she was on a stage. It took John a moment to catch up, but he fell into step with her. He pulled her into a waltz embrace, and their bodies fit perfectly. They moved together like they had been dance partners for years. For a few minutes, the other guests watched in silence as the two septuagenarians moved across the grass. When the first song ended and another by Lady Gaga started, other couples joined them on the lawn.

Marti and Peter joined in the dancing. Their hold was more contemporary than the waltz hold Gloria and John kept, but they moved around the grass with nearly as much grace as their elders. Cindy watched from the patio where she was setting out cookies for dessert. She wondered if they had been getting some dancing lessons from Gloria or at school or if they were learning from watching TV shows like *Dancing with the Stars* and *So You Think You Can Dance*. She was uncomfortable with how close and sensually they were dancing and fought the urge to stop them.

By seven o'clock, the party started to wind down and people were leaving. Cindy was drawn into the living room saying goodbye to her neighbors. William and Tabby Kentcher stopped to invite Cindy to come by their home. Tabby pulled Cindy into a hug and whispered in her ear, "Don't let the rumors about your house get you down. You've done a wonderful job with the renovations, and I'm so glad we're neighbors. Please drop by any time."

Before Cindy could reply, Randy tugged on her arm. Two of his new friends were at his side. "Would it be okay if Steve and Lee stayed over tonight?"

During the years they'd lived in the apartment, he'd never had a sleepover. Surprised and happy that his friendships were developing so fast, she waved goodbye to the Kentchers and replied, "It's fine with me. Let's ask their parents." Lee and Steve dashed off and reappeared minutes later with their parents in tow.

When Ralph and Jen Harrison had introduced themselves earlier in the afternoon, Cindy had been uneasy. Jen's stiff and perfect posture was unyielding, and even though she was at least six inches shorter than Cindy–including her perfectly coiffed brown hair – her confident and superior presence filled the room. Having come from a working-class background, Cindy felt certain they were looking down on her. She didn't know much about expensive clothing, but there was no doubt that she couldn't afford any individual piece of Jen's ensemble. Even if the ring on her finger was cubic zirconium, it probably cost more than Cindy's minivan. Somehow, Cindy doubted it was anything but the highest quality diamond. Cindy had heard that Lee's mom had been a gymnast and had just missed being in the Olympics. Maybe that accounted for the massive chip on her shoulder. Cindy was sure Ralph's suit didn't come off the rack, either. The incongruity of their displayed wealth with living in a decidedly middle class neighborhood piqued her interest. This was a family she would enjoy investigating. There must be a story in there somewhere.

"Lee says that you've invited him to spend the night?" Ralph asked.

"Yeah!" all three boys voiced. "And Steve, too," Randy added.

"Please, Dad?" Steve implored his father.

The father looked down at his son and ruffled his hair. He lifted his eyes to Cindy and raised a questioning eyebrow. She had no idea what his name was. She remembered that he arrived at the same time as two other couples, but they'd only had the chance to say hello. The next time she saw him was when she met Dawn on the porch. She had a vague recollection of him sitting in a lounge chair watching the boys play hockey. She was saved from embarrassment when he introduced himself as Darren Polk. He held her hand for an extra moment. She noticed he wasn't wearing a wedding ring. With his prominent forehead, receding hair, and bulbous nose, he wasn't what most women would consider handsome, but his intelligent blue eyes drew her in. She pulled her eyes away from his and looked at his hand holding hers. Though his nails were nicely trimmed, his skin was somewhat rough and tan; they were a working man's hands.

Cindy said, "We'd love to have Lee and Steve spend the night, if it's okay with all of you. I could certainly use their help cleaning up."

The boys groaned, drawing laughs from the four adults.

"Sounds good to me, then," Darren said.

"We have plans at eleven tomorrow morning," Jen said. "So Lee, you'll need to be home around ten."

The Harrisons left, but Darren hung back. "Would you like my help with cleaning up?"

"If you'd help me with the tables and chairs in the backyard, the boys can clean up the paper plates and such. We'd be done in a few minutes."

The clean up went faster than Cindy could have hoped. After-wards, she invited Darren to drink a glass of the white zinfandel that Dawn had brought. They took their glasses and sat in the chaise lounges under the pine tree in the backyard. It was a beautiful, warm fall night. The mild breeze gave a slight chill as a reminder that the warm nights wouldn't be around for much longer. The sky was clear, and the nearly full moon lit up the backyard.

"You've done a great job with this house," Darren said. "I'd heard that it was in pretty bad shape, but it looks great. Was it a lot of work?"

"Even with hiring contractors to do the roof and outside of the house, it took all three of us over a week of twelve-hour days to make interior repairs and paint. The rec room was just that... a wreck." Cindy described the mess and missing floor and walls.

"I would have expected the repairs to be made before the house was put up for sale," Darren said. "I'm glad you didn't make that room into a bedroom. I can't imagine anyone being able to sleep there."

Cindy told him the changes she had made to the flooring and the crawl space entrance.

Darren tilted his head and raised an eyebrow. "I'm impressed! How in the world did you learn to do that kind of work?"

"My father was a general contractor. By the time I was a teenager, I could wire a house, do most basic plumbing, and was pretty good with a hammer and saw. Just don't ask me about anything mechani-cal. If my van breaks down, I'll be the typical lady in distress."

Darren laughed. "Give me a call if you need help. I'm a pretty good mechanic."

They commiserated about single parenthood. Darren's wife had left him with Steve after being married for fourteen years. "One morning, she just up and left without saying goodbye. "The only way I knew that she hadn't been kidnapped was because she cleaned out the closet, our bank accounts, safe-deposit box, and took our only car. I didn't think a kidnapper would stick around long enough to let her pack first."

"That's horrible," Cindy exclaimed. "I can't imagine leaving my kids under any circumstances. I just don't see how a mother could do that. How old was Steve when she left?"

"It was four years ago. He was seven. It crushed him."

"Have you been in contact with her since?" she asked.

"Only through a lawyer for the divorce. She took everything she wanted when she left. She signed the house over to me, so at least that wasn't a problem." He sighed. "I'm not sure what she's doing now. Her parents died several years ago, and Steve doesn't have any contact with her side of the family at all."

After a few moments of awkward silence, Darren asked, "What happened with you? I can't believe you're single."

"I lost my husband to an industrial accident a few years ago." She drifted off for a moment. "There was so much bickering between the worker's compensation and his life insurance that it took until this spring to get the paperwork straightened out. In the meantime, I couldn't keep up the house payment. I'd been in journalism before we married, but stayed home to take care of the kids. I was lucky to be able to get back into the magazine business after he died. I worked my way up into the editing department, so now I'm able to work mostly from home. I'm blessed to be able to be here for the kids and for Gloria. I'm so glad to be able to be here for her as her Alzheimer's progresses. With the right care, we might be able to stop the progress of the disease."

Sometime while she was describing her situation, Darren had taken her hand in his. "When I finally got the payoff from worker's comp and the life insurance, I was able to get out of the apartment and back into a house. Dawn Thomas, my miracle-working realtor, worked her usual magic and got us an unbelievable price on this house. She was here earlier. Did you meet her?"

"A tall, pretty woman with brown hair?"

Cindy felt a rush of jealousy; it surprised her. "Yup, that's her. Too bad her husband wasn't able to make the party. He's a great guy.

Anyway, I feel like I've been lucky to have such a great friend."

"I think that you have been through some hard times and deserve some good things to happen. This house has a long history, and hopefully you'll bring the positive energy it needs," he said.

"Long history?" *Why do people keep saying that?*

He looked at her in surprise. "You don't know about the other deaths?" he asked.

"Please tell me you're just talking about the boys that were killed while the tract was under construction."

"Oh, there were more than just those." His eyes showed concern at how alarmed she was. "I'm so sorry I've upset you."

"Dawn felt something strange when we first checked out the house. She couldn't wait to leave. She was really upset. I'm afraid she didn't want me to buy it. But, you know, I can be pretty persistent, and I insisted. Anyway, the only thing the disclosures indicated was that someone had died of heart failure here. I didn't find out about the whole family being killed until we moved in." She took a deep breath. "Maybe I should hear about the rest."

"They just said one death? So much for full disclosure. Anyway, there's more to it than just the ones you mentioned."

Cindy thought about the bloodstain the carpet layers found. "Did something happen in the living room?" She described what was under the carpet.

Darren shifted uncomfortably and coughed. "Uh, yes. That's part of the house's history."

"How do you know about the history," Cindy asked. "Is it common knowledge?" She internally cursed the disorganization at the newspaper morgue. She should have been able to get the information.

"No, not common knowledge. We've tried to keep it quiet, but when you have long-established neighborhoods where families have lived since the houses were built, people remember things. The house is kind of an urban legend."

"You said 'we've tried to keep it quiet.' Who's 'we'? And why would you try to keep it quiet?"

"The Police Department." He looked at her, somewhat puzzled. "I thought you knew what I did for a living."

"No. Or maybe I've heard, but I can't seem to keep everyone straight. Too much information about too many different people in too short of a time." She looked at him questioningly. "What did you say your name was?"

They both laughed and he held his hand out to her. "I'm Homicide Detective Darren Polk at your service, ma'am." He didn't let go of her hand. "And police departments don't like to advertise that they have unsolved crimes. Do you want to hear about the rest of the history?"

She thought about it for a moment before saying, "No, not tonight. I'm afraid the stories will give me nightmares and I am so tired." She yawned as if in emphasis.

The yawn was contagious, and Darren followed with his own. "Well then, perhaps I should head home."

He continued to hold her hand as they stood up. "I hope I'm not being too forward, but I'd really like to see more of you."

Cindy's pulse quickened. "Really?" she blurted. "I'd like that, too." She was glad that the only lighting was the moon and the porch light because she was sure that her face was bright red.

They walked back to the house together where the boys were playing video games in the family room. "Steve'll be spoiled with that huge flat screen," Darren said. "I may find myself paying child support to you since he'll be spending all of his time here."

"Steve seems like a great kid. I'm glad that he and Lee befriended Randy. It's hard moving to a new place."

"Randy's a good kid. And he's a pretty decent goaltender, too. Steve is hoping that he'll try out for the ice hockey team. Steve and Lee have been playing defense on the team for a few years now. They usually complain about the goalies, but they have high hopes for Randy."

Cindy looked at Darren in surprise. "This is the first I've heard of it. I know he's been playing roller hockey at the park, but he hasn't mentioned any organized games, and definitely hasn't brought up ice hockey."

"Hmm. Maybe I shouldn't have said anything. But since I spilled the beans, I might as well finish. I coach my son's team. Randy has talent. Seriously. And we need a goalie."

She held her hand up to stop him. "Why don't we talk about this another time? I can only imagine how much it would cost."

They continued to the front door. He said, "Okay, now we have another topic to talk about another time. I think we should plan on getting together again soon."

"Yeah? How soon?" she asked.

"What are you doing at ten o'clock tomorrow morning?"

"I believe I'm sending your son home about that time."

"Then how about I come pick him up instead? We can all go to the park, and you can see your son play."

"That sounds nice."

After she shut the door behind Darren, she turned to the boys and said good night. They didn't even bother to look up at her, just muttered "good night." She watched the boys for a few moments longer before turning and going upstairs. When she passed her daughter's room she remembered that Marti was still out. It was a quarter to ten. It was times like this that she wished she had given in and gotten cell phones for her kids. It would be nice to send a text telling her to come home.

At precisely ten o'clock, Cindy heard the front door and came downstairs. Marti's hair was mussed and she scooted past Cindy without making eye contact. Cindy wondered how long the couple had been on the porch making out but decided not to say anything about it.

"Go to bed soon, you guys," she said to the boys.

"Yeah, Mom. Soon. We'll just finish this game," came the distracted reply from Randy.

Right, she thought to herself. They'll probably be in the same position when I come down in the morning. But she turned and headed to bed without saying anything else.

* * *

"Let's give them a few more minutes to go to sleep," Randy whispered to his friends when he heard his mom's bedroom door close. Earlier in the day, he had told them that he'd found stuff under the house, but he didn't tell them what it was. He wanted to take them down under the house to the exact spot where he found the blood-stained shirt and overalls—and the gun; it would be scariest to show them in the dark and cold. And he wanted to get even with Steve for calling him a pussy the other night when he was alone and thought someone was in the house.

Going upstairs, Randy could tell that his mom's light was off, but there was a thin strip of light still showing beneath Marti's door. Xena was asleep on his bed. He grabbed the bag from his closet and snuck back downstairs to the guys. They were waiting for him in the rec room. He only had one flashlight, so he gave it to Lee and opened the crawl space trap door. He jumped in and moved out of the way so they could follow him.

Lee dropped into the hole next. Randy saw him shiver and hoped it was in fear and not from the cold, damp air. Lee crouched and shined the flashlight around. The beam of light exposed only dirt and wood beams with concrete foundations and a lot of webs. "Where there are webs, there are spiders," Lee whispered, and Randy nodded. Lee let out an involuntary squeak and fell on his butt when Steve jumped down and landed beside him.

It was slow going for all of them, but Lee had more trouble since one hand was holding the flashlight. They scrambled on their hands and knees around the posts towards the opposite side of the house. Randy dragged the plastic bag behind him. It made a nerve-wracking scraping sound.

When they got to the area where he'd found the pile, Randy whispered for them to stop. He quietly pointed to the secret crawl space entrance that let out into Gloria's closet. With just the one flashlight and being so far from the entrance they had used, the mood was the creepiest that Randy could create. He couldn't see their faces clearly, but the flashlight beam was dancing around; Lee's hand was shaking. He could hear Steve's breathing coming in hitches.

First, Randy pulled out the old long-sleeved shirt. He put it on, even though it was huge, especially since he was on his knees. Next, he pulled out the overalls. He showed them the spots and whispered, "Blood stains." He heard Lee gasp and Steve gave the faintest of moans. The hat was too big, so he left it in the bag. His heart was pounding when he reached back into the bag.

"Are you ready to see the best thing?" he whispered.

Both boys nodded, but neither said anything. Lee pointed the flashlight at Steve whose wide eyes and open mouth showed that he was seriously freaked out. Randy knew they were all feeling the claustrophobia from the dark, cold, and cramped quarters, but he thought he saw a bit of respect in their eyes as well. He took a deep breath and pulled the gun out of the bag. He pointed it straight ahead, directly at Lee. His finger was on the trigger.

Lee screamed and threw himself down into the dirt. The scream startled Randy. His finger twitched, and the gun went off.

Chapter 12
September 3, 2011
Day 34

Boom!

Cindy was certain the noise was not a car backfiring. It was in her house. She jumped out of bed, grabbed the portable phone, and dialed 9-1-1. She ran down the hallway. Marti came out of her room with wide, startled eyes. Sherlock squeezed past the door and sprinted down the stairs, howling. "Get back in your room and lock the door," Cindy said to her daughter as the dispatcher answered the call.

"9-1-1. What's your emergency?"

"A gun shot in my house!" She continued down the hall to Randy's room. The boys weren't there. She headed down the stairs.

Cindy couldn't hear the dispatcher over the barking dogs, but she didn't hang up. At least she could keep him updated on what was happening so he could keep the responding units informed. At the midway landing on the stairs, Cindy stopped abruptly when a figure loomed in front of her. She screamed and jumped back, turning to head back up the stairs. The person screamed back. It was Gloria.

"Gloria, are you okay?"

"Shhhhh, you need to be quiet. The soldiers will hear us," Gloria whispered. Her mouth was close to Cindy's ear so she could be heard over the urgent barking of the dogs.

Cindy was confused. "Soldiers? What soldiers? Where's Randy?"

Gloria urged her niece up the stairs. "We need to find a place to hide."

She took her aunt's hand and led her to her daughter's room. She knocked on Marti's door. "Honey, it's Mom. Open up. I want Gloria to be with you."

Marti opened the door, and Cindy guided Gloria in. "Oh, this isn't a very good hiding place," Gloria said.

"That's okay," Cindy said. "I will make sure that no one comes up here. You'll be safe."

She whispered into the phone that she had located her daughter and aunt and told the dispatcher where she put them.

"We have units on the way," the dispatcher said. "You need to stay in a safe place."

"No. I need to find my son. I'm going back downstairs." As she reached the bottom of the stairs, she saw a light bobbing in the rec room. Anxiety roared through her body: who was in the rec room? She crept to the doorway and peeked around the corner. She could make out the shapes of three boys. She ran in and grabbed her son in a hug.

"What happened? Where'd the gunshot come from? Did you see anyone? Hear anyone? Are you all okay?" She threw out questions without waiting for answers. She felt her son trembling as she clutched him to her chest. The only relief she felt was that she could hear sirens approaching.

The boys were silent, and when she pulled away from Randy, Lee pointed the flashlight at him. What she saw stunned her. Her son was holding a gun.

"Where did you get that!" she demanded. She reached out and took the gun from his hand. "Did you shoot it?"

Randy pointed at his ear. "I can't hear anything, Mom."

The sound of screeching brakes announced the arrival of the first police unit. Cindy ran to the front door to let them in, flicking on lights as she went, the dogs leading the way. She opened the front door.

"Freeze! Police! Drop your weapon!"

She looked stupidly from the cop that was pointing his gun at her to the gun in her own hand. She released the gun like she'd discovered she was holding onto a viper and jumped at the thud it made when it hit the floor.

"Get control of the dogs, ma'am," the officer snapped at her.

She bent down and grabbed the dogs' collars. "Let me lock them in the backyard." The officer and his partner followed her in and watched as she pushed the dogs out the back door and covered their doggy door.

As soon as the police stopped pointing their guns at her, she asked if she could call the other boys' parents. The Harrisons arrived within minutes and, after curtly answering a few of the officers' questions, angrily whisked Lee away.

The sirens had woken up the neighbors. A dozen people gathered across the street, all chattering in loud voices. Standing at the front door, Cindy could hear them. "What happened now?" "How many more people were going to die in that house?" One of the neighbors called out to the Harrisons as the three left the house. "What's going on in there?"

Mr. Harrison walked over to the group and said, "That dipshit Randy found a gun. He fired it at my son." There was a collective gasp in the crowd. "Lee could have been killed. That house is cursed!"

Dismayed, Cindy turned away from the door. Tears filled her eyes when she saw that Steve was huddled in the corner of the couch in the family room. She could see his shaking from across the room. A police officer stood near him, leaning against the marble fireplace. Randy was in the kitchen with an officer who was jotting down his notes for the incident report he had to file. Cindy had instructed her son to not say anything until she was seated with him.

When Darren walked into the house, he hugged his son and whispered to him. Then he switched from parent mode to being a detective. The other police officers let Darren take the lead. He questioned Randy and his own son separately.

Two hours later, the uniformed police left, taking the clothing, hat, and gun. Darren stayed behind. Sitting at the kitchen table with Darren, Cindy couldn't decide which emotion was strongest: fear, embarrassment, relief, or anger. She seemed to be cycling through them at a rapid rate.

Pride in her daughter warred against mortification of what her son had done. Marti was her hero of the night. While Cindy was dealing with the police and the boys, Marti had stayed in her room, comforting Gloria. Gloria's Alzheimer's left her in confusion, unable to understand what was going on. Marti recognized that arguing with someone who couldn't truly comprehend a situation wasn't going to be helpful, but neither could she play into that delusion. Instead, she allowed Gloria to hold her, giving the older woman a feeling of control – something that Alzheimer's victims lack. As soon as the police had the situation under control downstairs, Marti brought Gloria down to her own room, hoping that the familiar surroundings would ground her in reality of the current time. She turned on the radio to a soft jazz station, letting the music soothe her great aunt.

At the other end of the spectrum was Randy. Cindy was shaking with anger at him. She had never raised a hand to her children, and tonight was the first time she wanted to strike him. Never before had she seen him be afraid of her. His shoulders were slumped, and he cringed away from her, keeping his distance. His expression was that of someone who had lost everything, one of complete despair. As soon as he was allowed, he ran to his room, unable to look at his friend curled up on the couch.

Cindy fought for her own self-control and focused on Darren. His strong presence soothed her nerves, but she saw a hesitation, an uncertainty in the way his eyes kept dropping to the table. "Is there something you're not telling me, Darren?"

"Unfortunately, yes," he replied. He stood up and moved to the doorway to the living room and looked at his son who was finally asleep on the couch. "When the Fremont family was killed in 2008, the house was thoroughly searched. The gun was never found—"

"Yes, I read that in the reports," Cindy broke in impatiently. "Obviously they didn't do such a thorough job, did they?" she said. "If they'd done their jobs, tonight wouldn't have happened!"

"That's my point," Darren said. "They *did* check under the house. The gun was *not* there."

"Oh, I see. You're saying that someone has come back since then and put the gun there." She got up from her chair, disgusted. "Why would someone do that? I think your cops just didn't bother looking under the house, and now you're afraid that we'll sue you."

"Sue us?" he said. "You would have no grounds." He visibly forced himself to speak gently. "But no, that's not what I think at all." He walked over and put his hands on her shoulders. When she wouldn't look at him, he lifted her chin and made her meet his eyes. "Cindy, there was a massive investigation, and the main suspect ended up dead. The Chief killed him. That was the end of the investigation. The evidence was overwhelming. But if the gun that Randy found is the one that was used to kill the Fremonts, then it means...hell, I'm not sure what it means. As you suggested, he must have come back to the scene of the crime at least once before Chief Atwater shot him."

Cindy pulled away. She was confused by her emotions. Part of her wanted him to hold her, though they had just met—had it been just a few hours ago?—but she was still too angry to give in to the attraction she had for him. "*Why* would someone do that? Why come back here and leave the murder weapon?"

"What better place to hide the weapon than someplace the police have already checked? Think about it. Do people actually look under their houses? No. When a house is up for sale, inspectors go down there, but they're not looking at the crap that's around. They're looking at the structure, wiring, plumbing."

Her stomach turned over. She told Darren about the night that the crawl space doors appeared to have been opened. That was more than a week *after* Randy had found the gun. Had someone returned to get the gun only to find that it was gone? "Can you have someone come out and look for fingerprints on the crawl space door?"

"Yes, if the gun turns out to be the murder weapon."

An even worse thought hit her: she had installed an entrance to the crawl space in the rec room, but she hadn't done anything yet to block off the entrance in the backyard. When she mentioned that to Darren, his brows furrowed.

"Okay, I'm not going to wait for the ballistics to come back. I'll have the forensics unit come out in the morning. You *must* block that entrance. From the inside. Because right now not only can someone get under your house—and apparently they have been—but they can easily get *into* your house."

Chapter 13
September 4, 2011
Day 35

Cindy couldn't fall asleep after Darren left. When exhaustion finally pulled her under, her dream was just as terrifying as her night had been. She found herself in the rec room with an air hockey table and piano. There was a dartboard on the wall. The darts were spread out on the target, and quite a few were on the corkboard outside of the target. Whoever played last was just as bad as she was. She noticed one dart on the floor near a leg of the air hockey table. Blood covered the entire tip of the dart, and small droplets of blood were on the floor around it.

Cindy turned back towards the door. Five people walked in, their steps hesitant. They lined up in front of her. On one end was a cute little girl in pigtails, maybe nine or ten years old. Her green eyes were wide with fear, tears streaming down her face. Beside her was a teenage boy in jeans and a Mr. Zog's sex wax T-shirt. Next was a man who was the same height as the teenager. He held a little girl who was about two years old. He pressed her head to his chest, shielding her eyes. His tight California Department of Forestry shirt showed muscles that were flexing with repressed tension. Last in the line was the woman from Cindy's previous nightmares.

As Cindy watched, one by one, blood started pouring from their heads, and they fell to the floor. Cindy tried to run, but her feet were stuck. Waves of blood swept over her feet. Horrified, she looked around for help. She sensed another person and looked up. It was a shadowy figure with a gun standing in the doorway.

Cindy screamed but still couldn't move. She was shaking and weak. She gasped for air. She managed to get one foot free, but she was off balance and slipped in the blood. She fell onto the pile of bodies, her limbs entangling with the arms and legs of the dead family. Blood splashed around her, in her eyes and mouth. Her scream finally pulled her from the nightmare. Waking up, she still couldn't move her feet. She'd tumbled from her bed onto the floor, her feet twisted in the sheets.

It took several minutes lying on the floor to get her breathing under control. She got up and went to the bathroom. Standing at the sink, she ran her hands under cold water and splashed it in her face. She lifted her head and looked at herself in the mirror. Her tired eyes were sunken and dull. Worry lines spread from her eyes to her hairline, and her hair was lank without any body. She barely recognized the woman in front of her.

When Cindy got back in bed, sleep came immediately. So did another dream. She was sitting under the pine tree in the backyard, having a glass of her aunt's special sun tea. A woman sat down in the chair next to her. It was the woman from her earlier dreams, but her face was composed and happy. The woman smiled at Cindy, her soft brown eyes crinkling. She said, "You have a beautiful family."

Cindy didn't know what to say. She was strangely drawn to the woman, perhaps a shared bond of love for their children. But as Cindy watched her, she realized it was something more. This woman needed her help.

The woman looked down at her hands clasped in her lap. "He's still out there, you know."

"Who is?" Cindy asked.

"I don't know," the woman replied. She sprang up out of the chair and pushed her face into Cindy's. Her breath was fetid, and Cindy felt like she was going to choke. "He's going to kill your family, too," she snarled.

Cindy sat up in bed, fighting down another scream. She wrapped her arms around her pillow, curled up, and pulled her blankets to her neck. She couldn't go back to sleep. She just rocked back and forth, fighting off hysteria.

At eight o'clock, Cindy dragged herself out of bed. She usually loved Sunday mornings. It was her weekly tradition to make a big, unhurried family breakfast, followed by a late-morning Mass. This morning, though, she had no enthusiasm for the ritual. After a quick shower, she went downstairs to check on Gloria. Her aunt's bedroom door was slightly ajar. Cindy poked her head in and saw that Marti was awake. She was sitting in the recliner doing homework. Gloria was still asleep.

Marti looked at her mom and gave her a weak smile. She put her book aside and followed Cindy out of the room, carefully closing the bedroom door behind her.

Mother and daughter embraced tightly. "I can't thank you enough for how well you handled everything last night," Cindy whispered. In her mind, she saw the woman from her dream and heard her words. *He's going to kill your family, too.*

Marti's voice startled Cindy back to the present. "I was cool to stay with Gloria out of the way of the cops. She wasn't really ...there. I don't know how to describe it. Maybe like she was dreaming while awake. It was really weird, but interesting, too."

"Hmm," Cindy considered her daughter's words. "I think that's what happens with Alzheimer's. We'll see her slip more frequently into that world now. We've been lucky so far."

"She didn't know who I was. I guess she thought I was someone from her past—probably her favorite niece." A hint of a smile touched her lips for a moment. "Anyway, she wanted to be sure that I was safe. She rocked me and hummed lullabies until I pretended to fall asleep. Then she put her head down and went to sleep, too."

"Very clever," Cindy praised her daughter. "I'm really impressed with how you handled everything. How was she when you brought her back to her own room?"

"She was still pretty freaked out, jabbering about having to hide from the soldiers. I didn't know she'd been in any wars.

"She wasn't ever in the military, but she was a nurse in some war-torn countries. She traveled all over and worked in small clinics in impoverished areas. I remember her stories about hiding small children from the guerillas. I'd bet she still has nightmares about those times. And that may have been the world she was in last night."

"You know what was really strange about the whole thing? Part of me was freaking out, but another part of me was fascinated."

"I think you may have just found a career path," Cindy said with pride in her voice.

Marti cocked her head in consideration and then looked at the floor and dropped her shoulders. "I dunno. How hard is it to become a psychiatrist?"

Cindy gathered her daughter in a tight hug. "The only thing that would prevent you from following your dreams is your own lack of belief in yourself. And I'm here to tell you, from the depth of my soul, that I *know* you can do it." She kissed the top of Marti's head and pushed her away. "Now go shower and get ready."

Marti came back downstairs in a half hour with damp hair and helped her mom make the Sunday breakfast. The aromas of coffee brewing and sizzling bacon filled the house, bringing Gloria and Randy to the kitchen, both still in their nightclothes.

There was no talk of the night's events during breakfast; they ate in silence. The air in the house was stagnant and thick, like a storm brewing in the distance. When Cindy was clearing the dishes from the table, she turned to Marti and asked, "Honey, would you take Gloria to church? I think Randy and I need to talk." Randy grimaced.

When Randy and Cindy were alone in the kitchen, he said. "I'm so sorry, Mom." He got up from the table and stood next to her at the sink, but his head was down, and he wouldn't meet her eyes.

"I couldn't talk to you about this last night, and I'm not sure what to say to you now," she said, keeping her voice low so that Marti and

Gloria wouldn't hear as they got ready for church. "I haven't sorted out my feelings yet." She took a towel out of the drawer, dried her hands, and handed him the towel. She waved a hand at the pans she'd washed that were sitting on the drain board. Randy took the hint and started drying the first pan. "And we obviously need to have a discussion about gun safety."

Randy cringed. "I've learned my lesson."

Cindy's voice was sharp. "Oh, no. You're not getting off that easy. What you did was wrong on so many levels. I'm not sure where to even start." She took a deep breath, held it, and let it out slowly. "But no matter what, I want you to know that I will always love you. That will never, ever change. No matter how mad I am." The tears she'd been holding back spilled down her cheeks.

Randy put the dried pan and towel on the counter and threw his arms around her, pressing his head to her shoulder. When did he get so tall? It wasn't too long ago that she was holding him on her hip. She felt his body trembling. She squeezed him tighter into the hug and whispered, "We'll work through all of this. Things will be okay. It may be rocky for a while at school. I'm not sure what kind of reaction you'll get, but I'm sure there were be some backlash. But no matter how bad things are, you *will* survive."

"I've probably lost all my friends." His tears soaked through her blouse.

Cindy moved her hands to his cheeks and brought her face even with his. Eye to eye and with a strong, grave voice, she said, "Why didn't you give me the gun when you found it?"

"I thought the guys at school would think it was cool. And you would have just taken it away from me."

"Ya think?"

He mumbled, "I love you so much, Mom." The doorbell rang, and he pulled away, wiping the tears from his face. He looked at her once more with apology in his eyes, dropped his head, and headed back to his room. Cindy went to see who was at the front door.

A portly man in his mid twenties was standing on the porch with his back to the door. He was wearing a black vest with "SCPD" stenciled in white letters on the back. He turned to look at Cindy when she opened the door. His expression was one of boredom and irritation, as if he were being put out by having to do his job. "Detective Polk requested that we fingerprint..." the crime scene technician paused and looked at his clipboard, "a crawl space door?"

It only took him a few minutes to find and take a couple dozen prints. "The lab will need a list of names: people who had access to this."

"That might be a long list. We had a party here last night. I saw several people sitting on the doors when we ran out of chairs. I couldn't even tell you the names of the people who were here."

He raised an eyebrow. "Must've been one hell of a party."

After the technician left and Marti and Gloria departed for church, Cindy sat on the chaise in the backyard where she had sat in her dream. She looked at the other chaise, mostly covered by the shade of the pine tree, and then closed her eyes. She could see the dream woman, feel her presence. *He's going to kill your family, too.* "Talk to me," Cindy whispered. "Tell me who he is." There was a distant chime and a cool breeze swept over her, making the hair on her arms stand up. The image of the woman disappeared. The dogs started barking in the house as the chime sounded again. The doorbell. She heaved herself out of the chair and headed to the front door. She was surprised to see Darren and Steve standing on her porch.

"Come in, come in," she said, opening the screen door. "You just missed the guy taking the fingerprints."

"I was hoping you and I could talk," Darren said. "And Steve wants to talk with Randy, if that's okay."

"Oh!" she exclaimed. "I was afraid..." she stopped, trying to figure out what to say. "He's in his room."

Steve looked up at his father who nodded his permission. The boy squeezed past Cindy and headed upstairs.

"I've got a pot of coffee on, if you're interested," Cindy said, leading the way into the kitchen.

"We only have a few minutes alone, I think," Darren said. "Steve wants to be sure that Randy is still his friend."

For the second time in a few minutes, Cindy couldn't hold back her surprise. "He does? I...I..." she stammered.

"You were afraid Steve wouldn't want to be Randy's friend?"

"Yes, exactly. After that stunt, I'm not sure *I'd* want to be his friend. I was afraid that you wouldn't want them to be friends either."

As Darren opened his mouth to reply, they heard footsteps pounding down the stairs. "Why don't we discuss it with the boys?"

Randy and Steve entered the kitchen looking like they were back to being buddies. Cindy let out a breath she didn't realize she'd been holding. "Okay," she said when they joined the adults at the table. "Let's have it. What's happened in this house?"

Darren looked down at his hands and fidgeted with his coffee mug. "The Fremonts lived here in 2008. A nice family. The oldest boy, Vic, was 14 and played PAL soccer, so I'd gotten to know him and his parents a little bit. On the day of the murders, the oldest daughter, Whitney, was 16 and had stayed home alone for the weekend while the rest of the family was camping. As best as we can tell, someone had accosted Whitney, and when the father had to cut their camping trip short because he got called in for an emergency—he was a Battalion Chief with the Forestry Department—they interrupted the attack. The intruder herded the entire family into the rec room and shot them. Something that wasn't released was that all of the victims were shot in the head. They were executed."

She shuddered remembering her dream. She saw them fall like dominoes. She closed her eyes. "First it was a little girl, about eight, then the brother, the father, the youngest girl, and finally the mother. She opened her eyes and glanced around. All three guys were staring at her. "What?" she exclaimed, annoyed.

"That information was *not* in any public reports," Darren said. "How could you possibly know what order they died in? We figured it out by the way the bodies were piled."

Puzzled, Cindy said, "Surely it must have been. How else would I have dreamed it unless I'd read about it first?"

"You dreamed it?" Randy asked, excited. "That's sick!"

"Sweet!" Steve exclaimed as he high-fived his friend.

"No, it's definitely not," Cindy said in disgust. She lifted her coffee mug off the table; it was empty. "Do you want more coffee?"

"Please," Darren said.

While she made a new pot of coffee, Darren continued. "Okay, let me tell you something else that was not in the papers. There was blood found in Whitney's bedroom."

"Oh!" Randy interrupted, "That wasn't in the newspaper, but I did find it online. Wasn't it a bloody handprint?" Darren scowled at him but nodded his head. Randy continued, "They got a fingerprint from it and proved it was Whitney's. But her body was missing."

"Yes, that's true," Darren said. "The blood type was B, but only the mother had that type. The rest were O. So some questions during the investigation that were never fully answered were why and how did Whitney leave a handprint in her room in her mother's blood, and where did she go? Was she killed and the murderer took her body? Or did she escape and we've never found her?"

"I think she was shot," Steve said. He seemed startled that he'd spoken. He glanced at his dad and flushed. He hurried on. "There were six casings found, but only five bullets. And each time people have been killed in this house, one person disappears, never to be found."

Cindy could feel the tension developing between Steve and Darren.

"Have you made it a habit of reading my files?" There was a sharp edge to Darren's voice.

Cindy broke in and tapped her fingers on the table. "What do you mean, 'each time?' How many deaths have there been?"

Steve and Darren glared at each other, but it was Randy who answered. "I heard at school the house is haunted; anyone who lives here dies. At least a dozen families have been killed."

Darren rolled his eyes and shook his head. "Don't you just love how things get exaggerated in the rumor mill? That's precisely why the police keep things quiet. No, there were three families who have lived in this house, and at least one person in each of the families has either died or gone missing with the presumption of death."

"Oh my God," Cindy whispered, slumping in her chair. "I remember from the paperwork during the sale that the house was built in 1967, and I've heard that some kids were killed during the construction. Does that tally include them?

"No. Including them, there were four different murder cases." He made quotation marks with his fingers. "The 'powers that be' did a good job of keeping it out of the press. It started with those kids. Then in the '70s, one woman was presumed dead, but her body was never found. She was the daughter-in-law of Larry Bell, the banker. That one was easy for him to keep quiet. He made it look like she'd run off with a lover. So there's no definitive connection between those two events. Then in the '80s, four children were killed. And you know about the Fremonts.

"Whoa!" Cindy exclaimed. "No wonder this house didn't sell. It would have been nice if someone had told me about it. How the hell is this not public knowledge? How could it be covered up? And why? It doesn't make sense."

"When the boys were killed in 1967, there was an uproar in town, but the owner of the development, Larry Bell, kept it out of the newspapers. This was still a farming town then with no local paper. He owned Valley Bank and had enough clout to do pretty much what he wanted. The Vietnam War was keeping the general public and the media occupied. They had little or no interest in a small farm community."

Cindy felt a little better about her wasted time at the newspaper morgue. If what Darren said was true, she would have spent a lot of hours trying to find stories that weren't there.

Darren tapped the table in front of Randy. "I'd like to see where you got the information. We must have a leak." He turned back to Cindy and said, "During investigations, we hold back information from the press for a couple of purposes. First, if you have information that only the killer thinks he knows, then you have a way to find and trip up suspects. Second, it can help discern repeat crimes from copycats. So if that information is out there, it takes away an investigative tool."

"But the case is closed because the chief shot the homeless dude," Steve said. "Right, Dad? So if it's closed, does it really matter if the info is out there?"

Darren shrugged. "In the long run, I suppose not. But since the case never went to court, most of the details were never released."

Their discussion was ended by the dogs barking and running to the front door. The group in the kitchen could hear Marti greeting the puppies.

Darren looked at Randy and said, "Would you go online and find out where you found the information?" Randy excused himself. Steve followed him upstairs.

"I think I smell fresh coffee brewing!" came Gloria's voice as she and Marti came into the kitchen.

Fixing a smile on her face, determined to look like nothing was wrong, Cindy hugged her aunt. "Want a cup?"

Darren was at the counter already getting mugs ready. He glanced back over his shoulder and waved to Gloria.

"Oh!" Gloria exclaimed. "Perhaps we should have stayed at church awhile longer, Marti," she said in a stage whisper.

Marti hugged her great aunt. "Would you like a croissant with your coffee?"

"That would be splendid, darling." Gloria sat at the table, fixing her eyes on Darren.

Marti stepped up to her mom and whispered low enough that Gloria wouldn't hear, "She doesn't remember *anything* about yesterday. She doesn't remember the party or... what happened later."

"Really?" Cindy thought about it for a moment. "Then she probably doesn't know who Darren is." Cindy crossed to the table. "Darren, I would like to introduce you to the most inspirational lady in my life. This is my Aunt Gloria."

Darren stepped over to Gloria and set the mug of coffee in front of her. Cindy continued, "And Gloria, this is Darren Polk. Darren is a detective with the city's police department. He lives one block over."

Darren took Gloria's hand. "It is an honor to meet you. Cindy speaks very highly of you." He gave Cindy a questioning look, but then his expression changed to one of understanding as he remembered that Gloria was afflicted with Alzheimer's.

"Well thank you, young man. I'm very happy to see that Cindy has made a new friend here." She gave him a mischievous wink and laughed when a flush spread over his face. "And a policeman to boot! How wonderful! Please sit. I'd like to get to know you more."

Marti whispered in her mother's ear, "Out of the mouths of the elderly with dementia."

Cindy covered her mouth to keep from laughing, and she and her daughter stepped away.

"After Mass we ran into some people from last night's party, but she didn't know any of them. Do you remember the older gentleman who sat with her?"

"John... John O'Conner."

Marti nodded. "Right. He was really patient with her when she didn't remember him. He was totally cool about it. He seems nice, but..."

"But what?"

"He lives across the street from Peter, and Peter thinks he's weird. He's always watching out his window."

"Some people don't have anything to do after they retire. Maybe he takes the neighborhood watch thing seriously."

"Peter says he gives him the creeps."

Marti finished fixing the croissant and placed the dish in front of Gloria. She asked Darren if he would like anything. When he declined, saying that coffee was all he needed, she turned back to her mother and said, "Would you mind if I took the dogs for a walk with Peter? There're some hiking trails in the foothills he wants to show me. His mom and brother are going, too."

"That's a good idea," Cindy said. It would be good for her daughter to have time away from the madness. She planned to tell Marti about the previous families in the house, but for now, her daughter needed to be a teenager. "I'm sure the dogs will love going out into the hills. Oh, and remember that I'll be leaving around two to pick up Laura from the airport, so I'd like you to be home by three."

"Um, about that," Marti said. "With everything going on here, hanging out with a medium isn't exactly what I'd like to do. I'd rather spend the evening with my new friends." As Cindy opened her mouth to reply, Marti continued. "Mom, come on. I know the ghost stuff doesn't bother you, but I really don't like it. It gives me the creeps, and Peter hates it, too. He doesn't even want to come over here. It's hard enough making new friends without them all hearing about you bringing in a psychic."

Cindy glared at her daughter. "Fine. Go hang out with your friends after the walk. Just make sure you call to let me know where you are."

Marti pulled a face. "Laura's a psychic. Couldn't she tell you that?"

"Hey! That's uncalled for, young lady."

The teenager sighed. "You're right. I'm sorry. I just... um... yeah, I'll call and let you know where I'm going to be."

Cindy hugged her daughter. In a voice too low for the rest of the people in the room to hear, she said, "We'll talk about your attitude later. Make sure you let me know where you are."

After Marti left the house with the dogs, Gloria finished her croissant and coffee. "I think I'd like to take a bit of a nap."

Darren and Cindy went out to the backyard and looked at the crawl space entrance. It looked like the storm cellar doors on a Midwestern house. They considered various ways of blocking the entrance and agreed that it should be locked from the inside. Cindy screwed in some hand brackets on the interior of the doors, and out of the scraps of lumber from other repairs on the house, she fashioned a bolt that slid through the handles. Taking a flashlight with her, Cindy crawled inside, closed the doors, and slid the lumber piece in place. In the darkness only relieved by the dim light of the flashlight beam, Cindy fought back her fear of spiders. Darren tried to open the door from the outside, but their locking mechanism worked well, and he couldn't budge them. The only way to open the doors would be from the inside.

Satisfied with the job they did and eager to get out, Cindy turned on her hands and knees towards the interior of the house. Flicking the flashlight on, she felt a wave of disorientation. Since the entrance in the rec room was closed, there was no landmark for her to follow, and everything looked the same. She wasn't sure exactly where to go. She tried to picture the layout of the house and started crawling in the direction of where she thought the entrance would be. The oppression she felt the other day down below the rec room was even stronger now. Her breath was coming in short gasps as she fought off panic. She shined the flashlight beam around and saw a small pile of debris on the ground. It was an empty water bottle and a deli sandwich wrapper on the ground. Irritated that Randy had missed them when he had cleaned up the area, her panic receded. She gathered the waste and continued her slow journey in the direction she hoped was her exit. A beacon of light appeared: Darren opened the hatch in the rec room. She scurried as quickly as she could on her hands and knees to the opening.

Darren helped her get out of the hole, and she lost her breath again when she stumbled into his muscular chest. She flushed and stepped back, almost falling into the opening. Darren grabbed her left arm, and his other arm snaked around her waist and pulled her against him. They stood in an awkward embrace for a few moments, long enough for Cindy to breathe in his scent and feel her knees weaken. This time it was Darren who stepped back.

Still clutching the bottle and sandwich wrapper in her left hand, she said, "Shall we go see if the boys have come up with anything?"

"We were just about to come get you guys," Steve said when the adults entered Randy's room. "We found it."

The blog was an unofficial history of the city that hadn't been updated in years. The page where Randy had discovered the information was one that outlined notorious events that had occurred since the founding of Santa Clara in the 1800s. There were gruesome photos of various murders, car accidents, and catastrophes. Some pictures, like those from the 1989 Loma Prieta earthquake, were well publicized, but others were crime scene photos that had not been made public.

"Go back to the home page, please," Darren instructed Randy. The boy scrolled to the bottom of the home page, and listed there was the site's author's name. "George Atwater. I bet he's related to our retired Chief Harry Atwater. It would explain where he got the information. The Chief'll be irate. He may be retired, but he still acts like he owns the place."

"George Atwater... that name sounds familiar. Or at least the name Atwater." Cindy pondered where she had heard it, but the more she chased it, the further away it got.

"Could he have been at the party?" Darren asked. "I don't remember seeing him."

"Hmm, I certainly suppose so. I'll never remember half of the people that were here. Oh, before I forget," Cindy said to her son before leaving the bedroom, "I found more crap under the house about ten feet from the old crawl space entrance."

"Really? I got all of it. What did you find?" She described it and the location where she'd found it. "No, Mom, I'm *positive* that I cleaned that area up."

The four of them looked at each other, each thinking the same thing. Someone else had been under the house.

Chapter 14
September 4, 2011
Day 35

"How much do you want to know about the house's past before you go inside?" Cindy asked Laura Lee as they pulled into the driveway. The psychic medium's flight had been on time, and they'd made it to the house before 3 o'clock.

"Very little, actually. I don't want anything to taint my perceptions." She ran her slender, manicured fingers through her long blond hair, not making a move to get out of the van.

"I feel funny about having you do a reading for me when you're here as my friend."

"I usually don't like to read friends, either." She reached out and took Cindy's hand. "But I think this is important. I got some pretty strong feelings over the phone. And if they're that strong at a distance, you'll be needing some help."

The medium closed her eyes for a moment. "The spirits will talk to me whether I want them to or not, whether we're friends or not. If I don't listen to them now, they'll be clamoring for my attention until I do." She squeezed Cindy's hand. "But before we go in, I'd like to tell you what I feel surrounding you. Keith is here. He's worried about you."

"My husband's here? He's worried? In what way?" Cindy asked. A mixture of emotions coursed through her: love for her husband, sorrow and loneliness at his absence, a pang of guilt for her developing feelings for Darren, and an uneasiness that Keith might be watching her with a new man.

"He's proud of how you've raised the kids, but he says you need to spend more time for yourself. He wants you to enjoy your life, to move on. He approves of someone you met recently." She paused, thinking. "The name starts with a 'D' but I can't quite get it. Someone in authority?"

Cindy felt her face flush. "That must be Darren. I met him at the party. He's a detective."

"Ah, yes. Keith is smiling. But he's also worried about your safety in the house. He's not alone. Others are here."

"Yeah, I've met at least one."

"Your dad says he's proud of you."

"Dad's here? Really?" Cindy clasped her hands to her chest and smiled.

Laura nodded, returning Cindy's smile for a moment before it turned grave. "He's showing me a gun. Does that mean anything to you?"

Cindy's eyes widened. She hadn't told Laura about what happened the night before. "Too bad you weren't here yesterday. I could have used that information. I don't want to go into it right now, but, yeah, there was an incident with a gun last night. Randy almost shot a friend of his."

Laura looked worried. "He's shaking his head no. I'm having a hard time seeing him clearly. There're a lot of others here. Your husband and father are here for *you*, but the others are attached to the house." She closed her eyes and breathed deeply. "Okay, let's go on in."

The dogs greeted Laura with enthusiasm as the ladies entered the house from the garage. Laura knelt down to pet them. Xena promptly dashed off and returned with a ball in her mouth, while Sherlock stayed by Laura enjoying a good scratching. Laura took the ball from Xena and tossed it down the hall . Xena chased with enthusiasm. Laura stood and said, "These two are...important..."

Randy appeared in the hallway, coming from the living room, and Laura didn't continue with the thought. "Has it really been that long since I've seen you? You were knee-high last time."

"Well, if you listen to Mom, that was just last week."

Laura laughed. "I think the same thing with my little girl, so maybe it's all mothers." Xena came back and dropped the ball at Laura's sandaled feet.

"Randy, would you mind taking the dogs away, please," Cindy asked.

"'Kay," he said. "Oh, Mom, Marti and Peter are going to the movies with Veronica. Veronica's mom picked them up here a couple minutes ago. They're probably going out for dinner after." He stood staring at Laura for a beat too long.

When he finally turned away, Cindy whispered, "I don't think he remembered how pretty you are. How have you kept your gorgeous figure? I'm so jealous."

Laura elbowed Cindy. "You're funny."

They took a tour of the house, but since Gloria was napping, they stayed away from that room. Laura didn't say a word during the tour, but let out a sigh when she sat at the kitchen table afterwards. "The rec room has the most power, and there's a lot of energy in Randy's room, but each room's had its share of grief."

"How so? What are you seeing?" Cindy held up a pitcher of iced tea, and Laura nodded.

"Does the name Ann–maybe Annie, Annabel, or something like that – mean anything to you?"

Cindy shook her head. "No. At least not in connection with this house." She put a glass of iced tea in front of Laura along with a saucer of lemon wedges. "I had a friend in college whose name was Anne. To the best of my knowledge though, she hasn't passed on. I just saw some friends from college who still see her. They didn't mention anything happening to her."

"This was Anne's place, the kitchen. It holds meaning for her." Laura's gaze became unfocused, seeing something that Cindy could not. "She's showing me trees. Pine trees. She keeps covering her face, like there's a bad smell."

"I'm sorry, I have no idea what that's about. Oh, wait. We have a pine tree in the back yard. Do you want to go out there?"

They went outside, but as soon as they sat on the chaise lounges, Laura shook her head. "No, this isn't right. It's not what she's trying to tell me. But..." Laura's voice faded as she looked around. "There's a mixture of happiness and fear out here, too. A little boy..." She drifted off again. "I'm sorry, I can't hear him very well. He keeps pointing at the back door and then the gate." She shook her head. "Let's go back inside."

"Laura, I don't know much about what happened here. I can tell you that the Fremonts owned the house before me. Patrick and Christina Fremont. Darren's a cop, so he might recognize the names of people you mention. Should I call him over?"

"I'd rather not, if you don't mind. At least not yet. Just remember the names I tell you. I think Christina went by Tina. She cringed when you called her Christina. She seems to be the strongest guide here." As they sat down at the kitchen table again, Laura continued. "Remember when we were on the phone, I asked you if there was anyone else in the house?"

"I do. It was just me and Gloria in the house. I checked."

"I'm feeling it again. There's a man. He's not here now, though. But he was here recently. He's upset about something. There's a lot of hostility in him." Laura crinkled her face. "He's a really nasty guy. Tina seems to be very angry with him."

"Is he the one that killed her?"

Laura slowly shook her head. "I can't tell. I think *she* thinks it's him, though. But she never saw his face clearly. I think he's a psychopath. People would see him as normal, maybe even a great, standup guy. But underneath, he's evil. Oh, how horrible!" Laura's face was pale.

"What do you see?" Cindy asked.

"She showed me what happened. Her whole family. Shot. Her oldest daughter almost made it."

"I dreamed about that," Cindy said. Her voice shook. *So there's at least one of Darren's questions answered: Whitney is dead.* "I couldn't see the killer's face. Could you?"

"No, no." Laura pushed away from the table and stood up. Her legs were shaky. "He's a big man. Tall. But that might be Tina's perception of him. Because she's short."

Laura walked into the living room and stood in the center, facing the front door. "It started here. I can feel him. He's not dead, but his energy is so strong that it permeates this room. He's been here recently."

"You said that before, too. How recently?"

"Very."

"Days? Hours? Is he here now?" Cindy's voice quivered near panic. Her knees felt weak. No, she thought. It couldn't be Darren. But he was the man most recently here. No way. Earlier Laura had said that her dead husband approved of Darren. Was he wrong?

"Not now, but within the last week. Maybe in the last day."

"Oh, God," Cindy whispered. "Do you think it could be Darren?"

Laura shook her head. "That's not what I'm getting."

Cindy felt a bit of hope. "Maybe he was at the party yesterday?"

"That should narrow things down," Laura said.

"I wish. Unfortunately, between neighbors, old friends, and the kids' friends, there might have been fifty people here throughout the day, and I don't think I actually met everyone."

Laura sat down on the couch. "The images I'm getting are difficult to make out. Fear does that to people."

"Do you think the same man killed everyone over the years? Darren said three teenagers when the house was being built—"

"Yes, those happened here. This room. No wait, not in this room, but they ended up here."

"I didn't get all the details from Darren, but he said that there were four different cases here. The three teenagers and the Fremonts are the only ones we really talked about. He started to mention others but we were interrupted. You mentioned an Anne, so that must be another. Who else do you see?"

"The little boy outside, but I felt him upstairs in Randy's room, too. And a little girl. Does the name Sue mean anything to you?" At Cindy's head shake, she continued. "The poor girl is riddled with guilt. She's a teenager. She blames herself for something. She's so upset, I can't figure out what she's saying. So much pain. I need to help them."

"Look, how about we get you settled in at your hotel and get something to eat. We can have Darren meet us, and he can give you more insight. Would that help you?"

"That's a good idea. Some distance right now might give me more clarity."

* * *

On the way to dinner with Darren and Steve, Laura told the boys about some of the cases she worked on with the police. Cindy enjoyed the stories, but the rapt attention Steve and Randy gave Laura amused her. They asked a lot of questions, and Cindy was impressed with their depth. Maybe her son would follow in her footsteps in the investigative journalism field.

Darren had reserved a table on the restaurant's patio. Steve and Randy sat at one end of the table, pretending to ignore the adults, although Cindy noticed that both boys kept stealing peeks at Laura.

"Darren, does the name Ann or Annie mean anything to you regarding the house?" Laura asked.

He thought for a moment. "Anne was the daughter-in-law of Larry Bell, the bank owner who also owned the house." He looked at Cindy. "She's the one I mentioned this morning from the '70s that was presumed dead even though her body wasn't found."

"And what about Sue or Susan?"

Their waiter put a platter of sizzling fajitas on the table for the adults, along with margaritas. The boys dug into cheeseburgers.

"Suzy... Dudley," Darren said. She was babysitting for the Eriksons back in the '80s. She was killed along with the oldest two kids, but the little boy went missing. There was evidence that he was killed, too, but, just like Anne, no body was found."

"Ah," Laura said, "that's why she feels so much guilt. She probably thinks that she should have protected them. And the little boy must be the one I saw in the backyard. He showed me a tall man in dark overalls. There was a straw hat covering his face."

Her description startled Cindy. "Hey, that's what the guy was wearing in my dream!"

Randy looked up, his eyes wide and excited. "Could that be the clothes I found under the house?"

Darren looked thoughtful. "Maybe. They're in forensics. We'll see."

"What about the name Eric?" Laura asked. She held up a hand. "No, wait...that's not quite right..."

"Enrico," Darren said. "He's the missing teenager from 1967. We have no evidence that he's dead. A lot of people thought he'd had something to do with it."

"No, I don't think he did," Laura said, shaking her head. "He's confused, and he's definitely dead. Angry. So angry. I need to help him move on."

"Dude," Steve said, his voice awed. "You can see them even now? When we're not even at the house?"

Laura nodded. "Once I've connected with them, I can sense them from farther away. I usually need some sort of tie to the location or the person they're attached to, like a telephone, but with really strong spirits, I can feel them after I leave. Enrico is strong. And angry," she repeated.

Cindy's eyes were wide. "Who's he angry at? Us? Does he want to hurt us?"

"I can't tell yet. Let me try to connect more with him when we go back. Tina is afraid of him."

Darren said, "Christina Fremont. That's who you mean?"

"Yeah," Laura answered.

He sighed. "That was a fiasco. Mrs. Fremont had come to the station and reported that there was someone in her house, but when she started talking about ghosts, the desk officer didn't pay any more attention. I've wondered if she and her family would still be alive if he'd listened or maybe if I'd been the one she'd talked to. Would I have passed her off, too, thinking she was a nutcase?"

Laura looked at him with hard eyes. "You think ghosts are only seen by crazy people? Do you even believe they can exist?"

"I'll be completely honest with you. I'm a skeptic. There are too many people out there trying to make a buck off of people's fears. A good observer can pick up on little things, give a little anecdotal evidence and build a good story, and *wham* you've got a ghost that people will pay you to get rid of."

Laura pursed her lips and then smiled. "You know, Darren, I think I like you. You're not afraid to tell the truth. You say it like you see it." She tapped her fingers on the table. "And you're absolutely right. There *are* a lot of charlatans out there. A disgustingly large amount of them. They've given psychics a bad name. That's one reason I prefer the term 'medium.' But there are a lot of people who are true sensitives, although most won't acknowledge it. Your Tina was one of them. Her oldest daughter was, too. She closed her eyes for a moment and when she opened them, she said, "Whitney. She's another one who's angry."

The server arrived with the check, interrupting their conversation. "Shall we head back to the house now?" Cindy asked.

"Definitely," Laura said. "I'm feeling stronger."

* * *

"Let's start in Randy's room," Laura said, looking at Randy for his permission. When he nodded, she headed up the stairs, and took one step into the room. Randy and Steve sat on the bed, while Cindy and Darren stood at the doorway. Laura closed her eyes, her face calm and expressionless. "This was Whitney's room," she whispered. She placed her hand, fingers spread, on the wall beside the door. Slowly her hand dropped to her side.

Darren whispered to Cindy, "Amazing. She just put her hand exactly where the bloody handprint was."

"She fought back," Laura said. Her voice was colored with a combination of sorrow and admiration. "She's the only one who ever did." Laura stepped across the room to the closet. "There's a gun here. No, it's gone." At Randy's groan, she turned to him, but her eyes were focused elsewhere, someplace no one else in the room could see. There were tears in her eyes. "There's a little boy. Aaron? He's looking for his older brother." A tentative smile touched her lips. "He thinks ... Chuck? Yes, he thinks Chuck is playing hide and seek, but he's not here."

Laura sat down on the floor and crossed her legs. She closed her eyes, and a calmness enveloped her. She held her arms out, beckoning to something unseen. Her lips moved in a conversation that no one in the room could hear. The room was silent as if all the air had been swept out. Finally Laura stood up. Her eyes were again focused.

"Whoa," Steve whispered to Randy.

"Okay, that's one soul crossed over. But there are still so, so many left." Laura looked at Randy. "Your soccer ball will probably stay put now."

Randy gasped. "How'd you know?"

"Aaron loved soccer. It was his favorite toy. He wanted you to play soccer with him."

* * *

"Say, do you think I could steal Gloria away for a few minutes?" Laura asked when they finished in Randy's room and returned to the kitchen.

"Sure," Cindy replied. She stood up and looked at Darren. "Would you like to take a walk?" She gave the boys a pointed look. They took the hint and went out to the backyard with the dogs.

As soon as they were alone, Laura said, "Okay, Gloria. Spill it. What's on your mind?"

Gloria attempted to look innocent. "What makes you think something's on my mind?" At Laura's raised eyebrow, Gloria said, "Okay, yeah, I'm a bit worried. I'm glad you've confirmed that there're ghosts here. It's not all in my mind."

"You were worried about the Alzheimer's?"

She nodded. "I'm afraid I'm not always sure what's real and what's not. I keep seeing movement out of the corner of my eye, but when I turn, there's no one there."

"How often does it happen?"

"A lot. I'm afraid to tell Cindy, although she took it better than I thought she would when I told her something feels wrong about the house."

"What emotions are you feeling? I mean, do you feel like there's a negative energy? Positive? Happy or angry?"

"That changes. In the mornings in my room is when I feel the most...I don't know how to describe it... the most tension or fear. It's not hatred or anger, I don't think. More like someone's lost and scared, maybe hopeless or helpless. But at night or late afternoons, I get the angry feelings. Hostility. It really worries me."

"Well, I think I can help you. I'm not feeling anyone here that wants to do *you* harm."

"What do they want, then?"

"Justice. Definitely justice. And I think what Tina wants most of all is to make sure nothing happens to you guys. She may be the one you're feeling. She's very worried about you."

With her voice trembling, Gloria asked the question that had been bothering her the most. "Laura, do you think that with my Alzheimer's, the ghosts could have a way into this world?"

Laura sat back and thought. "I'm not sure about that. If I were feeling a malicious entity, I might worry about your safety. But that's not what's here." Laura didn't tell her elderly friend that she suspected that the person who would do harm was still alive.

Laura also didn't want to tell her that one of the spirits was getting stronger, feeding on the fear in the house. She could see his face. He was the handsome Hispanic teenager they'd talked about at dinner, but his eyes held an intensity that scared her. He was looking for revenge, and would not cross over until his killer was dead. If he could use Gloria's ailment to his advantage, he would.

Laura needed more time to help the souls move on, but she was leaving the next morning; she would have to come back. Soon. She prayed that nothing would happen before she was able to return.

Chapter 15
September 6, 2011
Day 37

Tuesday morning started as usual, but after Gloria and Cindy worked out in the rec room, the first of the day's surprises arrived. After everything that had happened over the weekend with the gun, Cindy was apprehensive of what Randy would experience at school. She was half expecting to see a school counselor when the doorbell rang at 10:30, but instead, it was John O'Conner standing on the porch.

John was sporting a tweed coat and hat with a crisp white shirt. His posture was perfectly straight, not slumping in any way that would show aging or mask his six-foot height. His eyes were overshadowed by his drooping eyelids, the only sign of his age outside of his thinning silver hair. But the smile he wore lit up his whole face. It was hard to believe that he was in his mid seventies. His mustache was trimmed, and the rest of his face was freshly shaved.

When his smile faltered, Cindy realized that she had been standing there staring at him. She shook off her surprise and asked him to come in. "Mr. O'Conner, it is very nice to see you. Please, come in, sit down."

"Thank you, young lady," he said in his deep, melodious voice. The dogs herded him to the family room, sniffing everywhere they could reach. John was patient with the dogs' inspection and selected a seat on the couch near the fireplace where the sun shined in from the picture window. He sat down and held out his hand. Sherlock shrank away, backing up behind the couch. Xena backed up out of reach.

Cindy wondered if he had a cat. Or was the dog sensing something else?

"May I offer you some coffee? Something to eat? I made some croissants this morning."

"Just some coffee would be nice. Black, please." As Cindy moved towards the kitchen, he added, "I'm hoping that Gloria is available. At the party, we talked about going out today, but maybe she's forgotten."

"We just finished a workout, and she's resting at the moment," Cindy called from the kitchen. She came back with the coffee on a tray and set it on the table beside him. "Did you hear about the incident after the party?"

"You mean with the gun? I most certainly did. I heard the police sirens and came out to see what was going on."

Cindy grimaced. "My aunt had a hard time with it. Marti told me that she didn't remember you when you saw her at the church."

"No, she didn't. But we talked for a while after the service. I hope that she'll remember me from that."

"I hope you won't be offended if she doesn't remember." He smiled and shook his head. "Okay, then if you'd excuse me for a moment, I'll go see how she's doing."

Cindy left the dogs with John and went down the hall to Gloria's room. As she was raising her hand to knock, Gloria opened the door. Cindy found herself pulled into the room by her aunt who then gently closed the door. "Did I hear John's voice," she asked hopefully. "I wasn't sure who it was over the dogs' barking."

"Yes, he's here to see you." Cindy watched Gloria's face. The older woman definitely remembered him. That was one of the frustrating things about Alzheimer's. The victim might remember details with amazing clarity, but then have zero recollection about something that happened a few minutes later. And she didn't remember anything about a date today. Had there been an actual date? She tried to shrug off the uneasy feeling that was creeping up her back.

"Oh! You've got to help me pick something to wear," Gloria begged, breaking Cindy's line of thought.

It took Gloria about twenty minutes to finish with her hair, makeup, and jewelry, and the efforts were not wasted on John. He rose from his seat on the couch when she entered the room and held his hands out to her. She stepped up to him, accepted his hands, and shyly dropped her eyes as he gazed at her.

"I hope you'll let me show you around the city. There are a lot of historic sites, and quite a few parks. There's a Senior Center with a pool, too." John spoke with a lot of pride in his hometown. "There are some great restaurants in the old square, if you'd be up for some lunch."

John turned to Cindy as he escorted Gloria out the door. "I'll have her back by three o'clock, if that works for you."

"That will be good," Cindy replied. She made sure that he had her telephone number and waved goodbye.

Cindy had the house to herself for once. No children, workers, neighbors, or her aunt. It had been an exhausting weekend, physically, mentally, and especially emotionally. The house she'd thought would be the home she'd always wanted was a home to quite a few other entities. And while Laura said that the spirits didn't have any anger towards her family, there was still the living being that Laura also sensed who did not have such benevolent intentions. The medium had promised to come out again soon to help, hopefully in the next month or so. Cindy just needed to survive until then.

She thought of Laura's comments about Darren. On the way to the airport, Laura had again stressed that Darren would be important in her life. Laura wasn't sure in what way he was important, just that he was. He seemed to be a nice man. He made Cindy feel safe, yet conflicted. She was definitely attracted to him, and she didn't think it was one-sided, but Laura had indicated that her dead husband was watching. How in the hell was she supposed to have a new relationship knowing that?

She went upstairs to her office sat down at her computer, determined to stop thinking about Darren and Keith and get some work done. She logged into her work email and pulled up the first of more than a dozen articles sent in by her staff reporters for the magazine's next issue. The article was a well-written investigation into the trends of assaults on females in the workplace, but despite her best intentions, her mind kept returning to the mysteries of her house. Thinking that it wouldn't hurt to spend a short time seeing what she could find, she closed down her email and searched the journalism network using her address and the Fremonts' names for the query.

She printed out dozens of newspaper articles and several of the blog entries that Randy had found. While they were printing, she went downstairs and made a large mug of tea. By the time she came back to her office, they were completed. She took them to her room and stretched out on her bed. As she read, she took notes.

The Fremonts had purchased the house in 2004 for substantially more than she had paid for it. During the first half of the decade, house prices had been exorbitant in the Bay Area. The family had moved here from Southern California when Patrick Fremont was hired as a battalion chief for the state's wild land fire department. Both in their late thirties, Patrick and his wife, Tina, had three children when they moved to Silicon Valley: twelve-year-old Whitney; Vic, eight; and Gabby, four. In 2006, their fourth child, Kim, was born. The local weekly paper had several stories on Whitney who was by all accounts a beautiful young lady. For her sixteenth birthday in April of 2008, she had begged her parents to send her to a modeling and etiquette school in New York. She was scheduled to go in August —a trip that the killer had prevented her from taking.

Right before the murders, the family had seemed to be thriving, well respected in the neighborhood, and active in their social scenes. Cindy looked closely at a picture that showed the family volunteering at the Ulistac Nature Area in the spring, just months before their untimely deaths. The father was a short man, muscular but carrying a few extra pounds, with a receding hairline. He was dressed in shorts, T-shirt, and baseball cap. He was holding his two-year-old girl in one arm with the other hand resting on a shovel that was standing in the dirt. Next to him was a thin girl with her long blond hair pulled back in a pony tail and a gorgeous smile and huge eyes; her right hand was resting on her fourteen-year-old brother's shoulder who was kneeling in front of her. Cindy felt like an unseen fist punched her in the stomach. It was definitely the family from her dreams.

The remainder of the articles dealt with the aftermath of the slaughter, calling Police Chief Harry Atwater a hero for shooting the suspect, a homeless man who'd made his encampment in the creek by the school Whitney attended. Details were sketchy, but the article gave the man's name as Oscar Whitehead, 54, a Vietnam vet. The article stated, "Evidence at the scene indicates that Whitehead had contact with Miss Fremont, though sources cannot yet divulge what that evidence entails." Cindy looked through the rest of the papers she'd printed, but none mentioned the evidence found on Whitehead.

The strangest thing that Cindy found in the newspaper articles was what she *didn't* find. There were no references to the boys being killed in 1967, Anne in 1975, and the kids in 1982. If she hadn't been told about the other murders, she wouldn't have guessed that there was more to the story. Puzzled, she rested her head on her pillow and closed her eyes, trying to figure out why the past would be omitted. As a journalist, that kind of connection would be something that she would have followed. It would make one hell of a story. Like Darren had said, someone had managed to hide the past history and obscure any connections between the events.

* * *

"Fifty years ago, this area was mostly farm land." John O'Conner indicated the rows of houses as he drove Gloria down Kiely Boulevard, a beautiful tree-lined street. "Orchards of walnuts, peaches, plums, almonds, and apples kept this area alive. My father's family moved here in the early 1930s, and we worked the land for thirty years. Walnuts were our main product." He stopped his narrative as he turned into the parking lot of Central Park.

Gloria had been listening intently. John's deep voice touched deep inside her, giving her a peace she hadn't realized she needed.

The couple walked the winding paths and stopped at various points to enjoy watching the creek that meandered its way from one end of the park to the other. At the center of the park, they stopped at a picturesque pond, where dogs romped through the grass, chasing the young ducks and in turn being chased by the angry adult ducks. They found a vacant table at the pavilion near the pond. John used his kerchief to brush the bench before Gloria sat down. The hot sun filtered through a magnificent wisteria that had branched up and wound through the pavilion's structure creating a shimmering umbrella. The purplish-blue petals from the massive plant drifted down in the breeze, leaving a dusting of purple on the table and ground. The smoke from a family's barbeque overwhelmed the fragrant flowers that lined the pavilion.

"John, what did you do outside of the farm?"

"While I was growing up, other than school, the farm was it. I'd get up early and take care of the chickens before going to school. In the afternoon, my time was spent between homework and helping my dad. I was the youngest. I had seven brothers and one sister. When they got married, they left the farm and started their own lives. So as I got older, more of the farming was left for me."

"You just had one sister? Poor girl."

He nodded. "She was the next youngest, four years older than me. My brothers spoiled her. She could have anything in the world she desired. She helped my mother while we all worked the farm. I was much smaller than my brothers, mostly because I was so much younger. And Marybeth always watched after me, making sure that our older brothers didn't pick on me. She was my guardian angel."

John stared off into space before continuing. "War was brutal on my family. I lost four brothers to the Korean war, and two more to Vietnam." He paused again and looked at her, then shook his head in disgust. "Like my brothers, I went to war, too. But when my only surviving brother died at home in an accident on the farm, I became the last male O'Conner and was sent home. By that time, Father had pretty much stopped farming himself and left the majority of the land fallow. I'd seen more of the world and had no more interest in the hard labor of farming. The Army sent me to college, and I went into accounting. A few of the guys joined the police force when they got back, but I didn't want to do that as a profession. Too danger-ous...I'd had enough of that in the war. Besides, I had a new family. I ended up joining the PD as a volunteer. Back then in some areas, the police force was legalized brutality. But Santa Clara was better."

She reached across the table and took his hand in hers. She squeezed it and said, "I'm very sorry about your brothers. I can't even imagine how horrible it must have been for you. Or for your parents. What of your sister?"

"She married and moved to New York. She passed on a couple years ago. She was as happy as she could be, although she and her husband never had children. She enjoyed spoiling mine whenever she'd visit."

A sad look crossed his face, and he lowered his eyes to the table. Gloria watched him but stayed silent. He took a breath and let it out slowly. "But there was something else I wanted to talk with you about. Are you aware of what's happened in your house? The mur-ders?"

"Oh, yes. We had a medium come out. Laura Lee. She's a great gal, an old family friend. She crossed over one little boy and will come back soon to help the rest."

John's eyes narrowed. "A psychic? Do you really think that will help? I think you should get out of that house. You're not safe there. Bad things happen there."

"Oh, I think we're perfectly safe. Laura would have told us if we were in danger."

Glancing at his wristwatch, John stood up abruptly, his hand still meshed with Gloria's. "It's already past one o'clock. Shall we get some lunch? There's a wonderful diner in the old quad area."

* * *

At two o'clock, Cindy's second surprise of the day came like the first, with a knock on the front door. It, however, was not a pleasant one. When she opened the door, she was greeted with a very upset-looking Jen Harrison, the mother of Randy's friend Lee who was almost shot.

"We need to talk," Jen said. She opened the screen door herself, pushed past Cindy, and sat on the couch. It took a moment before Cindy could gather herself. The sound of the screen door clicking shut broke her surprise.

Cindy turned from the door and glared at the woman sitting on her couch. "Okay, come on in and sit down."

As they had earlier in the day with John, the dogs investigated the newcomer. Jen did not have the patience nor grace that the elder man had, and she shoved the dogs away from her. Xena growled her displeasure. Cindy wasn't sure if it was because of the harsh treatment or if Xena was giving a commentary on what she thought of the person invading her house. Either way, she agreed with the dog's assessment.

Cindy sat in the recliner directly across from her uninvited visitor and called the dogs to her side. "What's on your mind?" She knew it would be the shooting incident, but she wasn't going to start out on the defensive.

Jen glared at her. "Your son is at school today telling everyone about the gun—"

Cindy held up her hand to stop Jen's tirade. "Stop. I'm sure it's all over the school. It would be hard to avoid it. We've discussed the situation with the police, and the gun is no longer here."

"My son could have been killed! And now your boy is at school acting like some star because he almost shot Lee. Your son needs to be locked up. He's crazy and a threat to society. If you don't punish him, I'll make sure someone else does."

"Again, stop!" Cindy stood up, towering over Jen. "You are way off base to say he's crazy. It was an accident. One that *never* should have happened, for sure. Your anger is justified, but saying he's crazy and needs to be locked up? What the hell did you think was going to happen? There was a crowd outside because of the police cars. *Your husband* is the one who opened his mouth to tell everyone what happened. So the word is out. Not because my son was blabbing, but because your husband couldn't shut up!"

Jen jumped to her feet. "How dare you use that kind of language with me!"

Cindy stood, shaking, barely containing her fury. "You barge in here, uninvited, and threaten my son. I'll talk to you any damn way I want to!"

Mrs. Harrison crossed to the front door and paused with her hand on the screen. "There are rumors this house is cursed. I hope the curse holds true for your family, too." She stormed out of the house, not looking back.

Cindy was shaking with adrenaline. "Bitch!" She was still pacing the living room when Darren pulled into her driveway in an unmarked police car.

"Whoa," he said, when he entered the house and saw how upset she was. "What happened?"

It only took her a few minutes to tell him about her visitor, but when she finished, she was a bit calmer. He took her hand and led her to the couch. "Don't let her get to you. She thinks she's better than everyone just because she nearly made it to the Olympics. She's always had a chip on her shoulder, a conceited witch with a nasty temper. She's a has-been, and she can't let go of the idea that her dreams were never realized. Jen and Ralph are perfect for each other. They're both jerks. It's too bad that Lee has to put up with them. So far he's been a good kid, but one has to wonder with parents like them."

"She's on the PTA," Cindy said. "She could make life difficult for Randy. At least Marti is at a different school."

"So why don't you join the PTA, too? Even out the odds."

Cindy barked a laugh. "Are you kidding? Randy would *die* if I joined the PTA."

"Yeah, I see your point."

She sighed. "I'm sorry. I've thrown all of this at you. You must have had a reason for coming by."

"Can't a guy stop by to see the prettiest woman on the block?" he asked.

"Umm, yeah, right. So what brings you by? Honestly."

"I am going to stop in to see the retired police chief, Harry Atwater. He lives nearby. I did manage to find out that George Atwater, the author of the web page that Randy found, is his son. I know you're working here at home, but I thought that maybe you'd come up with questions that he might be able to answer. And it gave me a reason to stop by."

"I did do some reading this morning, but I still don't know enough to be able to ask decent questions. I'd like to hear more about the other incidents that happened here. Maybe you can tell me instead."

Darren looked at his watch. "It's almost three. The kids should be getting home from school pretty soon. How about this... I'll go talk with the chief and come back to see you after my shift ends."

"I'd like that." She paused for a moment in thought. "What about Steve? Would the two of you like to come for dinner?"

"You know the way to my heart! I am a horrible cook. If it can't be delivered or microwaved, it pretty much doesn't enter our house."

Chapter 16
November, 1975

Anne Bell opened the oven to check the turkey. It was golden brown, close to being done. The stuffing was good, the best she'd ever made. With her in-laws here, Francine and Larry Bell, she worried over every detail of the Thanksgiving dinner. The potatoes were ready to be mashed, the broccoli was ready to be steamed, and its cheese sauce was staying warm on the stove top. The cranberries were setting in the refrigerator. Her best creation, sweet French bread, was absolute perfection. Everything was under control. She sighed in relief.

The Bells didn't approved of her marriage to their son, Eddie. He was a big time banker, and she was just a simple girl from a small town in Minnesota, not the socialite they wanted him to marry. This was the first time since they'd married ten years ago that the Bells had agreed to come to dinner. Maybe this would be the turning point in her relationship with them.

Her own mother should have arrived at the airport several hours ago, but her flight had been delayed out of Minnesota. Eddie had gone to the airport to pick her mother up and should be back any moment. Her six-year-old daughter, Heidi, was keeping Larry and Francine occupied. They acted as though the delay was somehow Anne's fault, another sign that she wasn't good enough for their son.

Anne stood in the doorway between the family room and the kitchen and watched her daughter. Heidi was the most precious thing in the world to her. She had inherited her mother's Nordic features, another sore spot for the Bells, who were disappointed that their granddaughter didn't have their son's brown hair and eyes. They had the audacity to question if the baby was even their blood. They'd called Anne a tramp. Eddie stood by her through his parents' insults. Instead of tearing them apart, his parents' tirades cemented their bond deeper.

His father owned the only bank in town, Valley Bank, which carried most of the mortgages for the homes in this tract. And he owned this house as well. Mr. Bell took every opportunity to remind them that they lived in his house at his sufferance.

As the years went by, the elder Bells visited their son and granddaughter, but they ignored Anne—except to order her around as though she were a servant. As Heidi grew, Francine and Larry became entranced with the little girl. She had her father's intellect, but it was Heidi's positive nature that drew her grandparents past their shortsightedness.

"Can I refill your drinks?" Anne asked her in-laws.

Larry looked at his watch again. "No." His wife didn't bother to look up from Heidi's homework that she was reviewing.

Pedro, Heidi's beloved puppy, a pug mix that they rescued from the pound, bolted to the front door, announcing someone's arrival. His nub of a tail tried to wag, but instead, his whole body wiggled. Anne followed him to the door and was relieved when she saw her husband's car pull into the driveway. She'd been worried that her neighbor down the street might come by to visit while the Bells were here. John was a widower with a small son, and they'd struck up a friendship. If he stopped by with holiday wishes, the Bell's would think there was something lurid going on. It would be a catastrophe.

She turned to her in-laws and said, "They're here!" As she opened the front door, she heard Francine say under her breath, "About damn time." Anne slipped out the front door and ran to her mother's side. Mother and daughter embraced tightly, while Eddie got Nora's suitcases out of the trunk.

"You must be exhausted," Anne said to her mother. The two women, though they were twenty-five years apart, looked like sisters. Nora's light hair disguised the gray, and her face was like smooth porcelain. Both were slim, tall, and moved with easy grace.

Nora's stomach growled loudly, and she and her daughter laughed. "I'm hungrier than tired. I managed to sleep in the airport and on the flight. I slept right through the food service."

"Then let's get you inside."

The only time Anne's and Eddie's parents had met was at the wedding. The Bells had not made Mrs. Wilkinson feel welcome then, and it seemed that nothing had changed since. Nora found herself being stared at with open hostility by her daughter's in-laws moments before little Heidi jumped into her arms. She smothered the little girl in kisses.

"Gammy!" Heidi said, returning the kisses.

In twenty minutes, the family was seated at the dining room table. Eddie carved the turkey and passed around one platter of white meat and another of dark. Anne watched her in-laws as they tasted each bite. The pinched looks they had on their faces showed they thought the food would be awful, probably poisoned, but each bite brought surprised looks. They liked it!

Anne was proud of the pies she'd made for dessert, although she was afraid she'd gone too far. She'd made lemon meringue, apple, pumpkin, and pecan. She waited anxiously for her mother-in-law's response. With the first bit of pecan pie, Francine's eyes closed in pleasure. When she opened her eyes, she turned to Anne and said, "Where did you buy this pie? I simply must bring one to the next Ladies of Santa Clara meeting."

Anne ignored the implied insult that she wouldn't be able to bake a good pie. "It's Mom's recipe. We don't give out the recipe, but I'd be happy to bake one for your meeting, if you'd like. Please try the other pies. They're all Wilkinson recipes."

When Francine and Larry left forty-five minutes later, Anne's mother-in-law was laden down with samples of each of the pies. She also had containers of turkey, gravy, mashed potatoes, and stuffing. But most importantly, for the first time, she actually kissed her daughter-in-law's cheek with what appeared to be real affection.

With her in-laws finally gone, Anne sank down on the couch in the living room with her mother. Her husband was watching TV from the recliner, but shut it off and looked at his wife. "I think you did it," Eddie said. "You finally won over my mother. I didn't think it could be done."

They chatted happily for a while before Eddie suggested taking a stroll around the neighborhood. Pedro the pug, of course, was game for a walk, but Heidi was napping in her room, and Anne wanted to get working on the dishes. Arm in arm, Nora and Eddie left the house.

Anne turned the radio on in the kitchen and hummed along while working. She was quite proud of herself, happier than she could remember being in years. She finally won over the Grinch. She felt a warmth on the back of her neck and reached her left hand up to rub it. Her hair was seized in a strong grip from behind, and she was violently pulled back against a strong, tall body. A cold blade bit into her throat. She inhaled to scream. The knife slid across her throat, and the scream became a gurgling sound. There was no pain, just a disembodied fascination with the spurts of red that splashed across the sink and wall.

* * *

Pedro was the first to find something wrong. He stood at the entrance to the kitchen keening, hair on end. Nora stepped over him and into the kitchen. There was blood pooled in front of the kitchen sink, and crimson sprays on the walls and ceiling.

"Anne!" she screamed. "Heidi!"

Awakened by the screams and the barking, Heidi stumbled down the stairs. "Mommy? Daddy?" she called out, groggy from her nap.

She found herself swept up into her grandmother's arms.

"Where's your mommy, darling?" Nora begged her granddaughter. "Where is she?" She ran up the stairs, checking each room with Heidi riding on her hip. When Nora and Heidi came back down the stairs, her son-in-law was on the phone in the kitchen. "...blood all over the kitchen," she heard him saying. "But we can't find her! Please come, we need help!" He sank down on the kitchen stool and sobbed, holding the phone to his chest.

Chapter 17
September 6, 2011
Day 37

"Our retired Police Chief Harry Atwater was familiar with some of the cases involving this house," Darren told Cindy over a late dinner in her kitchen. Gloria, Marti, Randy, and Steve had taken their dinners outside. "He was a sergeant at the time of the 1967 murders and had just made detective in the 1975 murder or disappearance of Anne Bell. That was his first case as detective. He wasn't the lead detective in the 1982 killings of the babysitter and kids, so he didn't have many details about it. The murders in '67 and '82 had all been done with knives, but aside from the type of weapon and the location, there was no way to connect them. And since Anne Bell's body was never found, they couldn't tell what – if any – weapon was used. They remained separate investigations."

"So the only investigation that he has first-hand knowledge about is Anne Bell?" Cindy sighed. "Did he give you any details on that?"

Darren nodded. "We spent the majority of the time talking about it. It was Thanksgiving, and he was on call. He got a lot of grief from the first arriving officers because it took him an hour to get to the scene. His explanation was that he had just finished a several-mile run when he got the call, and he took a shower before responding.

"Most homicides are done by family members or someone the victim knows, and the main suspect is usually the spouse. Atwater grilled Anne's husband, but dismissed him pretty quickly. Anne's mother, Mrs. Wilkinson, had come out from Minnesota to visit, and she backed up the husband's story. Their alibi of being on a walk with the dog was verified by multiple neighbors. But Mrs. Wilkinson said her daughter's mother- and father-in-law strongly disliked Anne. They'd been cruel to Anne for the ten years she'd been married to their son, but that night, they'd been unusually nice to Anne. They even kissed her goodnight, something that was way out of character for them. Atwater said that it set alarms jangling in his head."

"Why would that bother him?"

Darren didn't answer right away. He took a bite of his burrito and washed it down with wine. "Let's say that you and I are married, and everyone knows we've come to hate each other. If you end up dead, guess who's the primary suspect."

"You."

"Exactly. So if I'm planning to kill you, I need people to think that we've mended our relationship and everything's great. I want people to think that there's no way I'd kill you. If people thought Bell hated his daughter-in-law, he would know that he'd be at the top of the suspect list if she ended up dead." Darren paused and spooned sour cream onto his burrito before taking a bite.

Cindy filled the silence. "Okay, he makes people think he finally likes his daughter-in-law because of one nice night? That seems kind of weak."

"Right. Ideally, I would try to set up a pattern over a longer period of time. You know, let our friends see a change. Convince them that all is good between us and you're the love of my life again. But if the opportunity to kill you arrived, I might get impatient and do it anyway."

"Makes sense, but still." Cindy shook her head. "What was the opportunity?"

"Anne had cooked a huge Thanksgiving dinner. Her mother and

her in-laws spent the afternoon eating, but the Bell's had gone home shortly before the murder happened. Francine's evening alibi of being at home was verified by the friend she had phoned, but her husband had gone out to a liquor store. He claimed that he drove around trying to find an open store, but he'd been unable to find one open on the holiday evening. He returned home empty-handed."

"So Atwater thought that Bell had returned to his son's house and killed Anne? I don't get it. How would he know that he could get Anne alone? Even if he'd seen her husband and mother leave, what about Heidi?"

"Good question, and one I can't answer. Atwater kept Larry Bell in the interrogation room for most of the night while he looked into the man's alibi, but was forced to let him go when his captain threw a fit that a man of Bell's stature was being held."

Cindy pursed her lips. "That's the kind of crap that really gets to me. Preferential treatment."

Darren nodded. "We're lucky in this city. I've never been put in that situation, but my friends in bigger agencies face political fallout continually."

"Did Atwater continue the investigation against Bell? Or did he give in to pressure?"

"To his credit, he kept digging. When you look at a suspect, you look for means, motive, and opportunity."

"I get motive and opportunity, but what's 'means'?"

"Basically, 'means' is the method or weapon available to commit the murder. We could get into a lengthy conversation about means, but that's the gist of it. Larry Bell had access to the house, and it was well-known that he disliked Anne and had tried to force his son to leave her. But would he go so far as to kill her to get her out of his son's life? If so, he had motive and opportunity. There was a lot of blood, but no body, no weapon. That would make means difficult to determine. So other than a gut feeling, he had nothing on Larry Bell."

They sat in silence while Cindy digested what Darren explained. "Let's go back to the rest of the murders that happened here. Surely the neighbors would have caught on that something was wrong, recognized that this house had too many bad things happen."

"Not necessarily. This area really boomed here in the '80s, and there was a lot of turnover in the houses. Not to mention, not many people seem to know much about their neighbors."

"Yeah, but surely there would have been rumors that the police would have picked up on. I mean, Randy said the kids at school all think something's wrong with this house."

"True," Darren said, "but those rumors really didn't start until the most recent deaths."

"Okay, then, what about the Fremonts in 2008? What did Atwater think then?"

"He was Chief by then, so officially he wasn't supposed to do anything on the case. But since he knew the oldest girl, Whitney, he'd gotten involved anyway. There was a lot of resentment on the force because of it."

Cindy was puzzled. "Why would they not appreciate the help? I mean, we know how it ended."

"First, having a supervisor butt in, much less a chief, is intimidating. In really small towns, the sheriff or chief might be hands-on, but in a city of this size, with more than a hundred officers, the chief is an administrative position. Second, it's not procedure. You can't have people going off in different directions doing their own investigations independent of the lead detective. Third, Atwater ended up shooting and killing a suspect, a transient, Oscar Whitehead. Atwater said he was following a hunch, so he hadn't told the detectives what he was doing. He said he'd been interviewed by Whitney for a paper she'd done earlier in the year, and at that time she mentioned some work with the homeless population. He decided to follow up on it. He claimed he didn't think it would pan out. But they found evidence in the Whitehead's camp. It closed the case and Atwater took the spotlight."

"Why didn't the press get involved earlier? I've found articles on the Fremont investigation, but nothing for the other deaths. I'd think it would have been a big deal."

"It's amazing what money will do. Look at what happened with

Larry Bell and the chief telling Atwater to back off. Until Bell retired from Valley Bank in 1990, he wielded a lot of power. Somehow, he kept everything hush-hush." Darren shook his head in disgust. "You'd think he'd do everything possible to find his daughter-in-law, and getting the media involved would have helped."

"Right. Sounds like he was more interested in his pocketbook than his family," Cindy said.

Darren agreed. "Something I found interesting was that even though Anne and Eddie lived in this house, Larry still owned it. His son worked at the bank with him, and whenever Eddie did something he didn't like, Larry would threaten to kick him and his family out on the street. "

"Wow, he sounds like a real charmer," Cindy said. "I'm somewhat surprised that he didn't end up on the wrong end of a weapon. After everything I've read about him, I might have been one of those in line to take a swing at him if he'd pulled his crap with me."

Darren nodded and his lip curled in a half smile. "I bet that's true. I kind of like that about you."

Cindy could feel the heat rise in her cheeks and had to focus on her burrito.

Darren reached out and lightly touched her hand, making her heart flutter. "You sure it doesn't bother you to talk about this stuff over dinner?"

"I'm glad we're not eating spaghetti and meatballs, but no, it doesn't bother me. What happened with Anne's case?"

"Two years went by, and her body still hadn't been found. About that time, Eddie pulled Heidi out of school and moved to the same small town in Minnesota as his mother-in-law. He contacted Atwater every few months over the next couple years, but the case had gone cold."

Cindy watched Darren as his eyes became unfocused in deep thought. "That was the only murder where not everyone in the house was killed or went missing. The daughter, Heidi, was upstairs asleep. I wonder if her being left alive has deeper significance."

"It does make sense in a horrible sort of way," Cindy said. "If it were Larry doing the killing, he might not be able to kill his own granddaughter."

After dinner, Cindy and Darren went out to the back patio to enjoy the cool evening air. "There's another topic you and I need to discuss," she said as she made herself comfortable on the lounge chair. She was wearing a long, loose skirt with a slit up the side, and it revealed a thigh until she pulled the edges together.

"We do?" Darren looked puzzled, and Cindy noticed that his cheeks had turned a little red.

Cindy wondered if he was feeling the same level of attraction that she was. She didn't think the chemistry she felt was one-sided. Every time they talked, though, it seemed to revolve around the murders... not exactly a mood-enhancing topic. Still, she was too nervous to approach that subject. "Ice hockey," she prompted him.

"Ah, yes!" he said with visible relief. "Tryouts for the next season are only a week away. Hmm, do you ice skate?"

"I've been on skates before, and I didn't break any bones. Both Randy and Marti have skated more than I have, both inline skates and ice. They have a lot more grace and balance than I do."

"How about we all go ice skating tomorrow evening and then let me take us out to dinner."

"That sounds good," she replied. "Well, all except the skating part, but I'm game. Only problem would be Gloria. I haven't left her alone in the house at night yet, and I doubt she'd be too keen on ice skating or even hanging out in a cold ice rink while we skated. She's been okay when I've had to run into the office or do errands. But what the heck, it's time to try."

"Okay, I should be home by 4:30. Pick you up at five? That's when public skate starts. We can see how Randy does on hockey skates. If he looks good, then I can take him to the hockey practice rink and see how he does with gear on."

They worked out the details with the boys, but Marti chose to pass. She asked if instead she could cook dinner for Peter, and Gloria offered to be their chaperone. Marti's face was lit up with excitement, and she clasped her hands together and chanted, "Please, please,

please!" Cindy couldn't resist that happiness in her daughter's eyes. Her little girl was growing up into a beautiful young woman. She gave permission, and Marti ran up to her room, cheering the whole way.

* * *

Marti was alone in the kitchen grating carrots when Peter arrived the following afternoon.

He took the carrot and grater out of her hands and put them on the counter. He turned her towards him and slid his arms around her waist. She stared into his eyes and felt lost, as though the rest of the world had disappeared. He lowered his lips to hers in a tentative kiss. Her hands were on his hips and she leaned back against the counter, pulling his body against hers. A tapping at the kitchen window made them both jump. Peter's head snapped up. Steve waved through the window. Peter pushed away from Marti, and she picked up the grater and carrot again. Both tried to look nonchalant, but their faces were flushed when Darren's face appeared in the window above his son's.

"Mom! Your date's here!" Marti yelled.

"It's not a date, dear," Cindy called down. "Would you please let them in?"

With a huff, Marti dropped the grater and went to the door with the carrot still in her right hand. She poked Steve in the chest with the carrot and whispered, "Not a word, little boy, not a word." She spun away from them and headed back into the kitchen.

Steve held his tongue until he was sitting in the back of Darren's SUV next to Randy. He told them what he'd seen. "Just wait until it happens to you," Darren warned.

"Ewwwww! Gross!" both boys chorused.

* * *

Gloria sat in her room looking at herself in the vanity mirror. Her bedroom door was open so she could hear the kids. She would never tell Cindy, but secretly she was thrilled for her great niece. Over dinner she'd watched the way they'd watched each other, the way they'd taken any excuse to touch. Marti needed to experience young love.

And that boy was a keeper. Gloria sincerely hoped that Cindy had had the sex talk with Marti. Falling in love at fifteen is a far cry from having sex and getting pregnant.

She let her hair down from the loose bun and began her evening ritual of 200 brush strokes. Her arthritic hands started aching, so she put the brush down, and as she clasped her hands together, she realized they were cold. She lifted her hands to her mouth to breathe on them, and when she blew out, she could see her breath. Out of the corner of her eye, she saw movement. Her head jerked up, and in the mirror, she briefly saw a black shadow before it shot towards the bedroom door. She stood up, knocking her chair over. The clatter startled her, and she started to scream but it stopped in her throat.

The kids! It was headed in their direction.

She hustled out to the living room where Marti and Peter were lying together on the couch. She didn't see the black shadow anywhere, but the kids' eyes were wide as they abruptly sat up.

"Did you see it?" Gloria asked, her voice shaking with emotion.

"See what?" Marti asked. "Aunt Gloria, are you okay?"

Gloria spun around, searching for the shadow. She was positive she'd seen it. "The shadow, did you see it?" she persisted. Neither of the kids responded, and she looked back at them. She could see a mixture of fear and something that looked like pity in their eyes. Despair fell over her. *They think it's my Alzheimer's. It's not, dammit, it's not!*

Without another word, Gloria turned away and went towards her room, but she stopped in the hall just out of their sight and listened to their conversation.

"Shadow?" Marti asked her boyfriend in a low voice. "Do you think she's losing it again?"

"No, I don't. Have you noticed how cold it is in here right now?"

"Yeah, my teeth are chattering and I've got goose bumps. Look."

"Ya know how me and my friends checked out this place before you moved in? And my friend fell through the floor? Well... just before we went into the room, I would have put my allowance on it that someone else was there, standing behind us. And it *pushed* him."

Gloria had heard enough. She wasn't imagining this. She tiptoed down the hall to her room and stood in the doorway, searching the room with her eyes for the shadow and with all of her other senses for a presence. The room was back to its usual temperature, and with a burst of speed, she rushed across the room and slipped into her bed.

* * *

At the ice rink, Darren handed goalie skates to Randy. He pointed out how the blades were designed differently than other hockey skates with the blades being flat rather than curved. The tip of the blade also did not have the serrated edge, the toe pick, that figure skates had. He spent the first half hour showing the boy how to maneuver on the different blades. Randy fell the first time he attempted a "hockey stop," but caught on quickly. He also discovered that it was harder to go fast in them. Even his mother was skating faster than he was.

"He seems to be getting used to the skates fairly quickly," Darren told Cindy as he skated around the rink with her. "I'd like to take him to the back rink and put some goalie gear on him."

"As long as he's up for it," she replied.

Darren spoke with the ice rink manager and got permission to use the back rink where the hockey leagues played their games. Even with Darren helping, it took fifteen minutes for Randy to get the goalie equipment on right.

On the ice, it was even worse. Randy complained at how little motion he had. Not only was he slow, but his range of motion was limited. The leg pads got in the way of crossovers, and the first attempt at a sharp turn put him on his butt. Worse still, he had a heck of a time standing up.

"I feel like a beached whale! I can't do this."

Darren was beside him with words of encouragement. "I remember how hard it was the first time I tried, too. Everything is different and awkward, for a while, at least. But you'll get used to it."

They spent the next hour working on movement, getting up and down, side to side. Once Randy was stable, Steve started lightly shooting the puck at him, while Darren gave instructions.

Cindy sat in the bleachers watching. She was torn between amusement at the awkwardness her son was showing and the motherly instinct to help him somehow. But as she watched how Darren worked with him, she found that she couldn't take her eyes off this man. Randy needed a strong man in his life to teach him and help him grow. And the stirring in her heart told her that she needed him, too.

At 7:30 they decided it was time for dinner. They brought a pizza home, but the boys still had homework, so Darren and Steve headed out after finishing their food. Steve went ahead to the car, and Darren hung back for a moment with Cindy. "I really enjoyed teaching Randy," he said. "But as much as I enjoy spending the time with the kids, I'd much rather get some time alone with you."

Their first gentle kiss made her legs weak. His arms slid around her waist, pulling her body close to his. She closed her eyes and surrendered. When he released her, she wasn't sure if she'd be able to stand.

"Good night, Cindy," he whispered. He touched her face one last time and turned away.

Chapter 18
September 8, 2011
Day 39

Thursday morning was overcast and humid. This area of California didn't get many summer storms, and a storm here in the valley would bring heavy rain and wind to the Sierra Mountains about 200 miles to the northeast.

Not long after Marti and Randy left for school on their bikes, gusty winds started, followed by a downpour. By the time Gloria and Cindy were working out, lightning and thunder made an appearance. Cindy was on the stair machine when lightning flashed close by, followed by a rumble that shook the windows. It reminded her of the day that she and Dawn had first looked at this house. She thought about the creepy feelings that had bothered the real estate agent so deeply and the things that had happened in this room. Her mood darkened to match the sky, and a sense of unease played at the edges of her mind, like there was a danger nearby that she couldn't quite see.

The storm passed quickly, and by noon, the sun was out. As Cindy had expected, the news said that the storm was hitting the Sierras hard. There were fallen trees blocking the highway to Lake Tahoe, and there was a surprising amount of damage in Santa Clara, too. Branches from the pine tree in the back yard were down; one had smashed the patio table, and Cindy swore as she threw it away. The rest would have to wait until Peter could come by to do the yard work.

Cindy's mood hadn't improved by evening. She couldn't get her mind to stop thinking about the mystery surrounding the house, and the feeling of foreboding was deepening.

"Earth to Mom!"

Her daughter's voice brought Cindy back to the present. She was sitting at the kitchen table with Gloria and Marti. "Huh? What?"

Marti sighed and rolled her eyes. "I was just saying that Peter asked me to the prom and Gloria is going to sew my dress."

"Oh, that's lovely," Cindy said. She was still distracted by her dark thoughts. She noticed the glance between Gloria and Marti, and her irritation went up a notch.

Cindy was relieved when the two went upstairs to Marti's room to look for dress ideas online. When she heard Darren's SUV pull into the driveway, she rushed to open the door. The boys passed her without pausing their conversation, but Darren stopped, waited until the boys were out of sight, and gathered Cindy in a hug. When he didn't immediately let go, she relaxed into his embrace and rested her head against his chest, pressing her body to his. How comfortable it was. She felt like she could stay there forever. She was tired from her sleepless night and wanted to put herself to bed—preferably nestled in Darren's arms. Embarrassed by her thoughts, she pulled away, but she noticed that his body had responded as well.

After dinner, Darren asked Cindy if she would sit on the porch with him.

"I have some bad news," he said. "You know how the city's had some financial difficulties? We've had to cut our budget, and the Cold Case Squad got axed. Detective Larson is the entire division now."

Cindy had a bad feeling about what he was going to say, and she snuggled closer, trying to somehow stave off the news.

"I brought Detective Larson up to date on what we found here and offered to look into this house's previous cases. No sooner did I get back to my desk when my phone rang. The chief wanted to see me."

"Uh oh. That doesn't sound good."

Darren shook his head. "Basically, the chief told me to butt out. He wouldn't give me any details, but he made it abundantly clear that my career would be impacted if I didn't leave the cases alone — I have my own cases to work. Anyway, Larson can be a real jerk, and I suspect he's throwing a fit about me poking my nose into the matter when it wasn't assigned to me. I think he has a bit of a Napoleon complex. He's a tiny man with a conversely large—and undeserved—ego."

They sat in silence for a few minutes. "I don't understand," Cindy said. If the Fremont case is considered closed, why does it matter if you look into it? Why would it impact Larson?"

"The Fremont case is closed, but the others aren't. It can be hard to get a closed case reopened."

"I see," Cindy said, shifting in her seat. "If a case is reopened, then it indicates that a good job wasn't done the first time?"

"Right. Well, sometimes. No one wants to admit they made a mistake, especially if a suspect was killed. The ramifications of killing someone only to find out later that the person wasn't the perp..."

"Can you introduce me to Larson?"

"He promised to swing by to see you," Darren said. He handed her a business card. "I got his card for you, just in case he doesn't show up in the next day or two." He tightened his arm around Cindy.

"Is this detective any good? Can I count on him? Even if he's a jerk?"

"He's new to the department. He came from out of state recently, so he doesn't know the area or its past. That could be a good thing... or a bad thing. He doesn't know the area, but it also means that he won't have a prejudice. Time will tell."

"Were they able to find anything on the gun Randy found? Fingerprints? Serial number?"

"The gun was registered to your neighbor, John O'Conner. But he reported the gun missing in March of 2008, months before the Fremont murders." He paused and took both of her hands in his, gripping them tightly. "And ballistics were a match to the Fremont case."

* * *

Cindy tossed and turned in bed. She felt abandoned. She knew that Darren couldn't go against his boss, but she felt like he let her down. Flopping on her back, staring at the ceiling, she tried to figure out why she felt deserted. She couldn't stop the flow of tears and heartache. It brought her back to the rollercoaster of emotions she'd had when her husband died. She was angry that she was left to raise their family alone. It wasn't Keith's choice to die and leave her, but it still happened. By dying, her husband had abandoned her. Now there was a spark with Darren, and she needed his help. And he couldn't — or wouldn't.

She shifted uncomfortably with that line of thought and changed her focus to the house. Was her family in danger? The police didn't seem to think so, yet Laura Lee and her dreams indicated that they were. And what about her dreams? Could she trust them?

Cindy thought back to what she'd been told in journalism classes in college about hunches: they were usually something that the subconscious had picked up that the brain hadn't figured out. Is that what her dreams of the shooting murders were? When or where had she seen things that would have caused her to dream about the details of the murders? Or was she somehow being contacted by the dead mother? A part of her resisted believing in the paranormal, even after years of friendship with Laura. On the other hand, Cindy felt comforted that there was someone in her corner, even if that person was dead.

Tina had made it clear in the dream that the killer wasn't dead. Cindy believed her. Instinct or intuition — she had a feeling that the killer was still out there. But what could she do to protect her family? After what Randy had done, she certainly wasn't going to get a gun. She would look into getting a security system.

In the meantime, without Darren helping, she needed to continue the investigation on her own. She didn't have access to the technologies the police used. She would have to organize the information she already had and see where it took her.

She rolled over and punched her pillow. It didn't matter what information she found if she couldn't do anything with it. The murder weapon was located, but that hadn't gotten the case reopened. How much would she need to bring to Detective Larson before he would open it back up? Chief Atwater had supposedly shot the killer, so why would they even consider opening it?

After midnight, she decided that she needed to organize her thoughts. Otherwise she would never get to sleep. She crawled out of bed and tiptoed to her office.

She started her records search with the transient who Atwater shot and killed, Oscar Whitehead. There was almost no information to be found on him, even using the journalism networks. He was born in 1954, which would make him thirteen when the boys were killed during the construction of the house. He was in the Air Force from 1972 to 1983. She assumed that at least in the early years of his service he was in Vietnam, which would preclude him from Anne Bell's murder. If the same person committed all of the crimes in the house, then he wasn't it. But Whitehead was in the area for the Fremonts' deaths, so he could have been guilty of that one. There was nothing to prove that all of the murders were the work of one person, either.

She decided to lay out what she knew about the history of the house. Maybe if she had it in chronological order, she would see a pattern. She created a spreadsheet in Excel and started entering information. The first column listed the dates of the murders: 1967, 1975, 1982, and 2008. Next she put an M next to those who were missing but presumed dead. In the 1967 column, she put Roger Duran, Frankie Dellman, and Enrico Martinez (M). For 1975, the only entry was Anne Bell (M). The victims of 1982 murders were Suzy Dudley, and the three Erikson kids: Aaron (M), Barbie, and Chuck. The entire Fremont family was killed in 2008: Patrick and Tina, Whitney (M), Vic, Gabby, and Kim. Next she listed what she knew about them: ages, hobbies, jobs. As more thoughts hit her, she included them.

Once she had filled in as much as she could, she started analyzing the information. She scrutinized the dates of the incidents. There seemed to be no pattern. All the crime-drama shows talked about serial killers keeping their activities on a time schedule, which invariably became shorter as they "decompensated," needing to kill more often when the thrill didn't last as long. But that certainly didn't seem to be the case with these murders. There was an eight-year gap between the boys being killed and Anne, and then another seven years before the babysitter and kids were murdered. But the glaring difference was the twenty six-year gap before the Fremonts died. Could the killer have left the area or been in prison? Or was the killer a traveler? Could he have left victims elsewhere that just hadn't been connected? Or were there, in fact, multiple murderers?

She needed to go see Chief Atwater. How was she going to manage that? If Darren gave her the retired chief's information, he'd probably get in trouble. She didn't want to put his job in jeopardy.

She went back to considering the dates of the murders. She tried considering major events for the years of the murders, but nothing popped up. They weren't leap years, election years, Olympic years... nothing in common that she could think of. She tried the *Farmers' Almanac* and other references. They weren't *El Niño* years, either.

"Okay, if the dates are significant, I'm not seeing it," Cindy said to herself aloud. Xena lifted her head to look at her. When nothing more was said, the dog sighed and put her head back down on her paws.

Frustrated by that dead end, she typed "serial murders" into her search engine. The amount of data floating around in cyberspace was astounding, and it looked like TV shows took a lot of artistic liberties. There was a lot of information about DNA. Depending on the type of equipment used, Cindy learned it could take hours to extract DNA from samples and several more hours to type it. Some sites indicated that the time needed was getting smaller with new technology, but it was certainly not advanced to the point of having results within a few minutes. Having the DNA was great, but it was useless if there wasn't a match in the system already.

She remembered the water bottle that she'd found under the house. If the killer had returned to the house, then the bottle belonged to him and had his DNA on it. It wouldn't do much good now, but it could be used for comparison later and evidence in a trial. She had thrown it out on Sunday. A feeling of dread went through her. The garbage cans were out on the street for the morning pick up. She didn't dare wait until daylight to find the bottle. She pulled on her sweats and went downstairs.

She snagged a pair of gloves from the first aid kit and went out to the curb. She'd thrown the plastic bottle in the recycling bin, a huge, blue, 32-gallon container. It was filled with plastic and glass bottles and cardboard from the party. She pulled a collapsed cardboard box out of the bin and spread it on the ground. One by one, she pulled out all the glass bottles she could reach and set them aside, being careful to keep them from clinking. Once they were out of the way, she tipped the bin on its side, cringing at the noise it made in the still night air as the plastic bottles shifted. She got on her hands and knees and inspected each bottle's label as she took it out of the bin. She remembered that it was an Alhambra water, and within fifteen minutes, she'd gone through all of the bottles and found only one of that maker. She set it aside and refilled the bin.

Elated that she had found the bottle, she took it inside and put it in a paper bag and sealed it with tape. She marked the bag with the details of where she'd found the bottle and noted that she had thrown it in her garbage. She listed the date that she found it under the house and the date when she pulled it out of the garbage. She put the bag in her file cabinet and locked the drawer.

Back at her computer, Cindy moved on to bullets. Ballistics weren't run instantaneously, either. It would be fairly quick to compare a known gun to a known slug, but the computer search to look for a gun when only the bullet was available wasn't as simple as TV made it seem. If a close match was found in the index, the possibility would still need to be verified by a specialist. And depending on the workload that person had and the perceived importance of the case, it could be minutes or days before they were able to make the determination. She was surprised that the ballistics results were already back on the gun from the crawl space considering that it was supposedly a closed case. She was sure she owed Darren thanks for that. He must have called in favors. She felt a pang of guilt at her earlier anger at him.

Fingerprint comparisons got the fastest results. The Integrated Fingerprint Identification System could compare fingerprints in seconds. Police computers could compare a sample to 600 prints per second. That was mind-boggling to her. Even more mind-blowing was that the FBI's AFIS computer could examine three million prints per second. TV made it look like the computer would spit out an exact match, but the FBI's website indicated that a computer would kick out a "candidate list," and then a specialist would sort through them to make a match. Sometimes it would come down to a dozen names that the detectives would then have to eliminate. No wonder TV shows skipped that part. She wondered what kind of results she should expect from the samples that were taken from her crawl space door. She'd had high hopes, but it looked like that was too optimistic. The technician had found dozens of prints. She was glad that the doors had been painted with the rest of the exterior of the house, otherwise she would have had to figure out who all might have had a reason to touch them: real estate agents, inspectors, and anyone considering buying the house. Not everyone who is going to buy a house would take the time to look at the crawl space, but some might. As it was, she'd seen people sitting on the doors throughout the party, but she couldn't remember who they were.

Cindy was startled to hear Marti stirring down the hall. She looked at the clock. It was already after six. She'd worked through the night. Cindy had a terrible feeling that she was going to pay dearly for the lack of sleep.

Chapter 19
September 9, 2011
Day 40

Cindy saw Gloria out the door for a day trip with John and hit her workout alone. Her mind went back to the day last week at the County offices. She'd made a list of the people who had lost their houses to Valley Bank, but the names had not meant anything to her. She wanted to go over them again. It took every bit of her discipline to finish her workout and shower before getting out the notes and photocopies she'd made from the County. She sorted the copies into four piles: birth, death, and marriage certificates and property records. Then she alphabetized the records in each pile. There were a few names that were now familiar: Atwater, Harrison, Kentcher, and O'Conner. Her heart skipped a beat. Larson. Could it be the family of the detective who now had the cold case? If so, maybe he had a reason not to want anybody looking into all of this. How convenient that it became his investigation. But Darren said that Larson came here from out of the area.

She ignored the Atwaters for the moment. She would figure out a way to talk with him. As the investigator in one of the cases and as the chief during another, she'd be able to get a lot of information—if he was willing. The Harrisons were another matter. She didn't want to interview them about their family's past, especially since the loss of the land might be considered shameful. With the bad blood between the two families already, Cindy didn't think the Harrisons would be forthcoming about any information they had anyway. Jen's parting comment popped into her head: *There are rumors this house is cursed. I hope the curse holds true for your family, too.* Talking with Jen and Ralph wasn't going to happen anytime soon.

William Kentcher was one of the people at the party who had been interested in the rec room. He seemed like someone who would be willing to talk. Cindy pulled out the Kentcher birth, death, and marriage certificates from the piles. She compared William's birth certificate to the property records. William's parents were the property owners who had sold their house and orchard to Larry Bell. Cindy fumbled through the stack of death certificates. She remembered seeing something that had bothered her when she was making copies.

"There it is," she whispered to herself. In 1964, the senior Kentcher died. The death certificate indicated that it was a self-inflicted gunshot wound. Cindy compared the death certificate to the dates on the property transfer. The man had died shortly after losing the land. Had that loss devastated the father enough that he took his own life?

William Kentcher was born in 1948. He would have been nineteen in 1967, certainly old enough to remember what happened to the boys at the construction site — or to have been the killer. She noted that he didn't say anything about it when they met in the rec room at the party. His father had killed himself three years prior to the boys' murders. How would a sixteen-year-old boy handle his father's suicide? Would he blame the person who took the land, if that indeed was what had caused the elder Kentcher to take his life? Would he have waited three years to decide to commit murder to revenge his father's death? And why kill three innocent kids instead of going after Bell directly? Something had bothered her about this man, but she couldn't put her finger on it. She remembered thinking that he had a predatory look. She put him at the top of her suspect list.

Cindy got the phone book out and found the Kentchers' number. Tabby answered on the second ring. She was more talkative than she'd been at the party.

"Is there any chance your husband would have some free time to-day to talk with me about the history of the area?" Cindy asked.

"If you're willing to be put to work, you're welcome to come over and talk with him. He's getting the house set up for a poker game to-night."

Cindy walked the three blocks to the Kentchers' house, and when she arrived, William was struggling to move a large, round game ta-ble into position in the middle of the living room over the aging green shag carpet. She jumped in to help him. When they had it placed where he wanted it, Tabby walked into the room with glasses of fresh lemonade. "Oh, no. It can't go right there," she said. She indicated the side closest to the fireplace hearth. "The person on this side won't be able to get up easily. And there's not enough room for Bobby's wheelchair." She suggested moving it to the other side of the dining room.

The two Kentchers argued over the best spot, but they eventually settled on the place she suggested. Tabby came over and whispered in Cindy's ear, "This is where we *always* put it, and we've been doing this for years."

With the table in the perfect position, William set a couple of fold-ing chairs at the table and sat down. He waved at the second chair and said, "I need a break, and I don't think you came here to help me move furniture." Tabby put the lemonade on the table between them and left the room.

"Mr. Kentcher, did you know that I am a journalist?" Cindy asked.

"No, I hadn't heard that," he replied. "And please call us William and Tabby. Are you here to do a story on our poker party? I have to tell you straight away that it's a men-only game."

"No, no. I'm looking into the local history, specifically this neighborhood, starting when it was a farming community. I thought you might be able to give me some insight. I was told that you were raised in this area."

"That's right, I grew up about two miles from here. Is there anything in particular you want to know?"

Now that she was thinking that he could be a suspect, she needed to be careful on how she got him talking. "Right now I'm working on a story of the urban development of this area. I'm interested in how this area went from being farm land to a sprawling city. And, if you're willing, I'd like to hear anything you might know about what has happened at my house."

"I'm not sure how much I can tell you. My folks had a farm here, but when I was in high school, they sold it. I think I was about sixteen or so. Don't rightly recollect. It was hard work going to school and then coming home to spend the rest of the day in the fields. Can't say I miss it. And not working on the farm sure helped my studies." He pulled a cigarette pack out of his breast pocket. "Do you mind?"

"No, go right ahead," Cindy replied. There was a sound of disgust over her shoulder, and when Cindy turned to look, she saw William's wife glaring at him.

Tabby walked over and tossed an apple at her husband. "At least do something for your health."

He exhaled a plume of smoke, a look of pleasure on his face. "She doesn't like me smoking. Says it's going to kill me. I say it hasn't yet. Something will eventually, why not let it be something I enjoy." He watched his wife walk away and reached into his pocket. He pulled out a pocket knife and started skinning the apple. "Where do you want to start?"

Cindy couldn't take her eyes off the blade. She guessed that it was at least four inches long, and by the way it was slicing through the apple, it had to be wickedly sharp.

William noticed her fascination with the knife and stopped cutting. "Do you like my knife? It's a Smith & Wesson." He wiggled his eyebrows at her. "Perfect for around the house or survival."

"I didn't know Smith & Wesson made knives," Cindy said.

"Is he showing off again?" Tabby asked, poking her head into the room. "You should see his collection of guns and knives. I should buy

Smith & Wesson stock. Men and their toys, I tell ya."

His eyebrows lowered and he scowled. "Don't you have something else to do?"

His wife snorted and left the room again.

Cindy poised her pen, ready to write. "What was the general feeling around town as it started to develop? Do you remember? Were people happy about it?"

His eyes narrowed. "No. People were definitely not happy about it. I remember my parents dragging me to town hall meetings. People screaming and crying about the bank taking their land and not paying a fair price. Houses were being built, and we couldn't afford them. I was able to get a job working at one of the first construction sites when I was fourteen, and my dad was furious with me. Whipped me good. Said I was working for the devil."

Cindy couldn't have asked for a better opening. "Do you remember the boys that died when this housing tract was being built?"

"I do. Quite well. I was nineteen at the time. I'd fallen from a tree in our orchard when I was a kid and messed up my shoulder." He rotated his left shoulder and winced. "Saved me from being sent to Vietnam. I was the only man under forty at the construction site. Those men taught me a lot, and not much of it was about construction." He made a sound that could have been either a laugh or dying donkey braying. "Anyway, back to the kids. There was a lot of talk about it just being an accident and not a murder. They said the Mexican boy caused it and ran away."

"What did you think?" Cindy pressed.

He shook his head. He deftly sliced another piece of apple off and popped it in his mouth. "Two of the boys, Dellman and Duran, were little hellions, always in trouble," he said around the apple. "Pranksters. They beat the snot out of my little brother a couple times when they were younger. It didn't surprise me they got themselves killed. Might even say they deserved it. But not the other kid. He was polite. Studious. I think he would have tried to help if the other two were in trouble. He used to hang out at our tiny apartment with my brother until he made it onto the football team and became popular. No, he didn't run away."

"What about Anne Bell? Did she run away?"

"Now Anne was a piece of work. She was a beauty. There was a lot of men who wanted to keep her warm the nights her husband was stuck at the bank. Eddie's father worked him hard." He grunted as a thought occurred to him and he punctuated his next statement by pointing the knife at Cindy. "The Mexican kid that disappeared—Enrico Martinez—his father worked for Larry Bell, too."

Cindy made a note of it and brought the subject back to Anne. "Can you think of anyone who would want to kill Anne? How about her husband, Eddie?"

He didn't answer right away. He ran his thumb along the side of the blade, caressing it. "Do you know John O'Conner? His wife passed away when his son was born. Anne spent a lot of time with him or watching his son when he was working. Eddie told me he trusted her. I remember he said they 'only had eyes for each other.' But, in my opinion, that's how a man gets cuckolded. By having blind trust. And a cuckolded man is an angry man."

The anger in his eyes made her wonder if he knew what he was talking about from personal experience. "Do you think Eddie killed her?" Cindy asked.

He shook his head. "I don't think he had the backbone to do it. But I remember Anne was having a hard time with the senior Bells. I wouldn't be surprised if she faked her death and ran away. But my money's on a jilted lover killing her in a rage."

"Anyone in particular? Who do you think she'd been with?"

"John's my first choice, but Bobby Donaldson's right up there, too. John's got quite a temper on him."

"Really?" Cindy asked. "He seems so down to earth and friendly. He took my aunt out for the day today. Should I be worried?"

William's eyes narrowed. "Let me put it this way: I wouldn't want my daughter to date him." He finished the apple and wiped the knife down with a handkerchief. She expected him to fold it up and put it back in his pocket, but he left it on the table. When he noticed her looking at it, he said, "Apple juice is highly acidic. I like keeping my blades clean and sharp. I need to give it a proper cleaning."

Cindy was unsettled by his assessment of John and his obsession with the knife. "A babysitter and the three children she was watching were killed in 1982 in my house."

"That one was terrible," he said. "It got people saying the house is cursed."

"Do you think it is?" Cindy asked.

He shook his head. "No, I don't believe in that stuff. But my wife was sure of it."

"Not me," came a voice behind Cindy. Tabby brought another folding chair over and sat down at the table. "I wasn't around then."

"Tabby is my second wife. My first wife died nine years ago. She and her friends said the house was cursed and that anyone who bought it was doomed. And sure enough, the next family was killed, too."

"You mean the Fremonts, right?" Cindy asked.

"Yes, ma'am."

"We've been worried about you," Tabby said. "Especially the night of the party when the police arrived. What happened?"

Cindy explained that a gun had been found in the house and was accidentally discharged. Both Kentchers looked skeptical. "It was an accident, pure and simple," she persisted.

Tabby left the room again saying that she needed to check on her cooking, and William took the opportunity to light up another cigarette. After his first lungful, Cindy said, "Let's go back to the Eriksons and the babysitter. You said Enrico Martinez's father and Anne's husband both worked for Larry Bell. Was anyone in the Erikson family connected to Bell?"

William thought about it before replying, his fingers absently spinning the pocket knife around on the table. "No, I don't think so. I don't remember where Erikson worked, but I don't think it was the bank. The babysitter's dad was a cop. You can see why people think the house is cursed." An alarm on his wristwatch sounded. "Time for me to get ready for a doctor's appointment. I'm sorry we didn't get more time to talk. I'll think more about the old days. See if I can't dig out some of my old photo albums."

"That would be very helpful," Cindy said with enthusiasm. She thanked William for his time and stood up to leave. As they approached the door, she asked, "So who all's going to be at your party tonight?"

"Harry Atwater, John O'Conner, and Bobby Donaldson."

* * *

Cindy went back to her spreadsheet and reconsidered the dates of the murders. She still couldn't see any pattern. She felt sure that she could remove the dates as a factor.

Next she looked at the victims themselves. What did they all have in common? The first three were just boys in 1967: Roger Duran, Freddie Dellman, and Enrico Martinez. Two were white, one Hispanic. Racism was predominant in the '60s, and even though it was less obvious now, it was still a factor. William Kentcher had referred to Enrico as 'the Mexican.' California was an agricultural state, and most farms relied on itinerate workers. Many of those workers came across the border illegally to work the fields.

She moved on to the case of Anne Bell in 1975. A white woman. The FBI site indicated that serial killers tended to have a type of victim: race, gender, hair color or something like that. Three teenagers — one Hispanic and two white—and a thirty-year-old white female. Other than the house, Anne appeared to have nothing in common with the boys in 1967.

The investigator, Harry Atwater, had suspicions about the father-in-law, Larry Bell. Bell owned the house. He owned the entire tract. She thought about this for a bit. Larry had a lot to lose because of these two incidents. The construction on the tract would have been delayed, and he would have been losing money while waiting for sales. Having a murder take place in the house structure would have made it difficult to sell. Is that why he kept this house for himself? He couldn't sell it? That might have hurt him financially, except that he was reported to be wealthy, so maybe having to keep this house was just an inconvenience. If the construction had been completely stopped, it would have been a fairly serious blow, she was sure. Forty-something years later, it looked to her like Bell shouldn't have been a suspect, but Atwater sure thought he was. Perhaps things looked different then.

Then there was William Kentcher's theory of an angry lover, and his suspicions of John. She thought about Kentcher. Something wasn't sitting right about him. There was something creepy about the way he played with his knife, and Tabby said he had a lot of weapons. She didn't like the way he was pointing at John. Could he be deflecting her to keep her from looking too closely at him?

She looked at her watch. It was after six. Her aunt wasn't home yet. As if on cue, Cindy heard the front door open and the dogs barking. By the time she got downstairs, John was already gone. Gloria explained that he had to leave so he could get ready for a poker game. Her hair was windblown, her cheeks were pink from the sun, and she looked exhausted, albeit happy.

Gloria took a shower while Cindy put on a kettle of water. Thirty minutes later, the ladies were curled up at opposite ends of the couch with mugs of peppermint tea. Gloria's eyes were bright as she talked about the beach and then the drive up the coast to Big Sur to see the massive redwood trees. Cindy steered the conversation to John. Other than superficial information, though, Gloria wasn't able to say much and began to look confused and worried at all the questions.

Cindy returned to the peaceful topic of redwood trees. The confusion disappeared from Gloria's face.

Chapter 20
September 10, 2011
Day 41

Cindy decided to take the dogs for an early Saturday morning walk before heading to the ice rink to watch Randy's ice hockey try-outs. Randy had already left for the rink to help Darren and Steve with the other age groups' tryouts. As Cindy stepped out onto the sidewalk, she caught sight of Peter's mother, Nicole Wilson, coming her way. Nicole was walking at a swift pace in a pink skort, white polo-style top, and white cross-training shoes. Cindy waved at her neighbor and waited until the woman was close. "Are you out for a walk, or are you going someplace in particular?" Cindy asked.

"Just wanted to get some exercise. You?"

"I needed to get some fresh air. Want to walk together?"

The ladies took off at a brisk step. Xena's tail and head were high, signs that she was enjoying herself. Sherlock not so much. His head was down, and his stubby legs had to work hard to keep up.

"I usually weave through the streets here," Nicole said. "My route is about a mile and a half. Will that work for you?"

"That would be perfect."

"How are things coming with the house?" Nicole asked.

"Pretty good, but I'm wondering about the house's history. Do you know much about it?"

Nicole's step faltered and she cast a pensive look at Cindy. "Are you really sure you want to hear about it?" When Cindy nodded, she continued. "I was a baby when the houses were being built. My family didn't come here until afterwards."

Cindy's list of families that had lost their land to the bank had included a Wilson. She was relieved that Nicole's family wasn't around at that time. She didn't want her daughter's new beau's family to be part of the mystery. She forced her mind back to what Nicole was saying.

"My parents bought our house when it was brand new, but they didn't know about the boys being killed when they bought it. They didn't find out until much later when Anne disappeared. She used to babysit me. I don't remember her well, just that she was nice, and I thought that she was one of the prettiest women in the world. I remember being upset that she wouldn't be able to babysit me anymore. Nobody told me why. I was about nine or so, and you know how kids are at that age—everything's about them, right?"

Cindy laughed. "And it doesn't stop until ... ever?"

Nicole grinned. "Right! Anyway, I found out years later what happened to her. I remember Mom saying that Anne was rumored to be having affairs with various men. Everyone figured that she'd run away with someone, although no one could figure out who."

"That's so sad. I suppose back then, women were considered 'loose' if they were friendly with men when their husbands weren't around."

"Yeah. But there are people today who still think the same way."

"So true," Cindy agreed, feeling a surge of warmth towards Nicole. "So after the Eriksons were killed, didn't people start to think that the deaths were linked?"

"Actually, no. At least not in the sense of there being one killer. Instead, people thought it was the house. I'd babysat the Erikson kids a few times when I was fourteen or fifteen. I hated that house." She shuddered. "I'm afraid of it. Something feels wrong there."

"I've heard others say that. I've noticed Peter doesn't spend much time in the house. He stays in the yard," Cindy paused and touched Nicole's arm, "and does a great job gardening, by the way."

Nicole smiled at the compliment. "He said he was 'totally creeped out' by the house. He also said something strange." She slowed down to a stroll and then stopped. "When Marti was showing him all the painting she'd done, she said the house had *told* her to paint the roses in Gloria's room. She felt like she had to do it. 'Compelled' was the word she used. Strange, huh?"

"Wow, she never mentioned it to me. I was just happy she did the work. I was completely surprised by it. I had no idea she had that talent. You know, when I first saw the house, I felt like it was talking to me." She looked at Nicole and cocked her head. "I hope you don't think I'm a nutcase."

"Oh, heck no." They started walking again, silent with their own thoughts.

They arrived at Nicole's house. "Thanks for joining me on the walk," Nicole said.

"It was great timing!" They hugged, and Cindy continued towards home. She decided to go into the backyard from the gate on the side street so she could toss the dogs' waste bag in the garbage. She was annoyed when she saw that the gate was open. She needed to remind the kids that the dogs could wander away if the gate wasn't securely latched. As she stepped into the yard, both dogs started barking and pulling at their leashes. She let them go and watched as a man stood up suddenly from where he was crouched by the old entrance to the crawl space.

"John! What are you doing here?"

He greeted the dogs with affection and turned to Cindy. "I, uh, umm..." He coughed, and Cindy noticed that his hand was shaking and his face was bright red. "I came to fertilize Gloria's roses." He gestured to her flowerbed along the fence line. "I got a bit light-headed and sat down here. Well, I'd better be on my way."

"Are you feeling better, John? Would you like to come inside and have some water or iced tea? See Gloria?"

"Uh, no." He took a quick glance towards the house. "I'd rather she not know that I was helping her roses. She takes a lot of pride in doing the work herself. She told me she doesn't want the young man to touch them. Not because he couldn't treat them well," he added hastily, "but because she wants her hands on them. But I know that young roses need extra nutrition. Please don't tell her." At Cindy's nod, he crossed to the gate and slipped out.

* * *

Cindy, Marti, and Gloria got to the ice center a few minutes before ten. The center consists of two buildings, each with two rinks. By the time they found which rink Randy would be on, the boys who were trying out for the team were coming out of the locker room and gathering at the entrance to the ice. The Zamboni was resurfacing the ice for them. When Cindy looked up in the stands for a place to sit and watch, she saw Lee's mom glaring down at her. Marti noticed and asked in a whisper, "Who's that woman?"

Cindy whispered back, "That's Jen Harrison and her husband. Apparently she's still a bit upset about the gun incident last week."

Marti laughed. "I bet she's just thrilled to see that Randy's trying out for the team. Shall we sit by her and try to make amends? Or go over to the stands farther down?"

"You know, she has every right to be angry–I sure would be in her place. But I didn't tell you about her visit the other day. Let's just say that she's a bit over the top. I'm not one to let someone else's bad attitude get in my way. Let's sit a few rows behind her."

As they passed, Jen elbowed her husband and snarled something too low for Cindy to hear. Ralph's head snapped up, and he focused on Cindy. His face turned red and his eyes narrowed. Cindy was glad that Marti and Gloria were with her. She worried that just by being there she was prodding a caged animal, pushing it to explode. Cindy hoped the Harrisons would keep cool, but like a wild animal, she had no idea what Jen would do.

When they sat down, Gloria commented, "My, my. I see things haven't changed since my kids were growing up. There's still a lot of competition between the parents, eh?" The stress and tension Cindy had been hiding rose to the surface, and she felt a mixture of laughter and tears battling within her.

Jen stood up and said to Cindy in a low, angry voice, "I can't believe you have the nerve to show up here. Hockey's a dangerous sport, you know. Especially for goalies." Without waiting for a response, she turned and descended the stairs to stand by the ice where the boys were gathered. She placed a hand on a large boy's shoulder and motioned for him to follow her to the side. The boy was a giant, especially compared to Jen's diminutive figure. To be a Pee Wee, he had to be eleven or twelve, but he looked like he was in his mid to late teens. His jersey had the number 24 on it, but no name, and Cindy didn't recognize him. Jen pointed at Randy and said something to the boy. He glanced at Randy and nodded.

"I have a bad feeling about this," Marti said.

The drills on the ice started with skating, and several of the boys distanced themselves from the rest with their skills. There were no nets on the ice, just a lot of cones set up.

There were two other goalies trying out, and they, along with Randy, had a much harder time with the skating agility drills than the forwards and defenders. Cindy was relieved to see that the other two had the same problems that her son did. The assistant coach pulled the goalies away to one end of the ice, moved a net into position and ran them through special drills. Some drills showed off Randy's strong points, and others exposed weaknesses. But by the end of the session, Randy had made the most saves.

When the coaches ended the session, Randy turned to the net to fish the pucks out. Number 24 suddenly skated away from the group, snagged a puck with his stick and made a quick wrist shot towards the net, striking Randy in the back of his leg where there wasn't any protective padding.

Randy collapsed on the ice. He shook off his glove and blocker and grabbed the back of his leg, writhing in pain. The assistant coach was immediately at his side, working the buckles on the leg pad to get them off as quickly as he could. Darren grabbed Number 24 by the back of his jersey and hauled him off the ice.

Up in the stands, Cindy was on her feet with her hands to her mouth in disbelief. Jen stood up in front of her and said, "See? It's a dangerous game. People get hurt."

It was Marti who lost her temper. "You bitch! You set him up for that!"

Suddenly there were people tugging at Marti to keep her away from Jen, and others holding Ralph back.

Gloria watched the scene unfold with detached amusement on her face. "Now *this* is hockey!"

* * *

Darren and his assistant coach, Mike, met with Cindy, Marti, and Gloria first. He took them back to the administrative area of the center where there were four identical meeting rooms. They went into the first one and sat down. Darren looked at Cindy and went to a cabinet on the wall and pulled out a box of tissues. He handed it to her and sat down across the table from her. "Okay, so tell me what's going on here," he said.

Cindy took a tissue and dabbed her eyes. "You know the incident with the gun at my house?" Cindy asked. Everyone but Mike nodded.

"I'll explain that later, Mike," Darren said. "Continue, Cindy."

"The following Tuesday, Jen barged into my house and made threats against Randy, but I didn't think she would follow through."

"I remember. You were pretty upset about it."

"Yeah, I was pissed off. Anyway, I didn't see her after that, and Randy said that Lee was just fine with everything." She explained what had happened since they arrived at the rink.

Mike and Darren looked at each other when she described the interaction between number 24 and Jen. "If she asked Jimmy Smith— number 24—to injure Randy," Mike said, "that's pretty serious."

"Please stay here until we come back," Darren said as he and Mike got up to leave.

In the next room, Darren sat down directly across the table from Jen and Ralph Harrison, while Mike slowly moved to stand behind them. "Tell me what happened out there," Darren said to Jen.

"All I did was try to console the mother of a wounded child, and her stupid daughter attacked me!"

"Console her?" Mike asked harshly from behind her, making her jump and spin to face him. "What did you say to her?"

"I don't really remember. I think it was something about injuries happen in ice hockey. It's a dangerous sport."

"Uh, huh." Darren stood up. "Stay here. We'll be back in a few minutes."

The coaches went to a third room where Jimmy Smith and his mother were waiting.

Earlier in the locker room, Darren had handed out dismissal notes to those who would be cut first, and notes of invitation to return the following day for more tryout drills. Jimmy Smith had not received either notice. Darren had wanted to dismiss the boy outright, but he hadn't wanted to hurt the boy's hockey future without good reason. He'd coached Smith since the boy had started skating at the age of seven, and the boy had serious talent.

Once again, Darren sat at the table with them while Mike stood at their backs.

"Why are we in here?" Mrs. Smith asked. Worry lines etched her forehead. She had run errands while the boys were trying out.

"Your son injured another boy on the ice," Mike explained.

"That was an accident!" Jimmy said, turning to look at Mike.

"Actually, you had to go out of your way to have that 'accident,'" Darren said. "There were no pucks nearby where you were skating with the group. You had to intentionally go get a puck to shoot it at the goalie."

"Are you saying Jimmy meant to hurt that kid? He said it was an accident!" Mrs. Smith looked panicked. "Does he need a lawyer?"

"For Christ's sake, no," Darren responded. "Unless, of course, Randy dies."

Mrs. Smith gasped. Darren held his hand up and said, "I'm sorry, that was in poor taste. Randy's injury most likely isn't serious. We won't know until he sees a doctor, but I suspect it won't be a lasting injury." The woman looked relieved.

"However," Darren continued, his face grave, "we still need to get to the bottom of what happened out there. From my point of view, as well as what I have heard from witnesses, it was an intentional act. Purposely causing injury to another player is punishable by suspension from the League."

"No!" Jimmy yelled, his eyes welling up with tears. "You can't take hockey away from me! I'm one of the best players. You need me on the team."

"Yes, you are," agreed Mike. "You, Steve, and Lee are our most promising defenders. We don't want to lose you to something so stupid."

Darren leaned back in his chair and covered his face with his hands for a moment. "Why did you do it?" he said, his voice showing his exasperation.

"I shouldn't have listened to her, I know," Jimmy said quietly. "But she's always been so nice to us, taking me on the hockey trips when Mom can't go."

Darren sat forward. "What do you mean? Did someone tell you to hurt him?"

At the same time, Mrs. Smith turned to her son. "Jen told you to hurt him? Damn it! I wondered what she was saying to you before you got on the ice. I figured she was wishing you luck. But to tell you to hurt someone? What the hell was she thinking?"

"Yah," the boy said, nodding his head. "She said that Randy was a troublemaker and needed to be kept off the team. She said to 'introduce him to pain.' I'd forgotten when we were on the ice. It wasn't until I looked up in the stands to see if you'd come back to see the tryouts that I saw her watching me. Then I remembered. So I skated back, grabbed a puck, and flung it at his back. I swear I didn't mean to seriously hurt him! Just a bruise, ya know?"

Mike and Darren went from room to room, talking with Jen and Ralph Harrison, then to Cindy's group, and then back to the Smiths. He was concerned about the legal ramifications of a mother inciting another child to injure someone. At minimum it was assault. The best he could hope for would be that everyone would drop it and let it be done with sanctions against Jen and Ralph Harrison. For that to happen, though, it would be up to Cindy and Randy.

Back in the room with the Fairbanks, Darren asked Randy how he was feeling.

"My leg really hurts." He shifted in his chair, trying to find a comfortable position for his leg that was elevated on another chair. "Is it true that Jimmy did it because Lee's mom told him to?"

"That's the theory we're working with right now," Darren said.

Randy shook his head and looked at his hands on the table. "Guess I kinda deserved it. I think it makes us even." He gave Darren a pleading look. "Please don't take Lee or Jimmy off the team because of me."

"There are legal ramifications, Randy," Mike said.

"I know." He snorted. "It's kinda cool that I had a hit put out on me!"

"Randy," Cindy said firmly, "there's a big difference between an accident that missed and an intentional act that caused injury."

"But Mom! Can't we just get done with this? It's just like what you've said about gang wars and stuff. If we fight back, then they'll fight back. And it's not going to get any better. Jimmy's already been dragged into the problem. How many more people is it going to hurt before we stop it?"

Mike looked at Randy with surprise, but before he could respond, Marti spoke up. "As much as I want to kick that bitch's ass, I've got to agree with Randy."

Cindy sighed. "Okay. How do we work this? Where do we go from here?"

Darren thought about it for a minute. "Let me talk next with Jimmy and his mom. On one hand, they're probably more than happy to have the problem go away since Jimmy could be suspended for the season. The League could even impose a tougher ruling and keep him out permanently if they wanted to make a point. On the other hand, Mrs. Smith probably would like to go after Jen herself for dragging her boy into it. So let me see if they're willing to drop it, then I'll talk with the Harrisons."

The only hitch he ran into was Jen's refusal to admit that she had sent the boy after Randy. She backed down once Darren said that he would have no choice but to file criminal assault charges against her and Jimmy.

* * *

It was late afternoon by the time the Fairbanks made it home. The ladies still needed to go to the mall to get the materials for the ball gown that Gloria was going to sew for Marti's Homecoming Dance. Cindy made sure that Randy was comfortable on the couch with his leg elevated with an ice pack and a Wii controller in his hand. Then they headed out again.

Gloria and Marti went to the sewing store, and Cindy went to the phone shop. It was time for the family to join the "smart phone" era. A salesman with dark hair and thick glasses stepped up to help her. His name was George, and he looked familiar, but she couldn't place him. He listened to what she wanted and helped her make the selections.

"Let's get the billing information into the system," George said. He typed in her first name and asked her last.

"Fairbank. Cindy Fairbank."

He looked up at her. "Oh! We met. You had a party at your house."

Cindy smiled. "When I first came in here, you looked familiar to me, but I'm afraid I lost track of everyone I met."

"I'm George Atwater," he said, holding out his hand to shake.

"Oh! I do recognize your name. Are you the author of the 'unofficial' Santa Clara blog?"

He looked surprised. "Indeed, I am!"

"You know, I'd really like to pick your brain about my house's past. Your website had a lot of information, and I hope that you can shed some more light on the subject. I work from home, so I'd be available to meet with you at any time that would be convenient for you. That is, of course, if you'd be willing."

"You bet I would."

She realized where she'd seen him at her party. He was the guy that she'd found standing in the rec room... the guy who ran away as soon as she said hello. She was about to offer an invitation when George's boss appeared behind the counter and cleared his throat. They quickly set up a time to meet during the next week.

When Cindy and the others got back home, Cindy called a meeting in the kitchen. Randy hobbled in, making a show of it. Cindy shoved an extra chair in his direction and told him to keep his leg up and iced.

"Okay, I've been giving our family situation quite a bit of thought. I'm concerned about our safety, and I want us to be able to be there for each other. So I thought that we could all use these." She pulled the boxes out and handed one to each person. Her kids cheered, but Gloria looked like Cindy had placed a snake in her hands.

"Gloria and I just have basic smart phones. We can access the web, but barely. But I thought you two would enjoy the more advanced stuff. I suspect you'll have to teach us elders how to use ours."

Chapter 21
September 11, 2011
Day 42

When Cindy arrived at the ice rink a little before ten for the second day of tryouts, Mrs. Smith hurried to greet her in the parking lot. A slight breeze ruffled her long hair, a golden light brown that showed reddish highlights in the sunshine. She stood a couple inches taller than Cindy, but outweighed her by fifty pounds. She had a cherubic face that endeared her to Cindy. "Thank you so much for not filing charges against my son!"

"It's in the past now. Let's leave it there. Randy's hoping they'll become friends. I don't want it to stand between us being friends either, Mrs. Smith."

"Please call me Amber. I hope we'll be friends, too." Her shoulders slumped. "But I'm really worried about Jen and Ralph. I just don't know how to act with them. I considered them friends, but..."

"Yeah, I understand," Cindy agreed, "although I didn't get the chance to know them before all this crap happened, so there isn't an established friendship for me to salvage." She shook her head in disappointment. "I've always been pretty good at getting along with people by just accepting them as they are. No judgments, no expectations. Just take them as they are. But I don't know if I'll ever be able to get past this with the Harrisons."

The ladies walked to the stands and watched as their boys skated onto the ice. Randy, Jimmy, Lee, and Steve were warming up together. Randy was favoring his injured leg, but still looked good. Cindy looked around at the stands and didn't see Jen. Amber noticed. "Jen and Ralph were asked to stay away."

"Thank God. I'm still fighting the urge to punch her."

The tryout drills went along the same line that they had the day before, but there were fewer kids on the ice. Cindy was anxious as she watched Randy stopping pucks, especially the slap shots, but it was even more stressful during the next hour sitting in the stands with Amber waiting to hear if he made the team.

Cindy jumped when her purse vibrated. It took her a moment to remember the new cell phone. It was a text from Randy. "I made it!" It took restraint to not leap up and shout for joy. Amber pulled her phone out of her purse, gazed at it a moment and turned to Cindy with a tentative smile. Cindy asked, "He made it?"

At Amber's nod, Cindy stood up and hugged her new friend. "Then we're teammates!"

Moments later, Cindy's cell phone rang. It was George Atwater.

"I've had a change of plans for this week," George said. My dad has a cabin up in the Sierras above Lake Tahoe. You know the storm that just came through here? It hit the mountains pretty hard. One of the neighbors called Dad to say that a tree came down on the cabin. Apparently the roof is caved in."

"Oh, no!"

"Dad's got appointments this week with his cardiologist I don't want him to miss, and the handyman he usually uses up there is away. That leaves me to take care of it. I'm heading up tomorrow. I have no idea how long it will take. Would you have a chance to meet with me this afternoon?"

"Sure. I'm at the ice rink right now, waiting for the boys to come out. We should be out of here within an hour. How about we meet at my house at three?"

"That would be great. I've got a date this evening, so I have to leave your place no later than five."

Cindy and Amber congratulated the boys when they came out of the locker room with Darren. The boys were jabbering with excitement, and Cindy couldn't understand what they were saying, using hockey jargon that she was going to have to learn. But she cherished the look of extreme happiness on her son's face.

"Mom, can I stay to help Coach with the other groups?" Randy asked.

"Me, too," Jimmy interjected.

Cindy hesitated. "I've got an appointment from three to five, so I can't pick you up then."

"I'll bring them home," Darren offered. "We should be out of here no later than six."

"Wish they'd asked earlier," Amber said as she and Cindy walked out to the parking lot. "We could've left a while ago."

At Amber's Honda, they exchanged phone numbers. Cindy continued on to her van, and as she got closer to it, she could see that something was wrong. The van was leaning to the side. Damn! A flat tire. She would have to hurry to get it changed to keep her appointment with George.

She had changed tires before and resigned herself to doing it again. But when she got to the van, she saw that both tires on the driver's side were flat. She only had one spare. She would have to call a tow truck to haul her to a repair shop.

Cindy estimated that it would be at least a half hour for the tow truck to arrive, another half hour to get to a repair shop, and probably an hour wait while they put new tires on. There was no way she was going to make her appointment with George. She called him and gave him the bad news.

"I'm so sorry to hear that. We'll have to reschedule for when I get back. Right after we talked earlier, I told my dad I was going to be meeting with you. He said he still has some stuff from the case he'd show me."

"I'd like to see what he's got," Cindy said.

"He had to run out and hasn't come back yet. Would you like to meet with him? I could set it up."

"Actually, I'd love to. Can you give me his number? Or give him mine."

"Will do." He gave her both the home number and his dad's cell number.

"Oh, by the way, he said he met you when you had the welcome barbecue, but you were probably so distracted that you don't remember. He only stayed a short while. Enough to say hello and leave."

The tow truck hadn't shown up yet, so she sent texts to Randy, Marti, and Gloria letting them know what happened and got into the van to wait.

A sharp rap on the window jolted her from her daydream. A scruffy-looking man in dirty mechanic's coveralls was peering at her through the closed window. "Someone mustn't like you," he said as she got out of the van. The tow truck driver showed her something she hadn't noticed about her tires. They had been deliberately punctured on the sidewalls. She felt the blood drain out of her face.

"You musta pissed someone off real good," he said. "Looks like a screwdriver to me. See the jagged edges of the hole? Them tires can't be fixed."

Cindy's eyes welled up with tears. Why wouldn't the Harrisons leave her alone? "Would you mind waiting here for a couple minutes? I have a friend in the rink who's a cop. I think maybe he'd better come look."

"No problem, ma'am. I ain't ate lunch yet. You go right ahead."

Cindy hurried back to the rink to find Darren. One of the kids working in the pro shop saw how upset she was and paged him over the speaker system. Darren appeared a few minutes later, looking irritated. When he saw Cindy, though, the harshness in his face was replaced with worry.

"What's wrong?" he asked her, taking her in his arms.

She rested her head against his chest and mumbled, "Someone intentionally punctured my tires."

He pushed her back to arms' length so he could see her face and said, "Are you serious? How do you know it was intentional?"

"The tow truck driver pointed it out. The punctures are on the side of the tires. Would you mind coming to look?"

He pulled her into his arms again. "Of course. Where are you parked?"

Chapter 22
September 12, 2011
Day 43

John O'Conner was early on Monday morning, and Gloria wasn't ready for their day trip. Cindy sat with him in the family room with a mug of coffee and a croissant. He was dressed for a warm day in light slacks and a cotton floral shirt. Cindy was envious of the energy he exuded.

"Gloria told me that you lived in this neighborhood for years," she said. "Your family had a farm here?"

"Yes, we did. When I was a boy, this area was just orchards and farmland. In fact, this house is built on what was my family's land."

"Oh! Really? Truly? What did you have growing here?"

"Most of the farm was a walnut orchard, but this section had a variety of fruit trees. There were a couple more pine trees back where yours stands. I had a fort between them."

"How did it come to be a housing development?" Cindy asked.

John's eyes narrowed and a scowl changed his whole look, from a gentleman to something ominous.

Cindy was suddenly nervous to be near him. "I'm sorry. That was rude. I used to be an investigative journalist, and the questions just pop out of my mouth. Please forgive me."

His eyes cleared a bit. "No, that's quite alright. I can see why you'd be curious. Like in a lot of large farming families, the farm was passed on to the eldest, but one by one, each of the boys in my family either died or chose different occupations. As my father aged, he wasn't able to work the farm as well, and he didn't have much help.

"The wars were brutal, and most of my siblings were killed. Without people to work the farm, taxes and mortgages couldn't be paid. The bank took some of the land, and eminent domain gave the city a little more of it. It was a downward spiral from there, with the bank leading the charge. Larry Bell." The warmth she'd seen in his eyes when he first arrived was gone. His hands curled into tight fists. "That man was ruthless. He wanted everything. He took the land in the name of the bank, then bought it from the bank for pennies on the dollar. This housing development was one of his bright ideas. There were a lot of us who wanted to see the project fail so he'd be ruined."

"I can see why," Cindy said, disconcerted by the anger in his voice. "Do you remember Anne Bell?"

"Yes," he said. His face softened and his hands relaxed, resting on his thighs. "She was a lovely lady. Her husband, Eddie, left her and their daughter home alone a lot. She'd come over to visit me, and our kids played together. She babysat for me when I had a shift with the police."

"It must have been terrible to lose her."

His shoulders slumped for a moment before he sat back up straight. "Yes, it was. She was sweet, but so many men mistook her Midwestern friendliness and innocence for flirtation. She wasn't that kind of girl."

"People say she ran off. Do you think that's what happened to her?" Cindy asked, preparing to gauge his reaction.

"Absolutely not! There's no way she would've left her daughter. It's not possible."

"You think she was murdered?"

His hands were in fists again. He didn't answer.

"Who do you think would have done it?" Cindy pressed.

"William Kentcher had a real thing for her. Bobby Donaldson did, too. They had a bet going to see who could get her in bed first. They all thought I was sharing my bed with her, but I wasn't. I warned her about the guys, but she laughed it off. Harry Atwater knew about the bet, and afterwards, I tried to get him to consider them as suspects, but he was focused on pinning it on the senior Bell."

"You mentioned Bobby Donaldson. That name sounds familiar."

"He's a poker buddy. Grew up here. Sad thing about him. He was a wrestler in school, one of the strongest guys I've ever known. Was in the Special Forces in the war. Now he's in a wheelchair."

"Oh! What happened to him?"

"I don't really know. He had a spinal injury and had surgery, but the pain kept getting worse and worse. He says it's some kind of spinal degenerative disease. He could still get around pretty well until a couple years ago. Just this last year he started using the chair."

"So your poker group's been around for a long time?"

"Members have come and gone, but Harry, Bobby, William, and I have always been in the group." The old man shook his head sadly. "It's funny looking back how often our lives intersected, Harry and me, especially. We both raised our boys alone as widowers. He had a hard life. As kids, Harry used to work on the farm with me after school and on the weekends. He helped support his parents. His mother had rheumatoid arthritis by the time she was in her forties, and his father had lost an arm in the second World War.

John was warming to his story, and Cindy leaned forward, intent on his words.

"Harry, Bobby, and I joined the armed services in 1964 to go to Vietnam, but William'd been injured in an accident and stayed home. Harry saw the war as an opportunity to send money home to his family. He was an M.P. and didn't expect to see any real fighting. Then his base was infiltrated. He was on KP duty—kitchen duty, that is—when the attack came. He took out six men with just his RTAK survival knife before being shot in the shoulder. He was sent home, and after a few months of recuperation from his injury, he joined the police department."

Cindy saw that John's mug was empty and offered to get him more. He followed her into the kitchen and sat at the table.

"When I got back home, the Army sent me to school," he continued. "I joined the volunteer police department, more to see if I wanted a career in law enforcement than out of civic duty. I'd seen enough 'civic duty' already between the war and the eminent domain taking our land. I studied during the day and patrolled the streets at night, usually with Harry." John stared off, remembering his past.

"Harry married before leaving for the war. A year after he came home, his wife died in childbirth while he was on a police stakeout, trying to take down a drug ring. Little George was born before the paramedics could get her to the ambulance."

Cindy cringed. "Was the baby early? I'm surprised Harry wasn't home if his baby was close to being due."

"They didn't expect the baby for another couple weeks. Harry was taking any shifts he could to pay for the new house they'd bought. He was mortgaged to the hilt, and lived just down the street from Larry Bell, a couple miles from here. He was also hot on his career path. He took the dangerous assignments and usually took me along with him. Volunteers like me weren't supposed to be going on those jobs, but somehow I always ended up with him."

"So did he end up raising the boy by himself?"

John O'Conner nodded. "My wife took care of the baby while Harry and I were on patrol until she passed on, too. Here's something strange: my wife also died giving birth. We were both widowed fathers."

"It's good that you two had each other to lean on."

John agreed with a curt nod. "I left the police force and focused on my job with the accounting firm. We were contracted by the Treasury Department to do an audit of the bank. That's how I found out what Bell was doing." The anger that had shaded his face earlier returned. "How I would have loved to kill that bastard! Making his fortune on the backs of destitute farmers. If I couldn't see him dead, I would have settled for seeing him in jail or losing his fortune."

A feeling of dread made its way down Cindy's spine. John just so-lidified the possibility that she'd considered: the murders of the boys could easily have been a way to hurt Larry Bell. Was he the only one that felt this way? She thought about the list of names she'd made who'd lost their land to Bell. But what about the later murders? That reminded her of the ballistic report. "Did you hear that the gun that Randy found under the house was registered to you? I was told your house had been robbed and the gun was taken."

John paled. "Oh! I'm glad it's been found, but how the hell did it get under your house?" His eyes misted. "I feel horrible that my gun almost shot a child."

Cindy scrutinized his face as thoughts raced through her head. The ballistics showed that the gun was the one used to kill the Fre-monts, but John wouldn't know the tests had been run, or if he did, that the results were already back. He truly looked stricken. Was it because, as he said, the gun almost killed a kid? Or was it because the connection to the Fremonts' deaths might be known? Sharp pains hit her stomach as she struggled with the idea that the man in front of her, a man dating her aunt, could be the killer. *If he is the killer, then he's a sensational actor, too.* Too many thoughts collided in her brain, and she couldn't sort them out. *If I were a real detective, I'd know how to follow this up.*

She noticed that he was now carefully watching her face. She took a deep breath. "Now that it's been found, hopefully you'll get it back. Was it your service weapon?"

He shook his head. "I haven't much use for it now, and frankly I don't care to have it back. But no, I was one of the few who left the Army without taking my weapon. I was issued another with the PD, but I kept that in the locker at the station. I bought that gun around the time construction was going on. There were too many people hanging around, and I wanted to be sure my son and I were safe."

"Did you teach your son to shoot?"

He nodded with a faraway look in his eyes. "In the 70s, we spent a lot of time at the police gun range shooting targets, and sometimes we would go up towards the bay, the area that's now Alviso, to hunt.

Back then, there were deer and elk, wild turkeys and pheasant. There were a lot of hunters. Hard to believe, eh?"

"Wow, that area is totally developed now. It's hard to imagine big game in this area. I didn't know you were a hunter. Did you shoot game with your gun?"

"No, I borrowed a gorgeous Remington rifle from William. He had quite a collection. Still does, I think."

"I don't think I could hunt," Cindy said.

"I wouldn't do it now, but back then, it put food on my table."

"I doubt I could shoot a deer, but cutting it up would be absolutely outside what I could do. I could cook it, but I'd have to imagine it was beef from the butcher's shop."

John said, "We would have gotten along fine. I could shoot it, clean it, cut it, package it for the freezer, but I made a mess of it cooking. I even made boots out of the hide. We used or sold everything. No waste. Anything else would have been a disservice to the animal. I think there's a special place in hell for trophy hunters."

"I'm really glad to hear that. I have a real problem with animals being killed just for sport. She changed the subject. "What will you and Gloria do today?"

"I thought we'd go up to Santa Rosa to see the Snoopy museum. Then maybe over to Napa, if she's up to it."

"That will be a full day."

"I'll be careful to watch her. I know stimulation can be good for Alzheimer's, but there's a line where it becomes too much and detrimental."

"I'm glad you recognize that," Cindy said. "Have you been around others who were afflicted by the disease?"

"A couple of friends have had it. Poker buddies, friends from the Senior Center. I tried to learn as much as I could..." He broke off whatever he was about to say and stood up.

Gloria was standing in the doorway to the kitchen. She was wearing a lavender sundress with a white blazer. Cindy caught a whiff of Gloria's favorite perfume—one she sometimes said put her 'in the mood.'

Chapter 23
September 12, 2011
Day 43

Cindy's talk with John gave her a lot to think about, and she sat at her computer in her office and wrote down her conclusions. Everyone despised Larry Bell. The local men wanted to get Anne in bed, and William Kentcher and Bobby Donaldson had a bet on who would succeed first. The house was cursed. She'd already decided that Larry Bell stood to lose the most–if the development fell through he would be hit hard financially. She still had a nagging feeling that the murders involved him and his business dealings, somehow. She thought about Harry Atwater. Why would he have been so suspicious of Bell when he was investigating Anne's murder? His family wasn't on the list of people who lost their land, but he was close friends with John, who had. Was it just a hunch? A bad feeling? Something Atwater couldn't quite put his finger on, like her reaction to William Kentcher?

John had admitted motive to hurt Larry Bell. Ex-military and cop–even if it was just volunteer–he was no stranger to violence. And he was a hunter, so he wasn't afraid to kill a living being. If he cut up the animals he killed, would that translate to the know-how and the tools to do it to people? Not that it takes much experience to lop a head off or gut someone when you aren't concerned about protecting the meat. And what exactly was his relationship with Anne?

On the other hand, Cindy hadn't seen anything to connect John with the 1982 murders of the Erikson kids and the babysitter, and he'd reported his gun missing before the Fremonts were killed with it. But then again, he could have filed that report and hidden the gun to use later. That would make the Fremont massacre premeditated by several months. She shivered at the thought. It would take a very cold person to plan it that far ahead. She didn't want to think John could do that.

William Kentcher had pointed at John, but John had in turn pointed back at William and Bobby Donaldson. Both of those men were on her list of families who lost their property.

And what about Bobby Donaldson? She pulled his birth certificate from her pile. He was born in 1943, so he was the right age range. He would have been in his 20s when the boys were killed. He had a connection with Anne, or at least a crush on her, and a bet to see if he could sleep with her. John had indicated that Bobby had been physically fit back at the time of the first three murders. By the time the Fremonts were killed, his back had taken away his vitality, so switching to a gun would make sense.

She needed more information, but how was she going to get it? She dug through her purse and came up with the paper she'd scrawled Chief Atwater's phone number on. She wished she'd been able to talk with George Atwater more and wondered how he was doing up at Lake Tahoe. She dialed Chief Atwater's number and was disappointed when she got the answering machine. On a whim, she looked up Bobby Donaldson in the phone book. No listing. Nothing showed up online, either.

She decided that her next step would be a visit to Detective Larson.

At the station, Cindy dropped Darren's name, and was escorted up to the third floor to see Detective Larson. "I was told that you're new to the area," Cindy said as they sat down in his cubicle. The area was spotless. Not a single paper or file was out of alignment. The cubicle matched his tidy appearance. His short, dark brown hair was perfect, and his suit was immaculately pressed.

The detective looked at her with a puzzled expression. "Who told you that?"

"Detective Polk mentioned it."

He sneered. "Then he's not much of a detective. I was born and raised here. Played football in high school and got a scholarship to college. After that, I got a job in Corrections here and then moved to the east coast. But after twenty years, my wife decided she'd had enough of the cold winters and muggy summers. So we moved back here."

"Ouch. That must've messed with your pension."

He shrugged. "Not really. I was able to retire from the force there with a good pension. Now I'm working on another one here. It's actually a good deal."

Upright file holders sat on top of a lateral file cabinet. He fingered through the files until he came up with the one labeled "1492 Almond Way."

"Let's see here," he said as he skimmed the papers in the file. "I'm not sure if this will be good or bad news for you. The fingerprints came back with dozens of potential matches. We've narrowed down some of them. A few of your neighbors. They would have come to the party you had?"

"Yes, there were a lot of my neighbors there, and since we didn't have enough chairs, a lot of people sat on the crawl space doors. Would John O'Conner be one of them?"

The detective scanned the list. "Yes, I see his name there. Was he at your party?"

"Yes, he was."

"Hmm, here's an interesting one." He turned the paper towards Cindy so she could see. "Harold Atwater. Did you have the former police chief at your party?"

"I don't remember seeing him, but his son said he was there."

Detective Larson nodded. "I see George's name here, too. There were also seven other prints that we weren't able to match. That doesn't mean anything except that the people aren't listed in the system. They may be too young to have a driver's license, or somehow avoided getting their prints into the system another way."

"I read somewhere the FBI's database is extensive. But unless it becomes a law that each and every person must submit their prints, there will always be gaps."

The detective stared at her. "You've been doing research on this?"

"Well, yes. If this kind of stuff happened in your house, wouldn't you?"

His lips made a grim line. "I suggest you leave the detective work to me."

"Believe me, I would much prefer that you be the one to check into this stuff. I just found out the other night that you were aware of the case. It's out of my league. I'm just a journalist. I used to do investigative articles, but I'm an editor now."

Cindy could feel the tension pouring off the detective. Darren was right, this guy was territorial and didn't want anyone around his work. "So tell me about the gun," she continued. "I understand it belonged to John O'Conner, but he told me that it had been stolen some time ago. Is it possible for him to get it back? Or was it the weapon that killed the Fremont family in 2008?" Darren had already told her that it was a match, but she didn't want Larson to know that Darren had said anything.

Detective Larson flipped through a few more papers before settling on the ballistics report. "It says here the gun your son found was a match for the murder weapon. And, by the way, your son's fingerprints are the only ones on it."

Cindy sighed. How had they matched her son's fingerprints? How was he in the system? Through school? "Then I suppose John won't be getting it back any time soon."

"No, we'll need to keep it in evidence." He stood up and held out his hand to shake, dismissing her. When she took it, he said, "Now you be sure to let me know if anything comes up. I'll keep the file on my desk, but it is considered a closed case. I can't devote time to it unless something compelling comes forward. That said, though, do *not* go out investigating on your own. At best, you'll only get evidence destroyed, and at worst, you'll end up hurt." He was still holding on to her hand. His eyes said he expected something from her so she nodded to show she understood what he was saying. Only then did he release her.

Cindy left the police department with more to think about, but more frustrated than ever. She wasn't going to get help from Larson. On one hand he said that unless she comes up with something that would spark the case, it would remain as dead as the Fremonts. On the other hand, he doesn't want her to investigate.

She was just about to start the car when her phone rang. Caller ID showed it was Darren. Her heart fluttered.

"Hi!" came the cheerful, masculine voice. "Would you be up for meeting for lunch?"

"I can't tell you how good that sounds," Cindy replied. "Seeing you is exactly what I need."

They met at the El Camino Mongolian BBQ, a small, family-owned restaurant on the far west side of town. It was one of Darren's favorite places. There was a buffet of uncooked meats, noodles, and vegetables. Once she had selected the ingredients she wanted, she took the bowl to the grill where the teenager stir fried it. When Cindy took her first bite, she closed her eyes and savored the flavor. "Oh! My! God! This is delicious!"

"You see why it's my favorite?"

"Oh, yes! Can't wait to bring the kids here, too."

"Now I have some strange news for you," Darren said. "I wanted to find out where the Harrisons were when your tires were punctured." When she nodded, he continued. "They claimed they went to the Monterey Aquarium while the hockey game was going on, which is about two hours from here. I have a friend who works security there, and he checked the videotapes for me. They were definitely there."

Cindy put her chopsticks down. "Damn. Please tell me you're kidding. If it wasn't them... then who could it have been?"

"I'm not sure. It seems like someone is trying to keep you from looking into the murders. But then I keep coming back to one thing: Someone also wanted to stop *me* from investigating your house, and try as I might, brass isn't telling who made the request. I suspected that it was Detective Larson not wanting me sticking my nose in his work and possibly seeing that he isn't quite as wonderful as the brass seem to think. But now I'm not so sure with this happening to you. I'm just glad it was punctured tires and not something that would have caused an accident."

"I saw Detective Larson today."

Darren raised his eyebrows. "How'd that go?"

"Somewhat strange, actually. He said that he grew up here and was a corrections officer in the area before going back east. He's got a pension from back there and is now working on one from here. He said he's already vested in the retirement system. How long does that take?"

"Five years for ours. Why?"

She shook her head. "I don't know. My mind hasn't mulled it over long enough. I just felt like something was off about him." She smirked. "Maybe it's because he's a neat freak. He gave me the impression that he doesn't want me looking into this, but there's no way he's going to do anything on his own. Very irritating! Before I get too pissed off again, let's go back to the tires on my van. Other than the frustration and expense and such, the only thing that happened because of the tires was that I missed my appointment with George Atwater. So from that point of view, yes, someone managed to keep me from getting information from him. But that tactic would only delay the meeting."

"Okay, let's run with that thought. Who knew that you were meeting with him?"

"Well, Amber Smith was with me when I got the call. She was with me the whole time we were at the rink. I don't remember her making any calls. Plus I don't think she holds any hostility towards me or Randy for what happened on the ice. She's really upset with Jen, though." She concentrated again. "Let's see... I sent texts to Gloria,

Randy, and Marti to let them know where I'd be. That's it."

"Would any of them have told anyone else?"

"I suppose so," she responded, then had a terrible thought. "Gloria has become pretty close to John O'Conner, and she may have told him. He seems to be very good with her. We all like him. But, like you told me, the gun was registered to John and it's a match to the 2008 murders.

Darren looked thoughtful. "I can't imagine why he would have had anything against the Fremont family."

"You're right," she said. "The Fremont family just doesn't seem to fit with the other killings. The change from a blade – up close and physical – to an impersonal gun bothers me. Their deaths might not even be related to the other three incidents. Just a wild coincidence. But I'm not one for such tremendous coincidences, and my gut says they are related. And in my dreams, Tina Fremont implies they are." She shook her head in disgust. "I really shouldn't put any weight on what Tina says in my dreams."

"No, you shouldn't. They're just dreams. I know they seem real, and Tina and her daughter claimed to be psychic, but I prefer to base my assumptions on facts, not surreal events." He smiled to take the sting away from the statement.

Cindy thought about what Laura Lee had said about the house. Laura had felt multiple spirits. They were in pain. The medium had explained to Cindy that the residual pain created an energy that would compound, creating more negative energy. Cindy didn't understand how it worked, but she trusted her friend.

"So let's look at the facts," Darren said. "The only things that the Fremont deaths had in common with the other killings were the location and the fact that one of the bodies was missing. But that doesn't mean that Whitney, the oldest girl, was a victim. She may have been the killer."

"But how would she have gotten the gun? Did she have any kind of relationship with John?"

"Hmm. Not that I know of. His son was grown and gone, so there wouldn't be any connection there. I can't think of any reason that she would have been in his house or have known where he kept his gun.

"Let's go back to her as the killer for this one case." Darren continued after scraping his plate to get every last bit. "They found a bloody handprint in her bedroom, and it was confirmed to be her hand. The blood was type B, and only the mother had that type. Everyone else had type O. So if you make the assumption that the blood was her mother's, then the girl was alive *after* her mother had been shot."

"Or it could have been the killer's blood," Cindy said, remembering the bloody dart in her dream.

Darren looked thoughtful for a moment before continuing. "Good point. Unfortunately, since it was just a print on the wall, there wasn't a sample saved in evidence. DNA matching wasn't performed to confirm that it was the mother's blood. Looking back now, it could have been the killer's and we have no way to prove or disprove it. Defense lawyers would have a field day with that."

Cindy nodded. She focused on her food for a few minutes. "A major difference is the way they were killed. All of the previous deaths were done with a knife. Why change to a different weapon? Do you think it's the work of two different killers?"

Darren shrugged. "There's quite a date range involved here. The first murders were in 1967, so the Fremonts were killed forty-one years later. That's a long stretch of time. If it was the same killer, he had to have been young in 1967, because otherwise, he would have been too old in 2008."

"Not necessarily. Let's say he was eighteen during the first killings. That would only make him fifty-nine in 2008. That's not that old."

"You're right," he agreed. "Then again, if he was older in 1967, say thirty, then the aging might explain why the killer changed from a blade to a gun. Much easier to handle. Don't have to worry about the victim fighting back at close range. I can't see a seventy-year-old killing a whole family with a knife. It would be too risky, and the strength needed wouldn't be there. He might be able to take down one of the girls in a blitz attack, but not five or six people. Mr. Fremont was a firefighter. He would have been in good shape."

Cindy told Darren about Bobby Donaldson's debilitating disease.

"Well, that might explain the change in M.O." But Darren did not seem entirely convinced. Doubt shaded his rugged face. "There's another angle to consider. Back in the early '70s, Herbert Mullin killed more than a dozen people in the Santa Cruz area, only a few miles from here. He was hard to catch because he changed up his weapons and M.O. He used a gun, a bat, and a knife."

"So we aren't any closer to figuring out an age for the person, and we can't even be sure it's only one person."

"Yeah, that's about it. It *could* be two killers. Generally, when you've got multiple killers, you've got three possibilities: First, an accomplice. But that doesn't make a lot of sense with the time difference. Second, a copycat. But copycats usually mimic the previous crimes as closely as possible. The M.O. was different, so I'd eliminate that. Third, the murders are completely unrelated."

"That one makes the most sense to me, if we are only considering this being multiple killers," Cindy said, "but I can't shake the feeling that they *are* related. Let's add a fourth possibility. If people think the house is cursed, any additional murders might just add to the urban legend. The killer might think that he—or she—could get away with it by casting blame on the previous killer. That idea would work if Whitney Fremont killed her whole family. But I just can't imagine it was her."

Darren thought for a moment, tapping his chopsticks on the empty plate. "Atwater was a pretty good detective. What if he was right about Bell? I've read that psychopaths will act on their antisocial tendencies by being brutal in business. That certainly sounds like what we've heard about Bell. Something I learned at the FBI training courses is that the first murder can be done to throw investigators off track, with the subsequent victims being the real targets.

"For example, let's say a man wants to kill his wife, but he knows that the spouse is always the first suspect. So he kills another person to get the investigation going and focused on someone else. Then, when his wife dies, it looks like a pattern, and he is hopefully dismissed by the investigators. But in our cases, with so many years between the killings, that scenario doesn't seem at all logical."

Cindy thought about it and said, "But it does make sense in another way. Let's say Bell finds out the boys are partying in the development, he goes out and tries to stop them. Things get out of control, and he ends up killing them. He manages to minimize it by keeping it from getting into the newspapers. He doesn't get caught. It's well known that he didn't approve of his daughter-in-law. He's already gotten away with murdering three kids, what's one more? Atwater might have been right. Bell didn't have a good alibi. Fast forward to 1982. It doesn't look like Bell would have had any motive for killing the Erikson kids and the babysitter, but someone did. If that person knew about the other incidents, then he might have imitated the first killings hoping that the Eriksons would be grouped with them."

They both considered the idea in silence before Cindy spoke again. "I've thought a lot about the first two murders: the boys and Larry Bell's daughter-in-law. But I haven't done much research on the Eriksons. When I checked the County Assessor's Office records, Larry Bell was the owner of my property when the houses were being built, and he still owned the house when his daughter-in-law was killed. But the Erikson's were the owners when their kids were killed. Doesn't that take away any financial motive? Or at least a motive to hurt the Bells? It could support the theory of two killers."

"Unless there's a connection with the Bells that we don't know about," Darren replied.

"I remember reading that he owned Valley Bank until 1990. Who knows who all he pissed off over the years."

"Let's go back to thinking of it as one killer," Darren said. "He may have done the first one out of need or whatever motive, and discovered he liked it. In those cases, though, the murders tend to be closer together. I could buy six and seven years apart, like we have between the boys, Anne, and the Eriksons, but not the twenty-six years between the Eriksons and the Fremonts." He shrugged. "There are exceptions, of course. But that doesn't feel right here, unless the killer has been committing other murders that we haven't connected here." He sighed. "Which, unfortunately, is a possibility. Since I've been told to stay away from the case, I can't have the FBI run a check for similar cases. We'll have to get Larson to request it."

Darren stared at his empty plate for a few moments before continuing. "What else did you find out about the Eriksons and the babysitter?"

"I haven't really focused on them yet. I'll go back through my notes to see if I've missed something or if there's another track I should take. But I think you may be onto something with the idea that the later murders were to cover his tracks. I remember reading that Larry Bell died shortly after the Fremonts were killed in 2008. It was a heart attack. Too bad we can't question him."

"Chief Atwater killed the main suspect in the Fremont case, Oscar Whitehead, so that's another witness we can't talk to," Darren said.

"Let's go back to John for a minute. I talked with him this morning when he came to pick up Gloria. When he talked about Larry Bell, there was a change in him so dramatic that I was really freaked out. He became extremely angry. He scared me. He said that there were a lot of people who would have liked to see Larry Bell dead, or at least ruined."

"Why so much hatred towards Bell?" Darren asked. "I know he was successful. I suppose that by itself would piss off enough people who were struggling. We've seen that he was brutal, which is what made the bank so successful. But would that be enough motive to kill him?"

Cindy explained what John told her and what she'd found at the County Records Office. "The Bells ended up with most of the land around here, including all of the O'Conner's property. My house is on land that was once John's."

Darren reached for the plate with fortune cookies on it. He held it out to Cindy, and after she took one, he broke into the other. He read his and laughed. "'You will be the strength a friend needs.'"

"Wow, that's perfect for you since you're my knight in shining armor." Cindy read hers. "'You will find what you seek, but not where you expect.'"

Darren looked at his watch and grimaced. "I'm sorry to say that my lunch hour is over." He picked up the bill and stood up. At the register he said, "Can I see you later?"

"I'd like that. How about coming over for dinner? John may be there, if he and Gloria get back from their day trip in time. It would be a great time to question him some more."

Their prolonged kiss was a definite yes.

Chapter 24
September 12, 2011
Day 43

Cindy paced around her living room until Harry Atwater showed up. He'd returned her call shortly after she finished lunch and asked if they could talk in person. She was feeling a bit nervous that by talking with the former chief, she might be getting Darren in trouble. She had to be sure to leave Darren completely out of the conversation. Chief Atwater arrived at her house within the hour. Cindy was a bit surprised that she didn't recognize him from the party. He was a handsome older man, tall and still well built. She brought him a glass of iced tea, and they sat at opposite ends of the couch in the living room. Cindy sat sideways and tucked her feet up under her. She decided to start with Anne Bell since that had been his case.

"Can you tell me... did you have any good leads? Any suspects? I've heard that Larry Bell was one."

"Right. He was my top suspect. Do you know anything about him?"

"I've read quite a bit. He was an unpopular man. But why would he kill his daughter-in-law?"

"Larry and Francine made no effort to hide they disliked their son's wife. They wanted him to 'marry up' or at least marry someone of his stature, but instead, he married a sweet girl from Minnesota."

"I've heard that a lot of men thought she was quite special. A few even tried to steal her away. Were you one that had an eye on her?" She smiled to soften the question, making it sound playful.

He laughed. "Oh, no. I was still grieving my wife. She was my true one and only. Besides, I wanted to move up the ladder. Having an affair with the daughter-in-law of the most powerful man in town wouldn't have been very good for my career."

"Everything I've read so far indicates that her body was never found. Is that true?"

"Unfortunately, yes. Without the body, we can't even say for sure she's dead, not just run off. Although with the amount of blood in the kitchen... well, it seems unlikely she could've lost that much blood with a kitchen injury. The coroner said someone her size couldn't lose that much blood and survive, much less run away. We watched the hospitals up and down the state anyway, but she didn't appear. And, of course, we can't imagine that she would leave her little girl behind. The two of them were very close. Thank God the killer left the girl alone."

Cindy agreed. "Can you tell me who the other suspects were?"

"I wish I could. Unfortunately, I can't point my finger at anyone without putting myself in danger of being sued for libel."

Cindy let that go. Naming potential suspects in a private conversation would not be libelous. It would only become a concern if anything false was published or publicly pronounced. This was Journalism 101 and something all police officers should know.

"I've heard that you had a suspect in the Fremont case and killed him?"

The Chief's face clouded. "Yeah. A transient, Oscar Whitehead. He'd been seen hanging around the high school, and someone said that Whitney was in the habit of giving him her lunch. She'd interviewed me for a paper she was doing months before and mentioned that she had a soft spot for the homeless and did whatever she could to help them. I went by the school and eventually found him hiding in the creek that runs behind the football field." He stopped to drink some iced tea.

"Did he have a shelter back in the creek area?"

"Exactly. When I saw the canvas and all the debris, I approached, calling out to him. I must have seemed threatening, because he came at me brandishing a knife. He was yelling, 'She'd figured it out!' I told him to stop, but he kept coming. I pulled my gun, but that didn't stop him, either. I pulled the trigger when he was only a couple feet away."

"How terrible! Thank goodness you were safe, though. Were you able to find out for sure that he'd killed the Fremonts?"

He nodded and was silent for a bit. "Because I was involved in the shooting, I was taken off the case. The other detectives came in and checked his camp. They found Whitney's school ring, homework that belonged to Suzy Dudley – she was the babysitter that was killed in 1982 – and a backpack that had belonged to one of the boys that was killed in 1967."

Cindy found it curious that he said he was 'taken off the case.' He was the chief and was not assigned to the case at all. "Was anything found from Anne Bell's disappearance?"

"No, but we know he had been in the area at that time. The farmers all complained about him stealing their produce. And with him dead, there wasn't any way we could get anything else. We also didn't think that her situation was connected. I honestly thought Anne's death was a solitary event."

Again, Cindy didn't like his logic. Oscar Whitehead was in the Air Force from 1972 to 1983. She didn't know where he served, but at least in the early part of his tour, he would most likely have been in Vietnam. Anne was killed in 1975. He would not have been the transient stealing fruit. The Eriksons and the babysitter were killed in 1982. Again, that would seem to preclude Whitehead from being the killer, unless he was stationed here. There was no way for her to get a hold of his military records.

"Just out of curiosity, what was your personal opinion of Larry Bell?" she asked.

There was a prolonged silence. "I can't say I liked or admired the man. And as I said, he was a prime suspect in Anne's case. But my family hadn't been affected by his schemes. In fact, the first house I bought with my wife was from one of his earlier developments. He lived just down the street from us. I suppose I benefited from his shenanigans by being able to afford to buy a home. Because I got my mortgage through the VA, he was never really involved. I had very little to do with him."

"What can you tell me about the babysitter and the Erikson kids that were killed in 1982?"

He shrugged. "I wasn't the main detective on that case, so I don't have anything to tell. I'd asked for the case, but it was assigned to another detective, and I was told to leave it alone."

"Do you think that's because you hadn't solved the Anne Bell case?"

The chief bristled. "Having an unsolved murder or missing persons case isn't unusual, probably a lot more common than most people realize. I could have forced the issue, but going outside the chain of command and doing my own investigation would have been a breach of protocol."

Like going after the homeless man, Cindy thought. "There seems to be very little in the press about any of the murders, except for the Fremonts, and nothing much at all anywhere about the Eriksons and their babysitter," she said. "I was hoping you would be able to help me with that one. I haven't had a chance to do any checking on that case. That's the next one I'll be looking at."

"You really want to keep pushing at this?" he snapped. Cindy wasn't prepared for the anger in his voice. She could see a vein pounding on the side of his forehead. "All right, then. There were three young children and a babysitter. Two of the children and the babysitter were brutally murdered, and the youngest boy was never found."

He took a deep breath and continued. "Sorry, this hits too close to home. The babysitter was the daughter of one of our police officers, Officer Dudley. When an officer's family is the victim of a major crime, it's standard to investigate the officer's record of arrests to see if there was any connection. None was found. At least that's what we heard. Not long after the investigation by Internal Affairs, though, the officer quit. Left the area. I think it was all too much for him."

Cindy imagined the terrible pain the officer's family must have felt with the loss of their child compounded by being subjected to an investigation on top of it all.

"My brain keeps trying to tie all of these deaths together. It seems like too great a coincidence that so many people would die in this house," she said.

"Really." He sighed like he was having to explain things to a school child. "First, the boys were killed at a construction site. Addresses hadn't yet been assigned. Next, a woman goes missing who was rumored to be having an affair, maybe several affairs, and may have just staged her death to escape. Then a babysitter gets killed along with the kids she was watching. They've got nothing in common. Even with the deaths in 2008, I'm hesitant to connect them."

It was Cindy's turn to sigh in exasperation. "But they have the location in common."

"In 2008 the M.O. is different. Using a gun instead of a knife is the biggest thing. It makes me think that it was an opportunistic killing. The family was away on vacation with just the oldest girl left behind. There was suspicion of gang activity, especially since it appeared to be execution style." He put the iced tea glass on the table and stood up.

"Chief Atwater, thank you for sharing information. I know bringing all that up is unpleasant, and I appreciate your time. By the way, Detective Larson is handling the case now that the gun was found. What's your opinion of him?"

"I knew him when he was young. Smart kid. Quick to learn, but lazy on the job. I was disappointed he went into Corrections instead of coming to us. I thought I could have guided him into a good officer. Break his bad habits, you know?"

They walked to the door together.

Putting her hand on the knob and pulling open the door, Cindy said, "I understand you're a long time friend of John O'Conner."

"Ah, yes. John. We go way back. Why do you ask?"

"My aunt has moved in here with me and my kids, and she's been seeing a lot of John. In fact, today they're up in the Santa Rosa area together. He seems like a very nice man. Unfortunately, I don't know him very well, and I really should know about anyone she's taking an interest in. Can you tell me anything about him?"

"We had some great times together. John has a horrible temper, though. I'd watch how he treats your aunt."

Chapter 25
September 12, 2011
Day 43

George Atwater loved the drive from the Bay Area to Lake Tahoe. No matter the season, the redwoods and pines shaded the roads. He could have taken Highway 80 instead of 50, but it wouldn't have been as beautiful. He preferred the scenic route to the quicker roads. The creeks that ran along the highway were low, as usual for the fall, but they would be full and treacherous in the next month or so when the heavy rains started to hit the Sierras. In spring time, the creeks often overflowed with the snow runoff and flooded the area. But for now they were shallow and clear.

George stopped along the way to take in the beauty, admiring nature's sounds and smells. Being out here was the most effective way for him to shed the stress of being his father's caretaker and feeling like a failure in his marriage and career. Here he was, forty-five, divorced, living with his father, and working in a dead-end job in a phone store.

His thoughts continually went back to the missed meeting with Cindy. When he was on his date last night, all he could think about was Cindy. His date noticed his distraction, and he claimed that he was worried about the cabin. She didn't look convinced, and when he dropped her off at her house, she was formal and distant. She wouldn't agree to another date, he was sure. Would Cindy?

It was early afternoon when he pulled into the grocery store parking lot in South Lake Tahoe. He picked up enough food for a couple days, along with some bottled water. Looking out the front window while at the checkout counter, he saw a familiar face in the parking lot. He paid and hurried out the door. "Mr. Alvarez?" he called out. The gentleman stopped walking and looked around. "Mr. Alvarez, it's me, George Atwater."

"Well, hello there! I didn't know you'd be coming up. If your dad had called me, I would've gone over to make sure your cabin was cleaned up and ready for you."

George was startled. "I thought Dad *did* talk to you. He told me you'd called him about a tree branch that hit the cabin. He sent me up here to fix it."

Mr. Alvarez shook his head. "No, I haven't talked with Harry since you two were up here in the spring. Perhaps someone else called him. One of your neighbors."

"Hmm, must have been. He said you weren't available."

"Actually, I have some free time. If you've got some damage, I'd be happy to help get it fixed up. What kind of damage is it?"

"I'm just on my way there now. I haven't seen it yet. Apparently a branch landed on the roof. It sounded urgent."

"How about I get my grocery shopping done, deliver it to the wife, and I'll meet you up at the cabin?"

"Perfect. See you shortly."

Tree branches were strewn along the highway that skirted the west shore of Lake Tahoe. It took George a half hour to navigate the narrow and winding road. When he drove up the cabin's driveway, he didn't see any damage to the roof. There were no branches down anywhere near the house. There was a lot of the normal debris from the summer storm, but nothing requiring urgent attention. The cabin sat on about a half acre of land, and the abundance of redwoods and pines prevented him from seeing his nearest neighbors.

What the hell was going on here? Was someone messing with his father? Or was his father messing with him? Or was he just over-thinking this as his ex-wife always accused him of doing?

After putting the perishables in the refrigerator and bringing in his overnight bag, he made a thorough tour around the outside. A slight breeze brought the faint and unpleasant fragrance of sewer water to his nose. He groaned. He was going to have to check on the septic system—one of his least favorite jobs. As much as he would never wish the problem on anyone, he fervently hoped it was some-one else's septic system issue.

He opened all the windows and doors to air the cabin out and hoped the sewage stench wouldn't make its way inside. He was look-ing for the paperwork on the septic system when Joe Alvarez an-nounced his arrival with a tap on the horn of his pickup. When George came out to greet him, Joe said, "I don't see anything wrong. Is it at the back of the house?"

"No," George replied. "I've checked all the way around. I haven't gone up on the roof or into the attic, but I haven't seen any problems yet. I thought I'd wait until you were here before I explored the roof. No sense doing that without someone watching for safety."

"Good thinking," Joe said. "I'm glad you learned something dur-ing those years of hanging out while I did all the work."

They decided to start looking at the roof from the attic. The chain for the pull-down stairs to the attic was within reach of George's hands, although Joe would have needed a step stool to grab it. The attic was large enough to be used as a storage area, but not tall enough for a bedroom. Joe was able to stand up easily, but George could only straighten up in the center of the room near the roof peak.

There were dozens of boxes haphazardly stacked around the attic. George was looking up at the roof and bumped into a stack, sending it crashing to the floor. He stumbled and fell. Two boxes tore open, spilling journals on the floor. George extricated himself from the mess and stood up. He opened one of the books. It appeared to be a work journal with details of his father's investigations. It was a great discovery; he might get more police cases for his website.

Leaving the boxes, George inspected the parts of the roof near the peak, while Joe went to the outer edges. Neither man saw any damage from the recent storm.

The only problem they found was an area around one of the vents that needed to be sealed better to avoid animal infestation. Joe went back to his truck for some steel wool and a caulking gun. He made the repair in minutes.

"Let me get the ladder off the truck, and we can check out the outside," Joe suggested.

Joe set up the ladder and held it in place while George went up. Other than the leaves clogging the rain gutters, there didn't appear to be any problem with the roof. George showered Joe with leaves from the rain gutter, getting a colorful response from the older man, including a threat to take the ladder away before George made it back down. Joe returned to the truck and got yard bags out and started cleaning up the debris Joe was tossing down. They completed the work within a half hour.

Joe put the ladder and the tools away while George got beers and fruit. "I know wine would be a better compliment for the fruit, but I didn't think to pick any up. I didn't pick up any other snacks, either. I'm trying to stay away from junk food."

"I'm glad to see that your dad's bad eating habits weren't passed on to you."

"I'm kind of worried about Dad. And not just the food issues. I'm confused why he sent me up here. First, there wasn't any damage, and second, he specifically said that you were unavailable. I keep going back to that. It bothers me."

"I guarantee you he didn't talk to either me or my wife. We were glued to the baseball games on TV this weekend. We bought a seventy-inch flat screen. Those boys look like they're swinging their bats right in our living room. It's spectacular. I'll be installing a sound system over the next week. I'm looking forward to watching *Apocalypse Now* on it."

"That'll be amazing, like having your own theater in your house. But if I remember your wife at all, I'll bet you'll have to watch a *Fried*

Green Tomatoes for every *Tora! Tora! Tora!* you want to watch."

"You've got that right!" After two beers, Joe decided that it was time to head home.

When Joe went to use the bathroom before hitting the road, George remembered that he needed to check the septic system. Joe agreed to help him, starting with a test of the flushing system. His test flush worked fine, which told him that the problem probably wouldn't be found in the pipes between the house and the septic tank.

Meanwhile, George found the records on the tank. It had been pumped out two years earlier and was given a clean bill of health at that time. Since this was just a vacation home, it shouldn't need to be pumped out for several more years.

The telltale odor was mild between the house and the tank, but it grew stronger as they approached the leach field, a grassy field-like area about thirty yards from the house.

"I hate to say it," Joe said, "but you may need to have a septic company come out here. I think your pipes in the leach field may be blocked.

"Leach field pipes? How bad is that?"

Joe took on the mentor's tone that George remembered from his youth. "The leach field is a series of underground pipes that distributes the sewer water out into the soil to percolate. Damage to the pipes can come from the sludge in the tank escaping into the pipes and blocking them, or roots from trees breaking or displacing the pipes, or even heavy vehicles that might drive over the field. A single pipe being damaged can be repaired easily, but if the sludge has contaminated the system, the entire field might need to be replaced. It would be a long and expensive job."

"Looks like I've got some digging to do before the sun goes down."

"Please don't take offense if I don't stick around to help you with that job. A handyman's got to draw the line somewhere, and leach fields would be one of my lines."

The men walked back to the front of the house to Joe's pickup. Joe drove away, waving out the window.

Back in the house, George decided that he would wait until the following day to start the digging. He relaxed in the recliner and watched the Monday Night Football game. At halftime, he tried to reach his father on both the home and cell phones, but there was no answer. What reasons could his father possibly have had for sending him out here? Did his dad have a date or someone coming over? Had he wanted the house to himself? Having the guys over for a poker party? He thought that was unlikely since his dad had just been to one on Friday night at William's house. Was there something more to the doctors' appointments than he was telling and didn't want him to know? That was a scary thought, one he didn't want to pursue.

George tried calling his dad again during the third quarter. Still no answer on either phone.

After the game ended, he researched repairing septic systems and leach fields on the Internet. Before he turned out the light at eleven, he tried calling home again with the same results. He hoped that his dad was out having fun with the guys and that nothing was wrong.

He said a prayer that his dad's heart was okay.

Chapter 26
September 13, 2011
Day 43

Marti modeled her gown for Darren, showing off Gloria's talents. It was a strapless, full length Greek chiffon-style dress with a gold sash at the waist. The vibrant violet made her gorgeous blue eyes stand out. The final stitching would be done the night before the ball, so the fit would be absolutely perfect. In the meantime, the sides were securely pinned together. When she went up stairs again, she stood in front of the mirror admiring herself, playing with her hair, trying to decide on a style. She imagined Peter's face when he would first lay eyes on her. She knew he'd be knocked out.

She carefully took the dress off and put it in the closet, making sure that nothing touched it. As soon as it was in the closet, though, she wanted to put it back on. She resisted the urge. Hugging herself, she spun around in anticipation of Saturday night. Sherlock watched her from the end of the bed, a space that he had commandeered as his special place. He seemed amused by her antics and wagged his tail when he noticed that she was looking at him.

Suddenly Sherlock's head popped up and he growled. He jumped off the bed and ran to the closed bedroom door. He scratched at it and begged Marti with his eyes. She quickly pulled on sweats and stepped over to open the door. As soon as it was open wide enough for him to get his head through, he dashed out. He raced down stairs, still growling.

Marti slipped on sandals and followed. She heard him go through the dog door to the backyard. His growling turned into urgent and angry barking. She was opening the back door when she was knocked aside by Xena in her rush to follow her fellow canine. Both dogs were agitated, trying to get through the gate that led to the side street, Grove Road. Marti pulled a patio chair over to the fence, stepped up onto it, and looked out over the fence. She couldn't see anyone or anything except a white van that she didn't recognize and Darren's SUV. As she turned away, a shadow moved alongside the van. She tried to see what it was, but she couldn't make anything out.

Sherlock had his nose to the ground following a scent. It led him directly to the outside entrance to the crawl space that her mom had blocked from the inside. Marti decided that the dogs had sensed a four-legged intruder and scared it away. That must have been what she'd seen by the van. "Good dogs!" she praised them. "Let's go inside and get treats!" Both dogs danced around when they heard the word "treats" and dashed in the house ahead of her. The aroma of a roast and fresh baked rolls hit her as she entered the house.

As she opened the pantry door in the kitchen to get the treats, her mom asked what had gotten the dogs so excited.

"I didn't see anything out there, but they were sniffing around the gate and then the crawl space." She noticed that her mom's eyebrows furrowed, but before she could ask what was bothering her, she saw that Gloria had made it home.

She gave the dogs their treats and hurried over to the kitchen table to hug her great aunt. "Where's John? Did you have a good time? What did you do?" She threw questions at Gloria.

"John is outside at the car sorting out the packages to bring in. He's been out there awhile. We bought an awful lot of stuff. Maybe I'd better go help him. We had a *wonderful* time. Shopping, walking, more shopping, and my favorite, the Snoopy Museum."

The dogs alerted everyone that John was approaching the door, and Gloria hurried to open it for him. His arms were full, and more bags were hanging by their handles from his hands. "What took you so long?" Gloria teased. "I'd begun to think that you'd run away with my treasures."

"Absolutely not. The only treasure I want is standing right in front of me."

Gloria took a couple of the bags from him and led him back to her room to drop them off. When they didn't come out of the room for a few minutes, Marti said, "They've got the door closed. It must have been a great date. I'm happy for her. I think she's falling in love."

Cindy agreed, but Marti thought something was off, like her mom was trying to hide her real feelings.

By the time the older couple came out, Cindy was putting the meat, potatoes, and vegetables on platters. The rolls had just come out of the oven, and Darren was busy putting them in a bread basket.

Cindy turned to her daughter. "Please get the boys and get washed up for dinner. We're about ready."

Marti took pleasure in smacking her little brother in the back of his head, interrupting his game of Guitar Hero. "Come on, brat, it's dinner time. Mom said to get washed up." She hurried away before he could put the guitar down and return the hit.

It was a tight fit around the kitchen table with seven people. The conversation centered around the day trip that the older couple had taken. Gloria talked enthusiastically about the Charles Schulz Snoopy Museum and the ice rink next to it. Darren mentioned that the ice rink is the home of Santa Rosa's ice hockey team, so the boys would be playing there at least once during the season. At Gloria's excited cajoling, John promised that they would go see that game.

* * *

After dinner, Marti and Randy did the dishes, while Darren sent Steve to go clean up the mess the boys had made in the family room with the console games. With everyone out of the way and busy, Cindy took the fork that John had used and put it in a paper bag. She hoped they would be able to get DNA from it. She wrote the identification information on the bag and put it in her file cabinet with the water bottle. She would need to see if Darren could do a DNA comparison, but without having access to the case, he probably wouldn't be able to.

Cindy stepped into the living room just as Gloria was kissing John goodnight.

"John, would you be up for a talk out on the porch?" Cindy asked when her aunt headed to bed.

"Certainly. Is there a problem?"

"No, not at all," Cindy replied. She sat next to John on the porch swing, and Darren leaned against the stud. "I'm just hoping you can tell me more about some of the people in the neighborhood. What do you know about William Kentcher and Bobby Donaldson?"

"Oh, we've been friends for years. I just saw them the other night for poker. We get together every month for a game." He turned to Darren. "Do you know George Atwater? Sometimes he plays if someone is going to be absent. Would you consider stepping in a time or two?"

"I'd love to. I'm sure I need another place to lose money."

John patted Cindy's knee. "William is a piece of work. He loves his cigarettes, and it drives his wife crazy. He hates having the game at his house because he can't smoke cigars. She'll know the second she walks in the door. Hellfire and brimstone! That woman can really bring the house down when she's upset. What would you like to know about him?"

Cindy decided to hit it straight on. "Did he know Anne Bell?"

John chuckled. "Oh, yes. He most certainly did." He retold the story about the bets about who could get Anne in bed. "They just didn't understand. She wasn't that way. They thought I had a thing with her, and the more I denied it, the more certain they became. Shortly before she disappeared, they had a fight."

"They? Kentcher and Bobby Donaldson?"

"No, no. William and Anne. She was at the park with her daughter. They went there most days, and everyone knew it. The park was near my work, and sometimes I would meet her there on my lunch hour. On this particular day, when I got there, William was there, too. I could see that their conversation was heated, and then he reached out and grabbed her. You should have seen the bruises he left on her arms. Little Heidi saw me and screamed my name and came running towards me. William took his hands off Anne and left."

"Did you find out what they were fighting about?" Cindy asked.

"Yes, ma'am. Anne told me that he asked her to run away with him. He said he would leave his wife, and she was too good for the Bells. They didn't respect her, and they didn't treat her the way he would."

Darren spoke up. "Did you tell this to Atwater when he was investigating?"

The older man shook his head. "No. William might have a big ego, and he's headstrong, but he wouldn't have hurt her."

"Wait," Cindy said. "You said that William bruised her arms. That's pretty violent."

John was silent. He brushed dog hair off of his pants. "I hadn't really thought about it that way."

"Was he in the armed services?" Darren asked.

"No, sir, he wasn't. Something medical kept him out, if I remember right. I think it always bothered him that he didn't go to war. He gets snippy when we talk about Vietnam at the poker games."

"You told me this morning that William loaned you his rifle for hunting," Cindy said. "Sounds like he made up for not being in the war by being prepared for one here."

John snapped his fingers. "You are right. After my gun was stolen, he showed me his collection. He let me borrow one of his firearms, a nice .45. It was in the 1980s, and we were all worried about the Commies, and people were stockpiling weapons. He had made the crawl space under his house into a reinforced bunker. He'd dug down, not quite deep enough to make it a full basement, but he swore that a nuke wouldn't be able to take him out unless it was a direct hit. And he had enough survival gear to hold off an army."

Darren and Cindy looked at each other.

Cindy said, "What do you remember about the kids that were killed in the '80s? It was a babysitter and three children. Do you know anything about what happened? Any details?"

John sighed. "It was a terrible thing..." He paused for a moment and looked at Cindy and Darren before turning his gaze to his hands. "I remember Harry Atwater saying the oldest boy was stabbed in the shoulder and back. The youngest girl was stabbed once in the chest, and the babysitter was mutilated. The little boy was never found."

Darren nodded. "That fits with what I'd seen in the files. What did you know about the family? The Eriksons."

"They were very nice, but I didn't know them very well except to wave and say hello. I did know the babysitter. She'd babysat for me a few times, too. I was away at an accounting conference when Suzy and the Erikson kids were killed. My son was staying with some friends in San Jose, and I couldn't help but think that if I'd brought a sitter to my house instead, it could have been my son that was dead."

Cindy shuddered. "What a horrible thought! What about the boys who were killed in 1967?"

John grimaced. "I was on duty that night. I remember responding to the scene. The two boys... Are you sure you want to hear this? It's grisly."

"I think I need to hear it," Cindy said.

"When I came in, two boys were hanging by their feet from the roof joist. One was missing his head. I barely made it outside before I threw up. I was in good company — even the captain tossed his cookies." He stood up. "I really need to head home."

* * *

Cindy slipped into Darren's arms as soon as the front door was closed.

"If John was on duty that night," she said with her head against his chest, "then he's not the killer. I'm so relieved."

"Right. That is great news. But 'if' is the key word there. I just wish I could pull the case file to see if he was listed on any report as being at the scene. It may be my suspicious nature, but I like to check alibis. Even if he was on duty, it's only a good alibi if he was with a partner or someone else who could definitively place him somewhere."

"Enough of that stuff," Cindy murmured in his ear. "Gloria's already cleaned up and in bed. The boys are upstairs working on their project, and Marti is at Peter's. We've probably got ... oh, say... fifteen minutes of privacy. What do you think we should do for that time?"

What she really wanted to do was to take him upstairs to her room and make love to him, but with the boys there, she didn't want to risk it. Instead, they sat on the couch in the living room. She sat on his lap and they spent the next few minutes kissing. They were interrupted by snickering coming from the hallway.

"We've been caught," Darren whispered. They both laughed awkwardly, embarrassed to be seen making out, and she got up off his lap.

Cindy closed and locked the door behind Darren and Steve. She leaned against the door, already missing touching Darren's body. She turned around to find her son smirking at her. They made sure the windows and doors were locked, the lights were off, and went upstairs to their bedrooms.

"Sweet dreams," Randy called to her with a laugh.

It was some time before Cindy was able to sleep. Her emotions were too overwhelmed with thoughts of Darren. When she did finally manage to drift off, it was with thoughts of him swirling around in her head.

Her peaceful sleep with dreams of being cradled in Darren's arms only lasted a short while before she found herself once again awake, staring at the ceiling. The room was slightly illuminated by the streetlight outside on the corner, but she didn't make a move to adjust the blinds to block it.

She thought about the conversation she'd had with Darren at the restaurant and the conflicted feelings she'd been having about John. He seemed like such a wonderful guy, certainly a godsend for Gloria. But he fit their suspicions. He was of the right age and obviously hated Larry Bell. If Larry was the reason behind the murders, then John certainly had motive. He'd lost his home and inheritance to the man. He had been in the military and was a hunter, so he knew how to use knives and guns.

Cindy trusted her gut instincts, but this time they were giving her conflicting feelings. On one hand, they were telling her that John was a good guy. If he was telling the truth, then she had nothing to fear from him. She desperately wanted it to be true. But she'd seen his temper and it wasn't a reach to imagine him in a homicidal rage.

She also had a bad feeling about Detective Larson. She estimated him to be in his sixties. If he was sixty right now, then he would have been about 15 in 1967. That would have put him at about the same age as the kids that were killed. He probably knew them. She suspected that he was a couple years older though, so he may have been a few years ahead of them. Didn't he say something about playing football in high school? Could he have been jealous of the new "up and comers?" Her heart quickened. *Could* he be the killer? He was in the area for at least the first one and probably around for Anne Bell. Suzy Dudley and the Erikson kids were killed around the time that Larson indicated he moved to the east coast. He said he was vested in the retirement system here. Darren said that was five years. If that was the case, then he'd come back to this area about the time the Fremonts were killed. That would explain the long gap between the murders. But did he have any kind of motive?

Chapter 27
September 13, 2011
Day 44

George took his breakfast out to the back porch and stared at the leach field. He noticed the grass was dead in some areas, which would indicate either toxicity or lack of water from the pipes. But throughout the entire area, the grass was short. He hadn't been out here since the spring, so it should have been overgrown. Who had been maintaining it?

After bringing his breakfast bowl in and cleaning up, he decided that he would start by walking all the way around the field. At the farthest side of the leach field, he found something that made his heart sink. Tire tracks. The website he'd looked on said that a vehicle driving over a leach field is the surest way to ruin the pipes. This was private property, so no one should have been driving back here. It had never occurred to him that he needed to install a fence around the field. That would be the next job, right after fixing any underground pipes that were damaged.

He continued his survey of the field. He was able to determine some areas that seemed likely to have damage because the soil appeared different. He would start digging in those areas and along the tire tracks. He stayed hopeful that he would find minimal damage, but he worried that he'd have to dig up the entire field. That would take weeks, and he couldn't take that much time from work. He would have to hire someone to come out and do it.

When his circuit brought him back near the house, he went into the garage and grabbed his shovel, gloves, wheel barrel, and a jug of ice water. The sound of a truck engine straining to come up the road caught his attention. He jogged down the driveway to the road and saw a white landscaping truck rumbling towards him. As it passed the house, he saw a sign on the door that read, "Neighborhood Fire Watch." There was a riding lawn mower in the truck's trailer. George groaned. That was exactly the kind of thing that would damage the field.

George went back to the area of the field that had tire tracks. It would be a good place to start. He'd read that pipes were placed at different depths, depending on the soil make up. Since he didn't know how far down his would be, he was careful with his digging. He found his first pipe at twenty inches down. It was nearly flat.

Disgusted, he put the tools down and went back to the house. He needed to talk with his dad about this.

His father answered the phone on the first ring. "Hey, I'm glad I caught ya," George said.

"How bad is the roof, son?"

"There's nothing wrong with the roof. You must've been given some bad information. Who told you that there was a problem?"

"I got a call from one of the neighbors. Sunderson, I think he said his name was."

"He must have had the wrong address, because our roof is fine. I don't recall seeing anyone else's damaged, but then again, I wasn't really looking. I ran into Joe Alvarez, and he came and checked out the place with me. I thought you said he wasn't available."

"No, I didn't talk with Joe. It was the Sunderson guy who said it. I just took him at his word."

"Did you happen to get a phone number for this guy?" George asked, his curiosity piqued.

"I didn't think to, sorry. I was just happy that someone had tracked me down when there was a problem. I didn't question it."

"Well there *is* a problem, just not with the roof. There's damage to our septic system. I smelled the stench as soon as I arrived, and I found a flattened pipe in the southernmost part of the leach field, near the tree line. Have you heard of Neighborhood Fire Watch?" George described the truck he'd seen.

"Yeah, I remember someone talking about the guys on the volunteer fire department occasionally doing some work in people's yards if they thought it was a fire hazard."

"Hmm. I think maybe they've been using the riding lawn mower to keep grass over the leach field under control. That may have crushed the lines. Until I dig more, I won't know the extent of the damage. Hopefully it's localized, but I'm afraid it's the entire thing."

"That doesn't sound good," Harry said. "It's starting to sound like you're going to be asking for a few dollars."

"More than just a few, Dad. We've got to assume the entire field would need to be replaced. We'd be looking at as much as twenty thousand dollars."

Harry whistled. "What would happen if we didn't do anything right now?"

"As long as no one uses the septic system, it won't be too bad. It should be able to handle the small amount I would use. I'll wait until I come home to shower. Anyone a mile or so downwind might not be too happy if we delay repairs. But I'd like to dig around to see the extent of the damage."

"Oh, don't do that," Harry exclaimed. "I mean, the ground is probably pretty hard, and that would be a lot of work. You'd get sweaty and need a shower," he added lamely.

George laughed. "Don't worry, I will do just enough to get us an idea of what's wrong, and then I'll come home."

"That sounds good. We can wait until the spring when the ground is softer and I've had a chance to figure out how to pay for it. You'll just work on the southernmost area? The area farthest from the house?"

"Yup, I'll make sure that you can't even see that I've been there."

"Good. Just to be clear...do *not* dig near the house or the septic tank. Dig only down the slope. I want to be sure that nothing can be seen by passersby. If digging can be seen from the road, I'll have all kinds of people complaining about the eyesore."

George laughed. "What? You don't want me to surround the spoils piles with fluorescent orange netting?" There was a sound of disgust on the phone and then a click as his father hung up.

* * *

"I didn't get the chance to ask you about the Fremonts," Cindy said to Nicole. Randy had woken up with a stomach bug and spent the morning throwing up. Just before noon he started feeling well enough to eat and thought he'd be able to keep chicken soup down. She took the opportunity to walk to the deli that Nicole Wilson owned. The deli had a homey feel with wood planked walls and red and white checkered table cloths. Nicole and the workers had adorable green and white aprons that somehow both hid Nicole's extra weight and made her look curvy. While the helpers were filling Cindy's order, she sat down with Nicole to chat. Cindy brought the conversation around to the problems at her house. "Can you tell me anything about the Fremonts?"

"I moved back here right before the Fremonts were killed. I was in the middle of my divorce, and Dad's health wasn't so good. My parents decided that they wanted to go to an assisted living facility, and I ended up staying in the house." She thought for a moment. "The oldest girl, Whitney, came by asking questions. This was shortly after I'd moved home, and my parents were still here. She wanted to hear about the history of the area. Mom suggested that she talk to a few other long-term residents."

"You wouldn't happen to remember which people your mom suggested, would you?"

"No, not for sure, but if it were me, I would've talked with the O'Conners, Kentchers, and the Donaldsons. Oh, and the Harrisons. Definitely them. They've got their noses into everything. If she wanted dirt, they'd be the people to talk to. Personally, I'd go to Harry Atwater. Nice guy and a fount of information. Both him and his son know a lot about Santa Clara's history." She shook her head. "I really don't have much to tell you. Wouldn't Darren know more?"

As she walked back home, Cindy thought about Whitney Fremont. People said that Tina and Whitney were 'sensitive.' She'd been looking into the history of the house. She may have asked the wrong person questions or gotten too close to the truth. If the killer was someone she'd talked with, could he have been worried enough to shut her up?

In Cindy's dream, Whitney wasn't one of the ones killed in the shooting. But there was a dart on the floor with blood on it, and a small puddle of blood that was smeared as if someone had put a hand in it. Was it possible that Whitney was the only intended victim and somehow got away while the rest of the family was killed? Was the handprint in her room from her mother's blood, or was it the killer's? Cindy played the possible scenarios over in her head.

When she got home, the house was quiet. She put the meals on the kitchen table and went upstairs to see how Randy was doing. She was pleased to see that he was sitting up in bed, and Gloria was sitting near his feet. They were engrossed in a game of gin.

"How's the patient?" Cindy asked. "Are you ready for lunch?"

"Heck yeah!"

She left the room and headed to her bedroom to drop off her purse. When she passed her office, she ran into a tall figure coming out of the room. Cindy let out a startled cry. Strong hands grabbed her shoulders as she stumbled backwards. It was John. The papers he was holding fell to the floor in disarray.

Cindy pulled away from him and knelt down to pick up the papers. Her stomach dropped when she saw what the papers were.

"What in the world are you doing with my wife's death certificate?" John asked with an angry edge to his voice. He was holding the paper in a shaking hand. His face was red, and his eyes were narrowed.

He snatched the papers that she had picked up out of her hand

and flipped through them. "Just what the hell are you doing with these?" he demanded.

Cindy yanked the papers back out of his hand and continued gathering the rest off of the floor, trying to think of an excuse. *Making a case against you as a serial killer,* did not seem like the appropriate response.

"That's none of your business, John," she said.

"Seeing as how you have my family's information there, I think it *is* my business!" He put his hand to his mouth and sucked on his index finger. When he took it away from his mouth, Cindy could see blood welling in a paper cut. She looked at the paper in her hand and saw a sliver of blood. This would be better for DNA than the fork she took.

Gloria appeared behind them in the hall. "Please, please! Stop fighting!"

Cindy stood up with the papers and pushed past John into her office. "It's research I'm doing on deaths of mothers during childbirth in the sixties," she improvised. "There's been suspicion that the deaths and fetal deformities might be related to either pesticides or drugs given during pregnancy. Since both you and Chief Atwater lost your wives in the '60s during childbirth, it seemed like a good place to start. I was looking to see if there were others around here who'd suffered the same fate."

She put the papers in her file cabinet and locked it. She turned to face John. "I didn't want to tell you about it until I had more information. If it didn't look like a story would come out of it, I didn't want to bring it up. I'm sure it's painful." She was surprised at how convincing her lies sounded. The best lies have a basis of truth.

John took a deep breath. "I see. I still wish you would have talked with me first. My wife had a weak heart. There were no medications involved. Don't bring my family into your article."

"Thank you for telling me that. I assure you that names of the patients would be confidential, and if I had found something, I would have discussed it thoroughly with you. But now you've saved me a lot of research. So thank you."

John looked somewhat mollified, and his normal color was returning. Gloria took his hand and pulled him towards Randy's room. "Come on, play a hand of cards with us."

Cindy followed behind them and stood in the bedroom doorway. "I'll be right back with lunch. John, is a roast beef sandwich okay with you?"

"Yes, ma'am. That would be lovely."

Cindy's appetite was ruined; John could have her sandwich. She put the soup, sandwiches, and drinks on a tray and brought it up to Randy's room. She set it on his desk and left the room.

Her purse vibrated. Reaching in, she pulled out her phone. She had a text message.

It read: "We need to talk. Harry Atwater."

She wrote back: "Home with sick son. Call or come by? Your friend John is here."

His reply came moments later. "John is there?"

"Yes"

"Be right there. Danger. Stay away from him. Do not tell him I'm coming."

Chapter 28
September 13, 2011
Day 44

Cindy paced in the kitchen. Had Harry come to the conclusion that John was the killer? If so, what was his reasoning? Last night she and Darren had decided that John was not a murderer. Violent tempered—she'd just witnessed that—and trained in the military, but he was on duty when the boys were killed and out of town when the Eriksons died. If John was the killer, she needed to get him away from her aunt and son. Despite the warning to stay away from him, she went upstairs, taking the stairs two at a time. She stopped at the top and took a couple deep breaths to calm herself before going into the bedroom. She couldn't think of a way to get John out of the room. She hoped something would come to her.

"How was lunch?" she asked. "Can I get you anything else?"

They said they were fine, and she loaded up the tray. She noticed that John wasn't dealt into the game. "Say, John. I see you're not playing this round. How would you feel about coming downstairs with me and telling me about your experiences as a kid growing up in the valley. I could use some historical flavor."

Much to her relief, John smiled. "I don't think I've got anything in my past worthy of your magazine, but I can certainly share some of the valley's history." He stood up and put his hand on Gloria's shoulder. "That is, of course, if this lovely lady will excuse me?"

Gloria nodded, her focus was on the cards in her hand. "Just don't run away without me."

Both dogs were napping by the bed, and Cindy wanted to keep them in the room. She wanted them to be there to protect Randy and Gloria. John followed Cindy out of the room, and she closed the door. They went down the stairs and into the family room. "Would you like to sit in the family room here? Or perhaps on the porch?"

"I'd prefer to stay out of the sun," he said. "I got a touch of sunburn yesterday." He sat in the recliner with his back to the window.

Cindy opened the front door to let fresh air in. It was warmer than she liked, but she wanted to be able to see Harry when he arrived. She sat on the couch across from John. This way she was between John and the hallway leading to the stairs. She was determined that he would not hurt her family. He would not get by her.

Cindy pulled a pad of paper and a pen out of the drawer on the end table to take notes.

"You must take your writing seriously," John said. "Do you have pen and paper stashed everywhere?"

"As a matter of fact, I do. I have notebooks in my car, my purse, nightstand, and even in the bathroom. You never know when inspiration will hit you or where it will take you. Sometimes it's just simply a word or phrase that catches my ear that I like. I even carry a digital recorder in my purse.

"Why don't you tell me about one of your happiest childhood memories," she suggested. "Sometimes those kinds of stories can give me the flavor I need." Her hands were shaking. Could she really be sitting across from a serial killer? A psychopath? She was torn. He was the perfect suspect. But her heart screamed that it couldn't be him. She'd been so happy when he'd seemingly been eliminated. Was it just wishful thinking? Her heart was thumping so hard that she was afraid he'd be able to hear it or see the pulse in her neck. She took a couple deep breaths to try to calm it down.

"Let me think a moment." He was quiet for more than a minute, his eyes staring at nothing. "I was the youngest of nine children. The one that was just older than me was my only sister. She was four years older. It was her sixteenth birthday, and we were having a grand party for her. Pretty much everyone from town was there. My daddy always did the parties up right, and this was a very special one.

"Marybeth was a beautiful girl. All the boys had crushes on her, and my older brothers were very protective."

His story was stopped by the sound of a car pulling into the driveway. It was going too fast and bottomed out on the curb before screeching to a halt.

"Who in the world is that?" John exclaimed. "Kids these days have no respect!"

The dogs were barking at the noise from Randy's room. Cindy was glad that she'd closed the bedroom door when she and John had come downstairs.

John's face registered surprise when his old friend rushed up to the door. "Harry! What are you doing here?"

Harry opened the screen door before Cindy could get there, and he stepped inside. "John. I was afraid that you would be here."

John wore a look of confusion. He stepped towards Harry with his hand extended but took a closer look at the man's expression and stopped. He dropped his hand to his side. "What do you mean? You know I'm dating Cindy's aunt."

Harry looked at Cindy. "Where are your aunt and son? Is anyone else here?"

"They're upstairs. It's just my aunt, son, and the three of us here."

"Okay. Why don't you go on up and stay with them for a few minutes while John and I talk."

She nodded and left the room. Out of their sight, she stopped and listened.

* * *

"Sit down, John," Harry demanded. "And keep your hands where I can see them."

John hadn't seen his friend this angry in years. "What the hell is going on?" He sank into the same recliner as before, and Harry sat on the edge of the couch.

"I've been doing a bit of digging," Harry said. "Cindy's been asking a lot of questions, and it got me thinking. I pulled out my old files from the homicides that happened here."

"And what the hell does that have to do with me?"

"You and I were close friends back then. No wonder I didn't catch on."

"Catch on? Catch on to what?" John couldn't keep his voice from shaking.

"It was you all along, wasn't it?"

"Huh? It was me all along? What are you talking about?"

"That bastard Larry Bell stole your property from you. It would have been your inheritance. I remember us talking about what you would do with the land when your dad passed on. You were the last male, and your sister had no intention of remaining here. You didn't like farming. You preferred books and numbers. You wanted to sell the land to developers. You stood to make a fortune. But Larry Bell beat you to it."

"Yes, I would have sold the property, and yes, I was furious that Larry Bell took it. But so were a lot of other people. What does that have to do with the murders that took place here? Nothing! That's what. Nothing!"

"I remember you saying you wanted to see Bell dead. But beforehand, you wanted him to suffer like your family suffered. And the other families suffered. You wanted to see him lose everything. I never thought you'd go this far."

"Just a minute—"

Harry continued as though John hadn't said a word. "You started by using murder to curse his new development. How perfect that this house was on the exact plot of land that would have been *your* land when your dad passed. A grisly murder would bring down the prices of the homes, maybe even stop the development altogether. That would be a great start to Bell's ruin."

"You're crazy!" Sweat beaded on John's forehead, and he felt wetness trickle down his neck. "You know it couldn't have been me."

"No, actually I don't." Harry's voice was calm, in direct opposition to the panic John felt. "I wasn't with you the night the boys were killed."

"I was on patrol."

"No. You weren't. It was a rare Friday night off for me. My wife and I were at the varsity football game. I didn't know about the murders until we were driving home and saw the flashing lights. The captain called all off-duty officers in. Even the volunteers like you."

"No, that can't be true," John whispered, memories bursting through his head, mixing together and getting jumbled.

"And then Bell's son moved into the house with his gorgeous wife. Remember how you used to lust after her? Our sons were just babies, and Anne would come over when her husband was working and keep you company. You played up that grieving, widowed father act. Her daughter played with our boys, and you sat on the back porch drinking wine and imagining making love to her. Imagine how that would kill Bell. You debasing his daughter-in-law."

"How dare you!" John yelled, jumping up out of his chair. "I'd fallen in love with Anne, but I knew she was in love with her husband. There was no chance for me. I would never have 'debased' her as you put it. And I certainly wouldn't have killed her."

"Oh, you really expect me to believe that now?" Harry stood nose to nose with him. "I think you waited until you saw her husband leave for a walk with her mother after their Thanksgiving dinner and decided you'd get some action. It must have been driving you crazy to hear William and Bobby betting who could get her in bed first. What happened? Did she turn you down? Did she say she didn't love you? Did she tell you to leave?"

"No! She didn't say any of that!" John stumbled over his words. "I mean, I wasn't there! I didn't see her the night she died. I wouldn't have risked going over to their house."

"Oh, bullshit. You would be just a friendly neighbor stopping by to wish the family a happy Thanksgiving. There wouldn't be any risk.

What did you do with her body, John? Huh? What did you do with it?"

Harry changed tactics. "I remember being completely baffled by the murder of the Erikson kids. That was just so unnecessary. It wasn't until Cindy and I talked that I realized that one of the major reasons a killer continues to kill is to cover up what they've done before. Those murders were excessive, especially for someone trying to clean up evidence or shut someone up. So it made me think. Who would need shutting up? Certainly not the kids. That left the babysitter. It occurred to me that the girl watched our kids on occasion. What did she discover at your house? Did she find the body of your lover? Do you have Anne Bell's body hidden at your house?"

"No! No, no, no! And again, NO!" John shook his head in disbelief. "I wasn't even in town when the Eriksons were killed. You think you've got this all figured out. And somehow, you have decided it's me." He took a step towards Harry, pressing his offensive. "You've found your mark, and now you're twisting the facts to fit your theory. Just like you did when you thought Bell had done it. Then the transient. Don't you recall you're supposed to let the facts paint the picture? You've gone completely nuts."

"You said you were at a conference when the Eriksons were slaughtered. I never questioned it. There never was a conference, was there?"

"Yes! I don't know how I could prove it now, but I was there! I remember being devastated when I got back and found out about the kids. I told Cindy all that."

"It all makes sense now," Harry said, ignoring John's argument. "You banked on our friendship to keep you from getting caught. You knew I'd tell you anything that came up. You were always interested in hearing all the gory details. You pumped me for information. Now that I think about it, I should have been suspicious of your involvement. The shame is mine. If I'd caught on, there would have been so many fewer deaths."

John exploded in anger. He grabbed his childhood friend by the throat. The two men struggled, knocking the lamp off the table. They stumbled and fell together on the floor. John managed to end up on top and straddled Harry, his hands around the man's throat.

Stuck on his back, Harry brought his left knee up as high as he could. He planted his foot near his butt and pushed off the floor, forcing his body to roll to his right, hard and fast. The motion toppled John onto his side, and Harry pounced on him. He punched John's mouth, cutting his knuckles on the man's teeth. He grabbed John's head, lifted it, and slammed it down on the floor.

John reached out along the floor, fingers searching for any kind of weapon. He found the cord for the broken lamp and tugged it to him. He finally managed to grab the neck of the lamp and swung. It connected with the side of Harry's head. The former police chief collapsed on the floor, rolling away.

Both men lay there, breathing heavily. When Harry groaned and started to stand up, John scrambled to his feet. They stood facing each other. In a quick, practiced move, Harry reached down and pulled a gun from an ankle holster. He straightened up and aimed the gun at John. "It all ends now. No need for a jury. This house deserves an end to your terror." He cocked the gun.

Chapter 29
September 13, 2011
Day 44

The digging was strenuous, and with the sun shining on him, George chose to stop for water and to rest every fifteen minutes. Even though he'd told his dad that he would just check the farthest area, he decided to keep going. He worked his way back towards the house and found that the pipes were more deeply buried there. He stood up and looked carefully at the grade of the land and realized that it wasn't that the pipes were buried deeper so much as the land sloped away from the house. The pipes were probably level, they just appeared deeper.

As he worked his way around, he discovered that not all of the pipes were damaged. A few were malformed but weren't bad enough to need replacing. Unless he found a lot more damage, he wasn't going to have to tear out and reinstall the whole field. But he would need to expose all of the pipes. No time like the present, he thought.

Shortly after eleven, he was about to break for lunch when his shovel hit something different. Figuring that it was a rock, but wary that it could be part of the controller mechanism, he used a spade to carefully dig around it. As he exposed more, he started to feel sick.

He moved slowly, making certain not to damage his find. Finally, when he had enough dirt removed to be positive of what he had, he sat down and put his head between his knees. He felt like he was going to pass out or throw up. There was no doubt that he had uncovered a human skull.

The nausea and dizziness passed, but each time he looked at the hole, he felt another wave of queasiness threaten. He finally stood up and made his way back to the house. He wasn't sure what he should do. As the son of a cop, he *should* know what to do, but his mind was in turmoil, and he couldn't think straight.

He picked up the phone and called his dad. When the answering machine came on, he slammed down the phone. "Damn it!" He stood there, staring at the phone. Finally he decided he needed to call the police. But what number? He didn't know the non-emergency number. And this certainly wasn't an emergency. The poor person was long dead. Lights and sirens weren't going to help.

Finally, at a loss, he decided to call 9-1-1 anyway. When the call was answered, he said, "This is *not* an emergency, but it is urgent."

"That's okay, sir. Go ahead and tell me what's wrong." The female dispatcher sounded young and bored.

"I found a human skull in my backyard."

There was silence for a moment. "A human skull? You're sure it's human?"

"As certain as I can be without continuing to dig, and I don't want to damage any evidence. And since I don't think we have many monkeys around Lake Tahoe, yes, I'm pretty sure it's human."

"Fine. Your address, please."

He gave her the information she requested, and she said that officers were on the way. She hung up, but he was in such a state of shock that he continued to hold the phone to his ear, listening to silence until it squawked, startling him into dropping it.

The officers arrived in eight minutes with lights flashing and sirens screaming. In the Sierras, George knew, there wasn't much crime. The officers didn't have much to do outside of the occasional party break up. Eight minutes was a good response time, considering the area the officers had to cover and the treacherous roads. It didn't compare to the three-minute response time for units in Santa Clara, but George was nevertheless impressed since this wasn't an emergency call.

He met the patrol car in the driveway. Two uniformed officers got out. George introduced himself and showed the men the way to his dig site. The cops were both young, maybe in their early twenties, and looked fit. George noticed sergeant stripes on the uniform of one of them. He reassessed the man's age. Even late twenties was young to already be a sergeant.

While they walked to the hole he'd dug, George explained why he was digging. Both officers grimaced at the thought of digging in a leach field.

They stood over the hole and stared at the boney, vacant eyes. "Yup," the junior officer said. "That's a human skull all right."

The sergeant nodded his agreement. "We'd better get the coroner out here."

Several neighbors came by to find out what was going on, and the officers sent them away. Instead of returning home, they stood watching from across the road. When the van from the morgue arrived, the spectators tried to follow it back around the house, and more officers were called for crowd control.

Several technicians continued the digging. It was nearly one in the afternoon when they had their first break in discovering the identity of the skeleton. It was a wedding ring. The coroner picked up the ring and looked at the inside of the band. There was a tiny inscription, and he retrieved a magnifying glass from his bag. He read the inscription aloud. *"Anne Bell, my belle."*

George's world spun. Anne Bell. Her body had never been found. Until now.

The officer noticed George's discomfort. "Is something wrong? Do you know her?"

Yes, there's a body in my backyard. There is definitely something wrong. "No, I don't know an Anne Bell." He was surprised when the lie came out of his mouth. "But I think I'm going to be sick. It's one thing to have a skeleton, but when there's a name attached, it becomes a person." He covered his mouth and turned towards his cabin.

"Hey!" the officer called after him. "Don't leave the house!"

George didn't know what to think. Too many things were going through his head. Anne Bell. He could only think of one reason that her body would be here. His father had killed her. A glimmer of hope came with another possibility. Could his dad have known who did it and was trying to protect the person? He'd been the investigator on the case. Could he have discovered who did it and later helped them dispose of the body? His hope crashed down. No. No way. The only reason he could think of for a person to bury the body of their murder victim at a place that would connect the crime to themselves would be if they thought it would help them get away with the murder. Burying the body in a leach field would help the decomposition. A perfect place.

Over the years, even before he retired, George's dad had come up to the cabin every chance he got. If Harry had two days off in a row, George knew his dad would be here. From the time George was sixteen and could stay home by himself, the elder Atwater would come here alone. Their trips here together were rare.

How many more bodies would they find? If his father was the murderer all along, then they would find at least three more, and possibly a decapitated head. They would find sixteen-year-old Whitney Fremont, four-year-old Aaron Erikson, Enrico Martinez, fifteen, and maybe the head of Freddie Dell. How could a police officer become a serial killer? How does a murderer become a police chief?

George frantically tried to think of what to do. His world was shattered. What was he going to do? He rocked back and forth on the couch, unable to think clearly. A thought made its way out of the fog. He had told Cindy to contact his dad. And with that thought, things fell into place. Her tires had been punctured. He had told his dad that Cindy was going to meet with him after she left the ice rink. Dad had been obviously upset...and then left the house. Then there was the sudden need for George to come up here to the cabin. There was no damage to the house. And he was absolutely positive that Dad had said that he had contacted Joe Alvarez, but Joe said he didn't. Then Dad denied it later. He must have made it up. Did Dad need to prevent him from comparing information with Cindy?

He felt a crushing weight on his shoulders. His father was a murderer. In gruesome ways. He felt another wave of nausea, and this time, he couldn't stop it. He put his hands over his mouth to hold it in and sprinted to the sink. Wave after wave took him until he was sure he'd lost everything in his stomach. He collapsed on the kitchen floor.

It was several minutes before George stood up, turned on the faucet, and splashed water on his face. He rinsed his mouth to try to get rid of the taste, and drank a few mouthfuls to soothe his stomach. He pushed himself away from the sink and stumbled down the hallway. The journals in the attic... maybe they could give him some idea of what was going on. He pulled the stairs down and slowly made his way up, dreading each step that took him closer to the knowledge that could confirm his suspicions and destroy his world.

The first two boxes he opened were files from his dad's cases. A quick perusal determined that none of them was about the murders at Cindy's house. Gruesome crime scene photos and witness statements. Could a serial killer feed his sick needs by watching what others did? The third box had journals. Some had dates written on the spine, going all the way back to the early 1970s. But the majority had nothing written on the outside.

George picked up the box, carefully maneuvered down the stairs, and went back to the living room where he could read in comfort on the couch. He flipped through a few and saw that they were notes about his father's cases, except from a personal point of view. No wonder he kept the journals here. Anything that an officer writes on a case can be used by the prosecution or the defense in court. Harry wouldn't want his personal feelings brought into the courtroom. George wondered if his dad had written these in anticipation of writing books after retirement. He'd never said anything, but there certainly appeared to be enough information here to do it.

The third journal that he opened had no writing on the spine. He let it fall open near the middle. The writing on those pages was frenzied, not his dad's normal block-letter printing. "I've done what you wanted," was scrawled over and over along with "What do you want?" George moved forward a few pages. "I made them pay!"

Towards the end of the journal, the writing was normal again, and between the purposeful, legible writing and the contents, George's blood ran cold. It was dated September 29, 1982. "Karen. I've done it. I've taken the daughter away from the dispatcher who ignored your pleas. Now he will feel the same desolation we have." Karen was George's mom who had died giving birth to him. She'd tried to get help and died on a neighbor's porch. George started shivering, and nausea threatened again. He didn't have the chance to get to the sink; he vomited on the floor between his feet.

When the heaves ended, George's frantic thoughts went back to Cindy. If Dad was worried that she was doing an investigation, then he would need her to be quieted. Obviously the man wasn't opposed to permanently shutting someone up. He'd shot the guy in the creek. He must've set the man up. Planted the evidence before the other cops arrived.

George realized he'd better warn Cindy to stay away from him. And keeping someone like Darren around would be a good idea, too. Yes, Darren would be good, especially if he was armed.

He picked up the house phone but realized that he didn't know Cindy's number. It was programmed into his cell phone. He went into the bedroom and dug through his bag until he found the phone and switched it on. He was impatient waiting for the phone to warm up.

He nearly screamed when he dialed her number and it rang through to voice mail. He left a message for her to call him immediately, no matter what time. He said it was critical, but didn't explain. How could he possibly explain? After thinking about it, he decided to send a text, too.

"U there?" he wrote. And waited impatiently for an answer.

It was a couple minutes before his phone vibrated. "Yes."

He replied, "Did u talk w/dad?"
"Yes. He's here now."
George couldn't breathe. It was the worst possible scenario.
"Get out! He's the killer!"
There was no reply.

Chapter 30
September 13, 2011
Day 44

"Get out! He's the killer!"

Still in the hallway by the stairs, Cindy read the words over and over. His dad was the killer? Chief Atwater? It couldn't be! He was accusing John and it made sense. Atwater had put together all of the pieces that she'd found, and John was the killer. How could a police chief be the killer? She couldn't wrap her mind around it, and the hysterical thoughts kept circling around, confusing her.

The men's arguing turned into a physical fight. A crash was followed by grunts and thumps. It sounded as though they were rolling around on the floor. From her position, she couldn't see anything going on, but it sounded like they were still in the family room close to the hall entrance. She was petrified in place. She had no idea what to do.

She had hit "ignore" when the phone vibrated a few minutes ago because she didn't want the men to hear her and know that she was listening. She didn't want to call Darren where she could be heard, either. Instead, she sent a text to him. "Help. Killer here." She hit "send."

Then came the terrible, unmistakable sound of a gun being cocked. Her paralysis was gone. She bolted up the stairs, no longer worried about being quiet. She stumbled into her son's room, surprising her aunt and Randy. Both dogs were agitated by the fighting they could hear and the fear on her they could smell.

Randy saw the terrified look on her face and said, "What's going on, Mom?"

She shushed him and whispered, "We've got trouble, but I've called for help. We need to barricade ourselves in here. The killer is downstairs."

Randy's eyes got wide; Gloria looked confused.

Her aunt spoke first. "Nonsense. Get a hold of yourself. Are you sleepwalking? There's no killer. And even if there were, John would take care of him."

* * *

The sight of the gun made John's legs shake. He held up his hands in supplication, backing away, trying to inch towards the front door. The warmth of the sunrays on his back told him he was close, but he didn't think he was close enough to turn and run. Harry was maybe fifteen feet away. Too close to miss. John's eyes were glued to the gun and Harry's finger on the trigger. When he saw the finger start to tighten, his legs gave out. At the same time, he felt an incredible, burning pain sear the side his head.

* * *

Cindy had heard the gun cock less than a minute earlier, but she still screamed when she heard the gunshot. The other two in the room instantly understood that she was serious.

Randy jumped out of bed when Cindy said, "Help me move the desk in front of the door." All three together managed to move it, and Cindy was cursing the thick carpet the whole way. They curled up on the bed together, waiting for help to come. The dogs got up on the bed with them, shaking, not understanding what was happening.

Cindy's heart missed a beat when she heard footsteps coming up the stairs. She whispered, "Get down on the floor in the closet. Go!"

This time, neither of them questioned her. She closed the closet door behind them. The dogs stood on the bed, shaking with tension.

"Mom!" Randy frantically whispered. "Mommy, get in here." His voice cracked into a whimper.

She whispered back. "Stay still. And stay completely quiet. No matter what. Do not come out until I get you. Understood?"

Without waiting for an answer, Cindy crawled to the desk that was blockading the door. It wouldn't take much for Atwater to push the door open by toppling the desk. Even though it put her in more potential danger, she crawled under the desk and added her weight to the back panel that was against the door. Her extra weight might help keep the door shut and prevent the desk from toppling over. She hoped he wouldn't start shooting. Or if he did, he would shoot high, not down where she was crouching.

Her phone buzzing startled her so badly that she cried out. The dogs started barking again. Sherlock jumped off the bed and sniffed at the bottom of the door. He growled and barked louder. Xena tried to join him at the door, but there wasn't enough room under the desk. She positioned herself at the wall, getting as close as she could to the edge of the desk and the door.

Atwater's voice was just outside the door. "I hear you in there. It's safe to come out now. I've taken care of John. He won't be killing anyone."

Cindy didn't respond. She looked at her phone and saw that it was a text from Darren. "omw sending units. U safe?"

She replied, "in rs room with r n g. Atwater at br door"

She hoped that he would understand.

Moments later a text came back, "confirm Atwater killer and you are in Randys room?"

She texted back, "yes. help."

"Come on out," Atwater called from the hallway.

This time, Cindy answered. "No, thank you. I think I'll stay right here for now. Did you take care of John? I don't want to see it."

Atwater's laugh was evil. "Oh, yes, he's dead. Now come out."

Her phone buzzed. "2 min." Cindy wasn't sure if she should be relieved that help would be there in two minutes or terrified that they were still two minutes away and the killer was at her door.

When she didn't reply, Atwater tried the door. It bumped against the desk. "It's okay. Come on out."

"No!"

He slammed his fist against the door. "Open this door right now!"

The dogs' barking reached a higher intensity.

Cindy screamed when the door slammed against the desk, making it rock, even with her body pushing against it. She braced her feet and pushed back against the desk. The next slam moved the desk an inch, and she scrambled to try to push it back.

She wasn't strong enough, nor quick enough. The next impact moved the desk farther. This time, the opening was wide enough that Atwater was able to push his arm through and grasp the wall for leverage. Cindy screamed as she pushed back, but she simply wasn't his match. The door inched forward.

Suddenly Sherlock darted into the opening, squeezing his body through the narrow area. He latched onto Atwater's leg. The man howled in pain and kicked. Sherlock yelped and went after the leg again, growling. Xena was too big to get through. She did the next best thing. She lunged up at Atwater's arm and bit down.

Atwater screamed again. He pulled his arm back and out. He left a spray of blood on the wall, door, and desk. Cindy could hear Sherlock snarling. It sounded like he still had a hold of the man's leg. Her world froze when she heard a sickening thud followed by an agonized yelp. She knew that Atwater must have kicked the puppy. Her heart sank lower when Sherlock's growling stopped; she couldn't hear any whimpering. *Noooooo!* Tears streamed down Cindy's face. Xena renewed her barking.

* * *

His solid kick sent the pesky dog flying. He felt a surge of power and satisfaction with the loud yelp from the dog. When it landed several feet away, it didn't move and stopped making noises. How had she figured out that John wasn't really the killer? What had given him away? Now she would have to die, too. And her family. He turned his attention back to getting into the room. The next hit against the bedroom door toppled the desk, and he pushed the door open another few inches. He pointed the gun at Xena who was crouched in front of him, ready to attack. Before he pulled the trigger, the dog jumped at his arm and clamped down on his wrist. He jerked his arm back above his head, and shook the dog loose. The gun fell from his grip behind his head. It went tumbling behind him towards the stairs. He turned, dropped to his knees, and reached for the gun. The dog jumped on his back. He fell forward, scrambling for the gun, but the powerful husky bit down on the back of his neck. He rolled as hard and fast as he could to slam her into the wall. She let go.

He reached out for the gun again but missed. His hand brushed it, and it bounced down the stair. He got to his hands and knees and crawled forward. As he reached out, slightly off balance, Xena slammed into his back. He tried the same roll again, but she leapt off before he could crush her. The sudden change of weight made him fall forward, and he tumbled down the stairs. He tried to grab something, anything. But his body continued down the stairs until he hit the midway landing.

He was stunned and couldn't move. Every part of his body hurt. His left arm was shredded and bleeding badly from the dog bites. His neck felt like it was on fire. The husky stood a few steps above him, growling, showing her sharp teeth. He guessed the gun was near the top of the stairs, but the dog was blocking the way.

He inched his way towards the next set of stairs leading downward, and the dog stayed where she was, still snarling. He continued moving down the stairs. The dog didn't move. She appeared to be content with protecting her pack. At the bottom of the stairs, Harry scrambled to his feet.

* * *

Sirens announced the approach of the police. It was the best sound that Cindy had ever heard. She scurried on her hands and knees to the window and peeked out. She saw Darren's unmarked car bounce over the curb and skid to a stop in the driveway alongside Atwater's car. Two black-and-whites pulled up behind him. She felt panic when no one got out of the cars. One of the cars backed up and sped around the corner. She figured that they were going to be blocking the side gate to the backyard. Yet still no one got out.

She looked at the bedroom door. It was open, and Xena was gone. She couldn't hear the dog growling anymore. The door was warped and the wood was torn around the hinges. No matter how hard she pushed, it wouldn't close. She cautiously looked out and covered her mouth with her hand. She bit down to keep from crying out. Sherlock was in the hall. He was on his side and not moving. She couldn't tell if he was breathing.

Atwater's going to pay dearly for this. Growling from her right drew her attention away.

She inched out into the hallway and moved quietly towards the stairs where the growling was coming from. There was a lot of blood on the walls and the carpet. The dogs had done a good job. Her heart stabbed with pain for Sherlock. When she got to the stairs, the husky turned and looked up at her with a wag of her tail. Cindy held out her hand, and Xena came back to her. She was limping, unable to put any weight on her right front paw.

"Good girl, Xena," Cindy praised in a whisper. "What a good girl you are." Cindy saw the gun three stairs down and moved to get it. Xena stayed right with her. With the gun in both hands, she inched forward to the midway landing and peered around the corner to see if Atwater was there. Other than more blood, the stairway was empty.

With the dog at her side, Cindy continued down the stairs and into the bottom hallway. The entrance to the rec room was on her left, and she stepped into the room with the gun in front of her. She glanced around quickly. She didn't see anyone there, and she came back out. There was no one in the hall.

She closed the door to the rec room to make sure that no one could come up from behind her. She had just started to inch down the hall when she heard the front screen door open and someone yell,

'*Police!*' Momentary relief made her legs feel weak. Then she realized that the officers might force Atwater right back in her direction. She gathered strength from the weight of the gun in her hands. If he appeared in front of her, he would be dead. There was no way he would get past her.

Movement down the hall caught her attention. It was the shadow of gun barrel slowly entering the hall from the front room. In a series of sharp moves, the holder of the gun stepped into the hall and spun both directions, ending with the gun pointed at her. It was Darren.

Cindy felt her strength give out as she collapsed, sliding down the wall into a sitting position. Another cop entered the hallway, and Darren ran over to her side. Xena started snarling again, and Cindy petted her softly. "It's okay, darling. Good girl."

"Where is he?" he whispered.

"I don't know. The dogs got him and...and..." The tears broke free. "I think Sherlock is dead. And John, too."

Darren shook her. "Hey. Look at me. Where is Atwater?"

"I don't know. Xena was on the stairs blocking the way. There's blood on the landing and along the wall here. He's got some pretty bad bites on his arm at least. Sherlock bit his leg, too. He's bleeding pretty badly."

Darren looked back down the hallway, and the other officer shook his head. They hadn't found him either.

"Stay here with the gun. I'm going to check the rec room." He stepped past her to the rec room door and opened it. He scrutinized the room. He came back out, leaving the door open. "No one there."

The officers gathered in the family room, but she stayed slumped at the bottom of the stairs. She could hear the radio communication to the medics. They were told to come in and evacuate the gunshot victim. She felt a surge of hope. *He must be alive; otherwise they wouldn't risk bringing the medics in.*

* * *

The officers checked all of the rooms, including the pantry in the kitchen, but there was no sign of Atwater. Darren radioed the officers who were guarding the outside of the house, but none of them had seen him either. A tall man in a suit holding a gun approached Darren.

"The door from the garage to the side yard is slightly open. There's blood on the knob. He must have gotten away through the backyard."

"Damn it!" Darren muttered. He got on the radio and gave the update. "Remember, our suspect is a former cop. He knows our procedures as well as we do. He wrote them. Stay sharp!"

Darren went back to Cindy, three officers trailing him with their guns drawn. She led Darren to Randy's room, and the others continued down the hall to check every other possible hiding place.

Cindy knocked on the bedroom closet door and said that everything was okay. They could come out. She gently opened the door, revealing a scene that wrenched her heart. Her aunt's arms were wrapped protectively around Randy, but both of their expressions were of pure fear. Before she could reach in for their hands, Xena pushed by her and gave Randy a face wash.

Detective Polk stood in the hallway, guarding the bedroom, but the officers didn't find anything in any of the upstairs rooms.

The Chief of Detectives appeared at the top of the stairs. "He has escaped, it appears. I've called for a widened perimeter. We'll catch him. I promise you that. We will catch him."

Darren nodded. "We'd better."

"I'll leave two officers here, and I assume you want to stay as well."

"Yes, sir."

"Fine. They will be downstairs. Come down when the family feels up for it. We need to get their statements."

Darren nodded again. "Yes, sir." He turned and went into the room. Randy emerged from the closet.

"Is he dead?" Randy asked as he stood up. He reached back into the closet and took Gloria's hand, helping her to her feet. Darren, Cindy, Gloria, and Randy stood in the room huddled in a hug for a moment before Randy pulled away. "I asked if he's dead."

"No," Darren said softly. "Not yet. He's escaped."

Cindy pulled Randy back into the hug, and they stayed that way for a couple minutes, each gaining strength from the love of each other. Darren was the first to pull away, but he waited until the siren announced the departure of John's ambulance.

The foursome slowly made their way down to the kitchen with Darren herding them like dazed sheep. He was careful to block their view of the dog in the hall. He didn't want to move the pup until the crime scene people had taken their photographs and whatever else they needed to do. They sat at the kitchen table, and Xena crawled under it, favoring her right front leg.

Darren excused himself when his cell phone rang and came back a few minutes later. He pulled Cindy to the side. "You all need to give statements at the station. We'll have an officer here shortly to take you there."

"Is there any way we can stay here?" Cindy asked. "I'm concerned about Randy. He's sick. He stayed home from school with a fever and nausea." She ran her hands through her hair and held her head. "And Gloria. You can see she's in shock. She hasn't said a word. I don't know what that's going to do to the Alzheimer's. She was locked in the closet with Randy, so she didn't see the horrible things, but she most definitely heard them. And Marti should be home soon. She can't find the house like this."

"Does Marti have her cell phone with her?" Darren asked. "Maybe you could text her and tell her to go to Peter's house."

Cindy blinked. "Okay. But I still don't want to move Randy and Gloria."

Darren considered his words for a moment. "The crime scene folks need to come in and go over every inch of the house, taking pictures, and whatever else they do. It's vital that they have the run of the house to do it. The things they find will help convict Atwater. Without their magic, it would be his word against yours. He was a police chief. His word would carry some weight."

Cindy nodded again. His argument was logical, even if it didn't feel right.

"Besides," he continued. "*I* have to go to the station, and I'd really like to have you there. I don't want you out of my sight." He pulled her into his arms and kissed her forehead.

"Okay," she agreed. "What about Xena? I don't want to leave her here. She's been traumatized and injured, too. And I'd hate to think that she might hurt one of your people. Locking her outside when strangers are inside would be too traumatic for her. And I don't want Animal Control to take her."

"Bring her. I'm sure she'll be good for Randy and Gloria." A thought occurred to him. "But I need one of the techs to photograph her since she has blood on her mouth. They can take the DNA. Your dogs may be the key to convicting this bastard. And you're right about her being injured. We can get the department's vet take a look at her. She's limping quite badly. She and Sherlock are heroes and need to be treated that way."

The mention of Sherlock's name started a new barrage of tears that Cindy couldn't stop. "Oh, God," she sobbed. "How am I going to tell Marti about Sherlock?"

Darren tightened his arms around Cindy. "Just make sure she knows he's a hero." He held her until the sobbing stopped and then went to the coat closet in the family room for Xena's leash. The husky heard the leash's rattle, perked up, and hobbled over to him, dancing around on three legs as he clipped the leash to her collar. He led her to where the tech was just finishing photographing the staircase.

The technician was happy to stop and take pictures of the beautiful husky. She claimed that it was much more satisfying than shooting blood patterns.

Xena squirmed when Darren held her mouth open so her teeth could be documented and swabbed, but she didn't move to bite them.

The woman moved up the stairs, taking photos of the splatters and putting numbered cards down. Before going into the boy's room, she stepped over to the basset hound, squatting down near his head to get a close up of the damage to the ribs.

"Oh, my God" she said. "This dog is still alive! Get me something to make a stretcher, and let's get him to the vet."

Chapter 31
September 13, 2011
Day 44

It was nearly seven before the Fairbanks made it home again. An officer entered Gloria's room and deemed the room was safe. He was a trim man of medium height, but his bulletproof vest made him appear buff. Once he deemed the room was safe, Cindy brought Gloria into the room and turned the radio on. Soft classical music filled the room.

"Did you want to stay in here, Gloria? Or would you rather come out to the living room with us?"

Gloria picked up her book from the nightstand, sat down on the recliner, and put her feet up. "I think I'd like to read a while." There was a mechanical tone to her voice that worried Cindy. Her reaction to today's events were different from those she had when Randy shot the gun. She seemed dazed, as though she were heavily medicated.

"Are you hungry?"

Gloria shook her head. "Just tired, dear. I'll come out in a bit."

Cindy couldn't bring herself to eat, but she reheated the chicken soup for Randy. He curled up on the couch, wrapped in a thick blanket that Gloria had hand sewn, and slurped his dinner. He was still feverish and completely drained. She hoped he'd be able to fall asleep soon and get the deep rest his body needed.

Peter Wilson brought Marti home at 7:30.

Marti and Cindy had talked on their cell phones throughout the afternoon, and Marti was aware of what had happened. Once she had come up with the phone number for the police department's vet who was caring for Xena and Sherlock, she checked up on their statuses frequently.

Xena's injury was a sprain in her shoulder. There were no broken bones. She'd been released to come home with a prescription for a painkiller and an anti-inflammatory. She had been sedated so that the vet could take the x-rays, and she was still groggy. Sherlock's condition, though, was serious. He would be hospitalized for a few days. He had multiple broken ribs, and one vertebra was cracked, causing inflammation along his spinal column. He needed to be sedated to prevent movement and to help with pain. He would need surgery once the swelling went down. The doctor wasn't sure if the puppy would survive, but he promised Marti that he would do everything he could to save the hero.

At a quarter of eight, the next shift of officers arrived and sent the other two back to the station. Officer Avenaire was a pretty woman, and Randy perked up when he saw her. Her partner, Officer Belvere, gave Cindy a feeling of safety. He looked like a strong man, both physically and in attitude. She believed they were in good hands.

The two officers made a complete tour of the house, including checking in on Gloria, to make sure that everything was secure. When they were satisfied, they positioned themselves in the kitchen, giving the Fairbank family some privacy.

Randy's room was torn up, the desk overturned and broken, the door twisted and hanging on by a torn bottom hinge. He didn't want to sleep with his mom or his sister, and there was no way he was going to be in his room. He lobbied to sleep on the couch, but Cindy wanted him closer to her. She pointed out that the officers would be downstairs, and they might keep him awake. They decided that Randy would sleep in Marti's room, and Marti would sleep with her mom.

By nine, Cindy had tucked both kids into bed and came back down to the kitchen. She made a fresh pot of coffee for Avenaire and Belvere. "Is there anything I can get you?" she asked. She wrung her hands as she paced across the kitchen.

Officer Avenaire stood up and stepped into Cindy's path. She reached out and took Cindy's hands in hers and squeezed them. "It's okay now. Chances are pretty strong that Atwater has split town. He'd be a fool to stay here where people would recognize him easily. It's been all over the news." She pointed out the window to where a TV news van was parked. The reporter and cameraman stood talking on the sidewalk.

Cindy squeezed the officer's hands back, but a sickly smile was all she could muster. "I'm sure you're right, but I can't get his voice out of my head."

"I can understand that," the officer replied. She nodded to her partner. "Just know that Belvere and I won't let that man hurt you or your family." She nodded at the husky. "And by family, I mean Xena, too."

"Oh, that brings up a question. Is it okay if Xena is left free to roam the house? She got agitated when I closed her into the bedroom."

Officer Belvere spoke up. "I think it's a great idea. I've worked with dogs before, and they seem to be happiest when they have a job to do. Right now, she sees that job as protecting you. She will feel better if she's doing her job."

* * *

Cindy expected to have difficulty sleeping, even though her daughter curled up and fell asleep immediately. She read for a short time and found her eyes drooping. She turned off the light and put her head down.

"Cindy." She was on a dirt path surrounded by redwoods. The smell of the pines was overwhelmed by a pungent smoke. She could see smoke drifting through the trees, coming towards her, carried by a breeze. Tina Fremont was standing well off the path, partially concealed by ferns. "Cindy," the dream woman repeated. "Listen to me. It's not over. He's not done." Tina's voice was garbled and distant like a weak radio signal.

"He's gone, Tina," Cindy replied. "The police will find him. They will catch him, I know it."

The dead woman shook her head. "Your son. He knows."

"What does Randy have to do with this? I don't want him involved anymore. He's just a boy."

The smoke was getting thicker and was swirling around Tina. Her face was suddenly lined with panic. "Your son. Talk to your son!" She pointed into the distance at a boy who was walking through the billowing smoke.

Panicked, Cindy looked back and forth between the boy and Tina. A heavy plume of smoke covered the woman and obscured her sight of the boy. She woke with a start. Careful to avoid waking Marti, she pulled on her bathrobe and slippers and tiptoed out of the room. She closed the door and stopped to listen to the sounds of the house. She could hear faint conversation from the officers downstairs, but other than that, the house was silent. At first she thought that she could smell smoke, but decided that it was just a lingering effect of the dream.

She slipped into Marti's room where Randy was sleeping and was startled to see a small candle burning on the nightstand. She sat on the edge of the bed and touched his forehead. It was clammy and hot.

Cindy watched him for a few minutes, admiring his innocence. She remembered watching him and his sister sleep as babies, wondering what they were dreaming and what their futures would hold. They had been through so much in their lives. It wasn't fair.

She got up from the bed, deciding that she wouldn't wake him after all. Tina's warning rang in her head, but she thought about Darren saying that she shouldn't put any stock in dreams. She turned away but stopped at the bedroom door, hesitant to leave.

"Mom?" came a whisper from the bed. "Is that you?"

"Yes, dear. I came to see that you were okay." She moved back to the bed and sat down at his side again. "You still seem feverish. How are you feeling?"

"I'm still achy, but the headache and nausea are gone." He paused for a moment. "I had a dream, Mom. Like the ones you told us about. A lady was calling out for help."

A shiver went through Cindy's body. Tina had visited him. "Want to tell me about it?"

"You know how dreams are...things don't really make sense. I was in my room and heard something in my closet. For some reason, I thought that maybe Sherlock had gotten closed in there. As I got up to let him out, this woman passed *through* the closet door. She was calling out for help, but it was like she didn't see me. She was looking around and seemed confused. She was crying and mumbling. I think she was saying my name." He shook his head. "I don't understand."

"How about if we go into your bedroom? Maybe that will trigger something for you." The two walked into his room, the bedroom door creaking on its bent hinge. Randy scooted around the toppled desk and went over to his bed, but Cindy stopped just inside the door. She couldn't breathe. It had only been hours ago that she had held the door closed against the man that wanted her family dead. Tears welled up in her eyes, and she started to shake.

In the darkness, Randy stood staring at the closet. "Something about the closet," he whispered. "She was in the closet when she started calling out for help. Do you think that might mean something?"

Cindy shook her head. "I have no idea. She was in a redwood forest in my dream. There was a lot of smoke, like a forest fire. I don't understand why that would be in my dream. So I have no idea why she would be in your closet." She walked over to him and took his hand. They both sat on the edge of the bed, facing the closet door.

"Okay, let's think about it. Let's start with what happened earlier today in here. That's the only connection to the closet that I can see." They went through what he had seen before she sent him to hide. He hadn't heard much on the floor of the closet because he and Gloria covered their ears.

"Ya know," he said, "there's something about the closet that's bugging me, but I don't see what it is." He didn't let go of her hand when they stood up and moved to the closet. His hand reached out to open the door, but stopped short. He dropped his hand and said, "I can't."

Cindy squeezed his hand and let go. She picked up a piece of wood from the shattered door frame and held it like a club in one hand. She took a deep breath and jerked the closet door open.

Nothing.

They looked at the hanging clothes and the shoes on the floor.

"That's it!" he exclaimed. He grabbed his mom's arm in panic. "I know what it is that I'm supposed to remember!"

"What, honey?"

"This is where I hid the stuff from under the house. The crawl space!"

"I don't understand. What does this have to do with the crawl space and the stuff you found?"

"I think she's telling me that he used the crawl space to get away."

Cindy was confused. "No, there was no sign that he had gone into the rec room. His blood trail showed he went down the hall and out through the garage."

"Right," he said urgently. "And like all good bad guys, he doubled back and went into Gloria's room. He entered the crawl space from there!"

"What? What do you mean?"

"There's a crawl space entrance in Gloria's closet!"

* * *

Officer Avenaire heard the boy pounding down the stairs and jumped up, afraid that something was wrong. She met the boy in the family room. Through his gasping breaths, he told the officers, "I know where he is! He never left. He's under the house."

Avenaire and Belvere looked at each other and back at the boy. "His blood was on the door in the garage," Officer Belvere said.

Randy shook his head. "That's what Mom said, too. But you're wrong. I know it. He's under the house. He used the crawl space entrance in Gloria's room."

Julia Avenaire thought about it. It would be better to humor the kid and prove that there was no one under the house than to ignore him and find out later that he had been right. She looked at Randy. "Where is the crawl space entrance?"

"The one that he would know about is in Gloria's closet, but there's another one in the rec room. We just built it, so he wouldn't have any way to know it was there. Oh, and the exit to the outside is blocked, but it can be opened from under the house. He could escape that way."

Belvere got on his radio and asked the policeman who was positioned outside to come into the backyard. He quickly explained the situation. They waited for him to get in the yard before approaching Gloria's room.

* * *

Cindy and Randy stayed back in the hall with Xena. Even with the dog, though, she felt unprotected. She went into the kitchen and grabbed a butcher knife, then resumed her place in the hallway with her son. She wished that she still had the gun that Atwater had dropped earlier in the day.

Randy saw what she was holding. "Good idea!"

* * *

The female officer entered Gloria's room first. She turned on the light and called Gloria's name. When the older lady sat up, Avenaire crossed the room and sat on the edge of the chair by the bed. After introducing herself, she told her, "We're here to keep you safe. My partner needs to check your closet, if you don't mind."

Gloria frowned sleepily at her. "You go right ahead."

Avenaire nodded to her partner, and he moved to the closet.

He grunted.

She got up and moved closer to him. He pointed at the door knob. There was a tiny smear of blood on it; it was too small to have been noticed casually. The officers looked at each other and drew their guns.

Officer Avenaire turned to Gloria and said, "Ma'am, would you mind stepping out into the hall?"

Gloria stood up and walked to the bedroom door. "Be careful in the closet. I have lots of presents in there, and some beautiful new dresses. Don't get them messy."

The officer cued her radio and requested additional units to come in the house and into the backyard. She poked her head into the hallway and asked Cindy to unlock the front door. She explained that additional officers would be coming.

Cindy hugged her aunt and suggested that she go upstairs and sleep in the master bedroom with Marti.

* * *

Officer Belvere waited until Cindy had gone to unlock the front door and Officer Avenaire had stepped back into position, her gun aimed at the closet door. When she nodded, Belvere turned the knob without a sound and yanked the door open.

There was no one in the closet. It looked like someone had hastily shoved the shoes to one side, leaving a bare area. Belvere looked closer at the cleared area and noticed a small handle. He looked back at his partner. They nodded at each other again, and he yanked the crawl space door up.

It was pitch black under the house. Belvere pulled his flashlight off of his belt and shined it down. When he determined that the immediate area was clear, he stuck his head down the hole and looked around. The beam of his flashlight didn't go very far, so he pulled back out and stood up.

"I'm going down there." He lowered himself down and crouched. He wasn't sure if it was a trick of the shadows, but he thought he saw movement at the other side of the house. He carefully aimed his flashlight around the area he thought he'd seen movement, but couldn't see anything out of the ordinary. He moved forward, shining his light around him, trying to see behind the posts. A few feet away, he saw a wet area on the ground. Moving closer, he saw that it was fresh blood. He felt a combination of dread and excitement course through his body. The boy was right. The killer had been down here. He either still was, or perhaps he had escaped out to the backyard. He was about to cue his radio to announce what he found, when there was a scream from inside the house.

* * *

Cindy, Randy, and Xena waited in the hall while the two officers went into Gloria's room. They couldn't hear the conversation, but the officers' voices were tense. The female officer came out with her gun unholstered but held by her side. She asked Cindy to unlock the front door and be ready for additional officers.

Cindy dashed to the front door, unlocked it, and hurried back to her position with her son and dog. Xena was trembling and growling, a low rumble in her throat. The dog inched forward toward Gloria's room, positioning herself between the room and Randy. Cindy was grateful for the dog's protective instincts.

Seconds and minutes ticked by, and with each one, Cindy's anxiety grew. She had a feeling that something bad was going to happen, and she had no idea what to do. She was frozen in place. She was so intent on trying to hear what was going on in the room that she felt rather than heard steps approaching from behind her. As she started to turn, she felt a cold blade at her throat, and she was yanked back against Atwater's chest.

Cindy's gasp made Randy turn to look at her. He let out a loud, terrified scream, but didn't move. He was paralyzed with fear. Xena, too, spun around when she heard the gasp. She snarled, crouching, ready to spring on the intruder.

"Get your dog or your mom dies," the man growled. When Randy reached out and grabbed Xena's collar, Atwater continued. "It was nice of you all to talk about the new crawl space entrance you installed. If you hadn't said something, I would've been stuck down there."

Harry Atwater pushed Cindy forward, forcing Randy and Xena to back up. When he was nearly abreast of the small hallway with the door to the backyard, he said to Cindy, "Open it."

Cindy closed her eyes and considered her options. The cops had to have heard her son's scream and would be moving towards them. She suspected that at least one, maybe both, officers were under the house. Her hopes for survival were based on the officer's statement that there were also supposed to be more officers coming in through the front door. If she stalled, they would be able to get into position and shoot him. She opened her eyes and looked at her son. He was looking at her hands. She had completely forgotten that she was holding the butcher knife.

She adjusted her grip on the blade in her left hand, preparing to thrust it behind her. She saw a shadow cross Gloria's bedroom door and felt a surge of hope that at least one officer was coming to help. Finally responding to Atwater's request to open the back door, she said, "Okay. You'll have to let me step that way." She moved her body a bit to the right towards the door, as if she were trying to reach the handle. The blade's pressure on her throat eased as Atwater let her make the adjustment.

"This is for Sherlock," Cindy hissed. She brought her left hand forward and then slammed the blade back behind her into his body as hard as she could.

Atwater groaned and pulled back, letting her go, but remaining on his feet. As he stepped back, his knife sliced across her throat.

Cindy fell to the floor. She'd lost her grip on the knife when it stuck in Atwater's body. She used both hands to try to stop the flow of blood from her neck. She couldn't breathe. She was choking on her blood. More blood was pouring over her hands.

Randy dropped to the floor beside her, crying. "Mom! Oh my God, Mom! Don't die, please don't leave me!"

Xena lunged, jumping over Cindy, and bit down on Atwater's thigh. The former chief of police brought the knife in a slash towards the dog, but a shot ripped through his chest, staggering him backwards. Officer Avenaire moved forward, ready to shoot again. Atwater tripped over his own feet and went down hard, landing on his back. The dog leaped on him, digging her teeth into the hand that still gripped the knife. There was no resistance to the dog's aggression. The man was dead.

In moments the house was full of uniformed officers again, most trying to squeeze into the hallway to get at the monster they'd once believed to be a hero.

Randy begged for someone to help his mom, and two uniformed men gently lifted her and carried her to the front room where they had more space to work. One officer used his hands to put pressure on the wound to slow the bleeding. Cindy's blood flowed in weak pulses through his fingers.

The fire department's paramedics arrived in less than three minutes and pushed the officers out of the way. In a practiced dance, one medic took over the pressure on Cindy's neck while the other got the gurney ready. Seconds later she was whisked away to the ambulance.

* * *

The jostling brought Cindy into consciousness for a moment. A short woman with black hair, loving brown eyes and a ghost of a smile on her face stood over her. *Tina.* The woman mouthed, "thank you," lifted her hand in a farewell wave, and melted into the crowd.

Chapter 32
September 25, 2011
Day 56

After a week in the hospital, Cindy was finally home in her own bed. She caressed her daughter's hair and let her cry. "I'm sorry that Gloria can't finish the dress for you." Cindy's voice was a weak whisper. "This has been devastating for her, too."

"I know, Mom. But what am I going to do? Peter should be picking me up in a few hours to go to the dance, and the dress isn't done." A new wave of tears flowed down her face. "Even if I could fix it, I don't know if I want to go."

"Darling, I know it's only been a week since… since it happened. But *I* want you to go. You were looking forward to this. It's important that you have this. Have you called Peter?"

With a deep sigh, Marti rolled over and picked up the phone. Through tears, she told Peter about the dress. After a few moments of silence, she mumbled "goodbye" and hung up.

"He's coming over." She buried her face in the pillow and sobs wracked her body.

Within five minutes, Cindy heard the doorbell and Marti went down to greet Peter. But it was Nicole Wilson's voice that stood out.

As they came up the stairs, Cindy was able to make out what they were saying.

"—been sewing since I was in high school."

"Really?" Marti's voice squeaked with hope.

Their voices disappeared as they entered Marti's room and closed the door.

Cindy drifted off again, but Xena's barking brought her back around. Another visitor? She couldn't hear anything, but when heavy footsteps came up the stairs, she flashed back to the sounds of Atwater mounting the stairs. She started trembling and couldn't pull in a breath. The footsteps stopped just outside her door. She tried to scream, but between her damaged throat and no air in her lungs, all she managed was a quiet mewing sound. The door swung inward and a dark shape filled the frame. Her eyes flooded with tears, and she couldn't make out any details of the man.

He stepped inside, and the light from her window fell on him. Air filled her lungs in a rush. *Darren.*

"Hi." His voice was the best and most soothing sound she'd heard all day. "Are you up for some company?"

Cindy beckoned him forward. "I still can't talk, just barely whisper."

He sat down at her side and took her hands in his. She gazed into his eyes, gathering strength.

"Shhh," he whispered back. "Don't talk, save your voice."

After a few minutes of silence, each simply enjoying the presence of the other, Darren spoke, his voice soft and gentle. "I suspect you want to know what's been going on, right?"

Cindy nodded and winced. Moving her neck muscles was still quite painful.

"I saw Peter downstairs. He said his mother is working on Marti's dress." He squeezed her hand. "That's one crisis averted. What did you want to know about?"

"Sherlock?"

"Now there's some good news. The surgery on his spine seems to be a success, but they won't know for sure for a while. He has to stay in his crate for the next week while everything heals."

"Potty?"

It took Darren a moment to figure out what she meant. "He can go outside to do his business, but Marti or Randy needs to hold his spine straight by lifting his back end by his tail. He's handling it surprisingly well. He looks like a stuffed animal with the incision down his back. It looks like a zipper, which, I suppose it is."

"Gloria?"

"I hope you don't mind, but I hired a nurse to help out. The nurse says she's doing okay. She's still hiding somewhere inside herself, but the nurse thinks that the music therapy is helping to bring her back. She warns that it might be awhile before we have her back. And, of course, we need to be prepared for the possibility that we may never get her back."

Cindy closed her eyes for a moment and tears slipped out. "I failed her."

Darren stroked her face. "No, you haven't failed her. I think the time that she has spent here has been worth more to her than years of living elsewhere. Alzheimer's is a tough disease, but she's a tough lady. That strength seems to run in your family. She will need more care, but if you're willing to have assistants, she should be able to stay here with you. The love that you and your kids give her will buoy her spirits."

"Thank you, Darren."

He leaned forward and kissed her gently. "I have some more good news. John came out of his coma and appears to have most of his memory and body functions intact. His son is here and will stay to take care of him. He's been asking to see Gloria. With your permission, I'd like to take her to see him. I think it will be good for your aunt, even if she doesn't remember him. At least he knows about the disease and is willing to love her regardless."

"George?" Cindy asked.

"I spoke with him several times this week, even earlier this morning. He's devastated by everything that has come to light. Do you think you're strong enough to hear about it?"

She squeezed his hand and tried to smile.

"Up in Tahoe at their cabin, the bodies of the missing victims from here were recovered, plus the boy's missing head. Wait, let me back up. When George started going through the attic in the cabin, he came across a box of journals. In them, Atwater talked about being haunted by his dead wife.

"Apparently Karen Atwater went into labor early while Harry was on a stakeout. The dispatcher, Dudley, didn't alert him. He only passed along a message to the captain saying that Harry's wife called. He didn't say why she called. The captain didn't want to interrupt the stakeout for a call from someone's wife, and let it go. Too bad they didn't have cell phones or pagers in 1967.

"Apparently Karen Atwater called dispatch, but got impatient and hung up. She went out searching for help. She wound up on the porch steps to Larry and Francine Bell's house. Dispatch—Dudley again—got a call from Mrs. Bell saying there was a woman in distress on the porch. By the time medics got there, Karen was dead. They managed to save the baby. George."

Cindy closed her eyes, tears fell in earnest down her face.

"That's what started this whole thing. Atwater was already angry with Larry Bell because of the land issues. You already know about that stuff. So Atwater decided that it would be a good idea to ruin the Bells. Just like you thought, he hoped that the murders during the construction of the tract would derail it. It was a huge investment for the Bells, and if it fell through, it would probably destroy them. His plan didn't work. Housing was desperately needed with all of the soldiers returning from the war, so only this house went unsold. It didn't affect Bell negatively at all.

"Harry's journals talked about his wife coming to his dreams and demanding retribution. She stopped coming to his dreams for a while after the first murders, but then came back, once again demanding payback. The journals aren't dated, but I would assume that's when he killed Anne Bell. Remember we talked about the little girl being left alive? He did that to cast suspicion on Bell. He thought people would connect the murders and assume that Bell couldn't kill his own granddaughter. The timing was perfect for Harry since he was the detective on first call for the holiday weekend, and he figured that he could stage things and drive the investigation towards Bell. But there was so much pressure from higher up that he couldn't make the case stick. The suspicion alone, though, was enough to cause Bell a lot of stress within his family. Bell started having heart problems after that, and it may have contributed to his eventual death.

Darren took a sip of water from Cindy's glass before continuing. "Now, the part that we couldn't figure out: The babysitter and the kids. The babysitter was Suzy Dudley, the daughter of the dispatcher who didn't pass on the whole message from his wife and later delayed sending out the units to help her. Atwater was certain that Karen was still demanding blood retribution. He planned to kill just Suzy, but the little boy saw him first. And if all the previous deaths weren't enough, how about four more?"

"Fremonts?"

"Ahh, that one was so tragic. The oldest girl, Whitney, was taking a journalism class. Over the few years they had lived in the house, she had been having dreams about murders here. Both she and her mom claimed to be sensitive. She started investigating the deaths and eventually went to see Atwater."

"Nicole was right."

Darren continued. "Atwater didn't want the entire thing brought up again, so he decided that he needed to quiet her. He came here when the family was away on a camping trip. Whitney had her report to write, so she stayed home with a neighbor assigned to watch out for her.

"He had the whole thing planned out. He cut the phone line, not realizing immediately that there were *two* lines, and then entered the house. He found her in the rec room where she was playing darts by herself. He shot her in her chest, and she fell, but she wasn't dead. He stepped up to her to finish her off, but he heard the garage door rumble announcing that the family had returned early from their camping trip. In that moment of indecision, Whitney stabbed and slashed him in his leg with a dart. That's how she got blood on her hand and made the hand print. He apparently bled quite a bit, so she must have done some damage. It wasn't her mother's blood on the hand print on the wall, it was Atwater's. We've confirmed that his blood type is B."

"Why... home?" Cindy asked.

It took Darren a bit to figure out that she was asking why the family came home. "The father was in the California Department of Forestry, and there'd been a fire burning in the Santa Cruz Mountains. He'd had to bring the family home so he could respond to the fire.

"Atwater didn't want to risk another gunshot, and figured that the girl would die within minutes, anyway, so he wrapped his injury with his handkerchief to avoid leaving a blood trail. But when he went to the door to the backyard, he saw that the father was in the yard bringing camping gear to the shed. With his exit path blocked, he went into the crawl space, using the entrance in the downstairs closet. He listened to the family from there.

"He heard the mother's dismay at the amount of blood in the rec room, but she started calling out for her daughter. That's when he realized that the girl hadn't died and was making an escape. He started worrying that the girl had another way of contacting people. He figured out that, as a teenager, she might have a separate phone line in her room, and he made the decision that the entire family would need to be cut down."

Cindy closed her eyes.

"She must have gone to her room, probably to make the phone call for help. If she had gone out the front door or to the garage, her family might have survived." He paused and squeezed Cindy's hand. "So that's what you saw in your dream. You saw him come in, wearing overalls, holding a gun. He herded the family in and shot them one by one. I'm sorry I doubted you.

"When you started investigating, Harry planned to frame John for the murders. If George hadn't discovered the problem with the septic system, Harry would have gotten away with framing John.

"I'm sure you can imagine how mortified George is at what his father did over the years. He's eaten by guilt that he never noticed. But he discovered something that really bothered me. Apparently Harry had been coming to this house for years. Under the house was his favorite place to think about his cases. His house has a slab foundation, no crawl space or basement. The dark and cold here would allow him to close out the rest of the world. He probably solved a lot of his cases by sitting under your house. George suspects that he was still coming here when you moved in, even after he left the gun and clothes."

Cindy remembered something and struggled to speak. Darren put a finger to her lips and left the room for a moment. He came back with a pad of paper and pen. She scrawled a few words:

Bottle+wrapper=DNA. Put in bag. John's fork+paper w/blood paper cut. File drawer.

Darren read her note and nodded. "We could definitely use the bottle that you found under the house, but we won't be needing John's fork or the paper that has his blood on it." He kissed her forehead. "Great thinking to get that stuff. Oh, and remember that Gloria commented that the dogs would bark and growl facing her closet. They must have sensed Atwater down there."

Cindy sighed and wrote:

Murderer to chief. How?

Darren shook his head. "I've been thinking about that, too. In fact, just about everyone in the department has been talking about it. How could we all have missed it? The best explanation I heard was that there are basically three types of people who become cops. First is the one who wants justice for all. Next is the bully who likes having a badge to make abuse legal. And then there's the poor schmuck who got beat up by the bully and now wants retribution."

Cindy raised a questioning eyebrow.

"From everything that's coming out, he was the kid that got beat up. He didn't start to fight back until Vietnam. People that knew him before the war said he was different when he came back. Then when his wife died, he became morose. It didn't last for long, though, and people remember that he seemed to come out of his shell and become a real charmer."

She winked and pointed at him.

"Which one am I? Which of the three types?"

She blinked to say yes.

"I guess I'm the justice-type of guy. I always wanted to be a super-hero."

He leaned over and kissed her forehead. She was surprised and touched to see his eyes wet.

He took a deep breath. "When you sent that text that the killer was here, I thought I would die. I couldn't breathe. I was so panicked. I was trying to drive, call out on the radio for assistance, and text you at the same time. In hindsight, I'm surprised I didn't wrap my car around a tree. But I had to get here."

He squeezed her hand and stretched out alongside her, cradling her body to his. "Cindy, I know you've been through a horrible ordeal, and right now, no one should be putting any demands on you. But I want to offer you myself. If you would have me, I would like to be a part of your life. Permanently. Our kids get along great, and —"

She stopped him and whispered, "Darren. No promises, no demands. Hold me?"

He nodded. "I want you to get used to my being here, with my arms around you, keeping you safe."

Cindy snuggled into his arms, finding a peacefulness that had escaped her for years. She closed her eyes, letting herself relax, knowing that her life was finally on the right track. Darren moved away from her when there was a knock at the door.

Marti poked her head in. She stepped into the room when Cindy smiled a welcome. She was wearing her ball gown.

Cindy gasped. Her daughter was gorgeous. The dress was perfection.

Marti grinned at her and spun around in a circle, showing off the dress. "Isn't it stunning?"

"Oh, yes!" Cindy whispered in awe.

Nicole stepped into the room and waved. "Your aunt did an outstanding job. I can't remember when I've seen such fine stitchery work. Her attention to all of the tiniest details is amazing. I wish I had her talent."

Marti put her arm around her boyfriend's mother's waist and hugged her.

Cindy's eyes filled with tears again, but this time of joy. Her daughter was safe and was about to enjoy her first formal dance. The people she loved had survived the madness, and she was going to be okay. A sudden yawn caught her, and Nicole and Marti backed out of the room.

No sooner had the door closed than Darren resumed his position at Cindy's side and said, "Laura Lee called. She said that all of Atwater's victims have finally crossed over. Your house is now *your* house.

About the Author

Eileen is an occupational health and safety specialist with a background in criminal justice, emergency medical response, and rescue. She lives with her comedian sister (retired but still so darned funny), two rambunctious dogs, and a continual flow of spirits and entities in her house. Though she's a California native, her heart is set in the Pacific Northwest.

Made in the USA
Charleston, SC
10 June 2015